I0683225

CAMERON

By
Lane McFarland

Please visit Lane McFarland's website at
http://www.romancingtheeras.com
to learn more about her and her books.

CAMERON

(The Daughters of Alastair MacDougall ~ Book 1)

Copyright 2013 Lane McFarland

ALL RIGHTS RESERVED. With the exception of quotes used in reviews, this book may not be reproduced or used in whole or in part by any means existing without written permission from Lane McFarland.

Published by Lane McFarland: October 2013

This is a work of fiction. Names, characters, places and incidents are products of the author's imagination or are used fictitiously and are not meant to be construed as real. Any resemblance to actual events, locales, organization or persons, living or dead, is entirely coincidental.

Dedication

This book is dedicated to my husband, Ken, and
my son, Kenneth. Thank you for your love, patience and
constant encouragement to reach for my dream!

A special thanks goes to Tessy, who was the first to read
my chapters and one of my final beta readers.
Without her gracious support and gentle coaching, I would
not be writing today. Thank you for believing in me, Tessy!

And many thanks to my dear friend, Ann, my final beta
reader who has encouraged me my entire life, and has
always been there for me.

I'd also like to thank Lexi (my editor),
Shirley, Sylvia and Sandra (my dear beta readers),
and my critique partners in Hearts Through History
and Celtic Hearts for their wonderful suggestions,
comments and tremendous support.

Chapter One

MacDougall Castle
Kilmarnock, Scotland
May 1297

Cameron MacDougall scrambled up the steep hill, her brown basket clutched in one hand and her woolen skirt bunched in the other. Heart skipping fast, she crested the summit and caught her breath. Her gaze swept the flat landscape carpeted with green grass and hundreds of budding yellow wildflowers. A brisk breeze whipped her hair across her face. She pulled the dark strands from her mouth and tugged her grey cloak tighter against the chill.

She made her way across the grassy mound to her mother's resting place under the shade of a large blackthorn tree, its branches filled with white spring blossoms. Trees swayed in the wind, and petals skittered across the ground.

Cameron set her basket down and knelt. Her knees grew cold and wet from the damp ground as she brushed leaves off the gravesite. Images of Mum's sickly face flashed through her mind. Deep purple bruises, symptoms of disease, marred her translucent skin, and dark shadows surrounded her once vibrant blue eyes. Dull and lifeless, the orbs sunk into her pale face, the sharp ridges of her cheekbones prominent. Her once crowning glory of thick blonde hair lay in thin grey strands against her scalp, and the stench of death hung heavy around her shriveled frame.

A sharp pain sliced through Cameron's heart.

She had not been able to cure her mother's wasting sickness. Although it had been many months since Mum's passing, Cameron would never forgive herself for her inexperience as a healer. She ran her hand over the small iron cross the blacksmith made in Mum's honor—the cold hard surface uncharacteristic of her mother's warmth.

How she missed Mum, her encouragement and unselfish love. Even in her darkest hours, Mum

4

implored Cameron to continue her quest to learn the healing arts. *Follow yer dream. Never give up, my daughter.*

Cameron spent fruitless hours combing through manuscripts, desperately searching for a cure. But each potion she tried was quickly discarded after either having no affect at all, or sending her mother into bouts of vomiting, further weakening her frail state.

Tears slid down Cameron's cheeks, but she rubbed the moisture away. Mum would be disappointed to see her immersed in self-pity. Her mother had longed for strong, independent daughters.

Promises made to Mum in recompense of Da's indiscretions granted her four daughters the rare privilege to live as their hearts desired. The spirited, yet gentle woman ensured each daughter was educated in reading, writing and even performing basic calculations. Cameron's heart tugged. Because of Mum, each daughter lived the life of her choice.

Cameron snipped a bunch of the wilted yellow blooms from her visit yesterday, plucked the dead ones from the container and replaced them with fresh clippings.

"I'm worried about Fergus's arm, Mum. What a shame he may lose it over the Grahams stealing Da's bull. Why did they have to fight over that beast?" She sighed. "Nay, the bull is not the problem. They fight over anything and everything. I've begged Da to end this feud. Perhaps with Fergus's severe injury, he'll change his mind."

She tilted her face to the sun. Puffy white clouds drifted across the blue sky. "Well, I promised Muire I'd be back by mid-morning, and I still need to gather more elder for Fergus." She rubbed the cold ground over her mum. "I'll visit ye again tomorrow."

She straightened, picked up her basket and headed back down the hill. She grinned at the ridiculous sight of the chestnut horse waiting with a long wooden ladder strapped to

5

his back. He nickered and tossed his head at her approach. Perhaps he felt a wee bit silly. She unwound the reins and patted his sleek dark neck. "I know. A dignified beast such as yerself should not be made to tote a ladder."

The two ambled through a field and along a path winding into the woods. The sun shone through the trees, casting its light on green ferns and awakening flowers. The atmosphere alone should have heightened her spirits, but her father's aging captain weighed on her mind. Fergus was unusually quiet. His pain affected his mood, and she was determined to collect more elder bark and its white flowers to alleviate the inflammation around his wound.

She ventured farther into the forest, down the worn path to the clan's southern border. Black elder trees flourished in the damp shady woodland at the edge of a large field covered in yellow rapeseed blossoms. The shifting wind blew through the unfurling plants, causing the tall stems to sway and spread their honeyed musky scent.

A large black elder stood tall amongst the pines and oaks. Fragrant white petals covered the ends of the branches. When made into tea, not only did elder ward off fever, it lifted the patient's spirit. Just what Fergus needed.

After tethering her horse, she wrenched the ladder off the animal and leaned it against the trunk. She stood back and examined the limbs. The tree must be thirty feet tall. Its berries were turning red, not quite ready for harvest. "If only I can climb up without killing myself," she muttered.

She looped her basket on her arm and pushed on the ladder to test its strength. Cautiously, she stepped on the first rung and bounced, then did so again, testing before she took the next step, and the next.

Her palms perspired. A deep breath helped quell her fear of heights. She held on tightly, hung her basket on a branch, and hoisted herself into the tree. The flowers blooming at the far end of the limbs were almost within her grasp. She raked her teeth across her bottom lip. *All I have to do is inch along...one step at a time.*

6

She stood while maintaining a death-grip on another branch. Rough bark scraped her hands, but her feet shuffled closer to the edge. Sitting on the limb, she stretched forward and retrieved the flowers. After filling her basket, she peered at the ground, and her fingers shook in nervous anticipation of climbing down.

Grasping a limb, she tucked her feet underneath her and clutched her basket. Gingerly, she made her way back to the nook of the tree and sighed with relief. But when she looked down, the ladder appeared much farther away than she remembered.

She let her basket fall to the ground and eased her bottom into the cranny of the tree, stretching her leg, feeling for the top of the ladder. Her foot slipped to the right, and she grabbed the tree and closed her eyes. The ladder scraped against the bark and fell with a thud.

"Grand! Now what am I to do?" She searched the trunk. Gnarled roots ran in different directions, creating a rough hard surface. She rubbed her sweaty palms on her gown and glanced toward the castle. Would anyone hear her scream? Fear twisted her stomach.

Her horse nickered, his head held high and ears pointed to the west. The jingle of bridles and the clop of heavy hooves grew close. Cameron eased her feet into the nook of the tree and stood on shaky legs to get a better view.

Several men on horseback rode in her direction. The one in front sported the Graham's crest on his saddle.

She inhaled sharply. Oh, Lord. Did they return for more trouble? What would they do if they spotted her? Vulnerable and unprotected, her pulse hammered, her body trembling. Perhaps, if she remained quiet, they would pass without noticing her perched high in the tree.

As if he heard her thoughts, the leader of the group turned his head and met her eyes. He held up a hand, and the men stopped. His brows drew together. He nudged his mount toward her and tilted his head to the side, puzzlement reflected in his brown eyes.

His gaze raked her from head to toe, before coming to rest on her breasts. Her back straightened. How dare he examine her with such boldness.

Dark, shaggy hair hung to his broad shoulders with a single braid on either side of his face. Black stubble lined his cheeks and strong chin. The opening of his tan tunic revealed dark, curling chest hair, and the grey trews hugging his thighs disappeared inside his worn boots. A black and blue plaid draped his shoulder and rested under his leather belt. He crossed his hands on the saddle and raised his brows, as if he expected an explanation.

Cameron swallowed hard. Could this be Robert Graham? Why was he here? Given his outrageous stunt with Da's bull, what more could he want? The Grahams had severely wounded Fergus over that beast. Her ire rose, and she looked down her nose at the men. She would do her best to regain her composure; however, it wasn't easy to remain dignified while stuck in a tree.

His gaze dropped to the fallen ladder. A grin spread across his handsome face. To her horror, he threw a leg over his saddle and slid to the ground. The twinkle in his eyes clearly displayed his delight in her predicament.

Her back straightened. "What do ye want? To cause more mayhem like yer dim-witted stunt of stealing my da's bull? Do ye know what harm ye did? Do ye even care?"

One of the men scoffed. "Mayhem? Did ye hear that, Robert?"

So he *was* Robert Graham.

He advanced toward her. "Aye, I heard. But yer da was the clever fool who caused the bedlam, mistress. He had no reason to strap on his sword."

Her breathing quickened, and her nostrils flared. "Da tried to recover his property. Ye were the ones who instigated the attack."

He shook his head. "I see ye think like the rest of yer clan. So it's fine for yer da to smear pig-slop over our new smokehouse and not suffer the consequences?"

8

"Consequences? That is what ye call yer senseless act?"

"Well, aren't ye the bold one?" the other man behind Robert jeered.

Robert paused, his hands firmly affixed to his hips. "Do ye think it wise to insult and berate someone who can help ye out of that tree?"

He did have a point. "I don't need yer help. I can get down whenever I want."

"Can ye now?" The man peered at the fallen ladder, the basket of scattered elder leaves and then back at her.

She lifted her head a notch higher, bobbing slightly with confidence she didn't feel. "When I'm ready to be down."

He propped the ladder against the tree.

Her hand clasped her chest. "I'm fine, truly."

He climbed the first couple of rungs, and the corners of his mouth tugged up, dimples pressing into his rugged face. "Aye, ye are that, but ye need my help, lass."

What should she do? She did need help, but that rickety ladder would not hold both of them. She glimpsed the bemused faces of the other men and turned her attention back on Robert. "Now that ye've propped the ladder back up, I'll get down on my own."

He stepped to the ground. "By all means, please come down."

Cameron wished he would take his men and leave, but evidently, he intended to stay until she was out of the accursed tree.

"Verra well." She turned, eased into the tree nook and felt for the ladder with her toes. She held on to the trunk and put her weight on the top rung. But when she stepped to the next, it started to topple. She lost her balance. Her arms flailed, frantically grasping at the rough bark. Before she plummeted to the knotted roots, the man caught her.

"Oh!" She gasped and gripped his powerful forearms.

He gently set her on the ground, and she turned to face him. A bit dazed, she ran trembling fingers down the front of her gown. His hands lingered at her waist, and when he didn't step back, she looked up to find him smiling.

"I believe ye owe me yer thanks, Mistress Cameron."

At his mention of her name, she searched his face. "How do ye know me?"

He chuckled, his deep voice rumbling throughout his thick chest. "I make it my business to know all the bonnie lasses in the area."

The men behind him laughed.

Her stomach tightened. She was no beauty. He obviously mocked her—in front of his men. Prickly heat tingled across her cheeks.

"I'll catch up to ye," Robert called over his shoulder.

"Oh, aye. Once ye've taken care of business," one man asserted.

"Important business to be sure," the other bantered.

The men chuckled as they nudged their mounts, then trotted down the path and out of sight.

Robert's gaze lingered on her mouth before he raised it to her eyes. "I believe it's customary to thank someone when they've helped ye."

Cameron cleared her throat. "Aye, I do thank ye."

He studied her lips again. "I had something more in mind. Ye know ye'd still be stuck in that tree if I hadn't come along, so ye owe me."

His warm breath caressed her face. He bent and placed his mouth on hers. His arms pulled her close, his muscular frame molding her body against his. Stubble scratched her skin, and she inhaled his male scent of leather, and aye, of horse.

She should be horrified at his advances. What was she thinking, allowing a Graham to kiss her so...so wickedly and deliciously? She should push him away and demand he step back, but somehow, she loathed the idea. Indeed, she reveled in the feel of his hard body pressed against hers.

Robert broke the kiss, and she tried to compose herself. He placed his hand on the side of her face and paused, gazing into her eyes. "I just returned from visiting yer da."

10

Cameron straightened. "Ye talked to Da?"

Robert searched her eyes, his thumb caressing her cheek. "We have sealed a truce."

Her eyes widened. "A truce?"

"Aye." He lifted her hand to his mouth. "And I look forward to getting to know my *neighbors* much better."

He kissed her palm, and his whiskers scraped her skin. Tingles shot through her belly, and her breath caught at his dark mesmerizing eyes. They stared at each other through stilted silence. Finally, he stepped back and bowed. "Good day, m'lady."

He leapt onto his horse. The large black animal pawed at the ground while Robert continued to stare at her. The appearance of his dimples and the sparkle in his eyes caused her stomach to flutter. He turned his horse in the direction of Graham Castle and galloped through the woods.

Her hands trembled. She pressed her fingers to her lips and stepped away from the tree, searching the path he took, but no one was in sight. Placing her hand on her chest, she fought to steady her nerves. Her legs shook, but she turned to her basket and gathered the spilt elder flowers.

My first kiss.

The desire lighting his eyes had both thrilled and horrified her.

He was a Graham—*Robert* Graham, no less.

A man who stole her father's bull and because of his reckless act, Fergus might lose the use of his arm. She should not feel such exhilaration over her father's adversary. But, no…he was no longer their enemy. Robert said they'd sealed a truce.

Her heart soared with happiness over an accord she had prayed for and envisioned in her dreams.

The sun shone directly overhead. It was time to return home. Muire would be waiting. She secured the ladder onto the horse and picked up her basket. With thoughts of her first kiss running through her mind, she led the animal down the path toward home.

~~~

Robert's pulse hammered in his ears. What was wrong with him? They had only shared a kiss. Something about the MacDougall lass intrigued him. He grinned. Her soft curves and plump lips stirred his blood, not to mention his cock. The strain against the front of his trews was a painful reminder of her full breasts crushed against his chest. How he longed to cup their fullness and taste their sweetness. He groaned and shifted from his uncomfortable position, his thoughts not helping the situation.

Robert squeezed his legs around Eton, spurring him forward to catch Lachlan and Kendrick, who road ahead.

Lachlan smirked. "Ye didn't waste time getting the lass in yer arms."

"Och, I couldn't leave her stranded in the tree."

"Nay, I suppose not. And of course ye wanted a reward for yer services," Kendrick asserted.

Robert grinned at his friends. "A token of my Lady's favor."

"Oh, aye. To be sure," Lachlan agreed.

What was she doing in the tree? Her spilt basket had been full of elder bark and flowers. She didn't appear a fanciful lass collecting fragrant flowers. More like willful and deliberate, berating him from her perch. Nay, MacDougall had boasted of Cameron's healing ways. Most certainly, her habit of climbing trees aided the rendering of her treatments.

She held him responsible for stealing her da's bull. He wanted to clear his name, tell her he had nothing to do with the raid. Hell, he wasn't even around when his father's men took the beast.

Why did he wish her to know he wanted no part of this feud? Did he desire her approval? The idea was absurd. Not since his former-betrothed had he coveted a lass's acceptance. Upon finding Jacqueline in another man's arms, Robert learned his lesson, no longer caring what women thought of him. He pleased them well enough and never lacked for bedmates, but he didn't lose sleep over them nor waste time on a lass's

12

frivolous emotions. Important matters—the English soldiers and Scotland's fight for freedom—demanded his attention. King Edward encroached on their land, getting closer to Graham Castle every day.

So why did he want Cameron's approval? He couldn't understand his caring what the lass thought of him. The idea was ridiculous and...disturbing. Well, all that aside, he definitely wanted to see her again.

This truce may prove to have advantages he had not yet considered.

~~~

Robert walked into Isobel's room at dawn to find his two sisters asleep in front of the hearth. A log rolled in the grate, sending sparks flitting up the chimney. Nichola cradled their baby sister in her lap, firelight dancing across them.

When he gently picked up Isobel, Nichola woke and rubbed her eyes. Robert laid the little lass on her bed. She yawned and turned onto her side as he drew a blanket over her shoulder. Relief poured through him. She had survived another bout.

Nichola rubbed her arms. "'Tis my fault she had another breathing spell. I shouldn't have taken her out-of-doors. I only wanted her to have a wee bit of fun."

He stroked Isobel's dark curls. "I understand, but we have to be more careful. She's fragile."

Isobel had stolen his heart the day she was born. Could it really be five years ago already? Because of her illness, she had not experienced the joy of running and playing, or having friends. The only life she knew was living inside her bedchamber walls.

He would give anything to find a cure, enabling her to live like other children. Da had brought in healers from around the country to treat her, but she continued to wheeze and cough, oftentimes gasping for air. At the healers' insistence, heavy draperies covered the windows, and stifling oppressive air hung heavy in the room. Did the healers know what they were doing?

Nothing they had suggested helped Isobel.

He clasped Nichola's shoulder. "I must start the drills. Ye will let me know if she worsens?"

His sister nodded, and her disheveled blonde hair fell over her shoulder, her blue eyes sad. "Aye, I'll be with her."

Robert strode across the room, down the stairs and into the bailey where sounds of clashing steel broke the early morning quiet. He marched across the line, inspecting his men's progress. Even his old captain, Duncan, and Robert's young brother joined in the exercises.

At ten years old, Androu had trained with Duncan for three years now and someday would become a fine warrior. His brother struggled to manage his sword, but what he lacked in stature, he more than made up for in attitude.

Robert approached the two sparring. "Well done, Androu. Watch for yer opening. Lunge in to take yer opponent out."

Androu parried blow for blow, but soon grew tired. Robert held up a hand and signaled Duncan to stop.

"Yer technique improves every day," Robert said.

Androu proudly straightened his shoulders.

Robert ruffled his brother's dark hair. "Ye deserve a day off."

Androu's eyes widened. "Duncan promised to take me hunting. Can we go tomorrow?"

How Robert would enjoy a carefree day. "I'm ready for a good hunt, too. Mayhap I'll join ye."

"Aye!" Androu jumped up and down while holding both arms in the air.

~~~

The next afternoon, Kendrick raced into Robert's solar. "Laird, the horses Duncan and Androu were riding came in without them."

Without them? Heart pounding, Robert swallowed the panic rising in his chest. He raced from the room, through the keep into the bailey with Kendrick following. To his left, Michael pumped the sharpening stone as Lachlan held his sword's blade against the grinding rock, the noise loud and grating. Several others stood by, joking and laughing while awaiting their turn.

"Lachlan, Michael, I need yer help."

Michael stood as Lachlan and the others turned to Robert. "What is it?" Lachlan asked.

"Duncan and Androu are missing," Robert shouted. "Brian, David, mount up. Kendrick, send runners to the clan families and have the men scour the area."

They ran to their mounts. Robert grabbed Duncan's horse and sprang onto his back. He dug his heels into the animal's sides, and the men thundered out of the bailey and into the woods.

Duncan and Androu had gone on a simple hunt. Had something happened to *both* of them? How he wished Laird McCarthy's untimely visit this morning had not prevented him from accompanying the two. If there had been an accident, he would have been there to help, perhaps prevent it.

His chest constricted. Androu had followed in Robert's footsteps, tagging along behind, mimicking and trying hard to become a man. He prayed they would find him alive and unharmed.

Robert called for his brother and Duncan repeatedly, but received no response. He had no idea which way the two went. Frantic, he raked his fingers through his hair.

Where would they have gone?

"Split up so we can cover more ground. Brian and David, search the south side of the woods. Lachlan and Kendrick, come with me. We'll head north."

Splashes of purple and red streaked the darkening sky. His shoulders slumped. Where were they? He searched the forest and the tall grass. He'd been over this area before, but as

15

he turned, he caught sight of the captain lying in a thicket of weeds.

"There's Duncan!" Robert jumped from his horse, hurried to the old man and knelt beside him. Two arrows fletched with characteristic red and black feathers protruded from his back.

MacDougall feathers!

Fury welled from the pit of his stomach. His nostrils flared, and his breath came hard and fast. Duncan lay on his stomach, his head turned to the side. He was cold, but air puffed against Robert's fingers.

"He's alive!" Robert called over his shoulder. "Can ye hear me, man? Where's Androu?"

Duncan moaned.

How could MacDougall look Robert in the eye, give his word on a truce and perform such a horrific act? The old laird had betrayed him, broken his oath with this treacherous attack delivered directly to Robert's gut.

"Here's Androu," Lachlan yelled, thrashing through the undergrowth.

Kendrick knelt beside Duncan, and Robert rushed to his brother's side. An arrow protruded from Androu's back and another from his thigh. Robert shook with rage.

Blood soaked his brother's tunic and trews. He lay on his stomach, his young face smeared with dirt and grime. Robert brushed his brother's dark hair off his neck, pressing his fingers against his pulse point. He held his breath. Aye, a beat, then another—slow and weak—but steady. He exhaled a sigh of relief and wiped the sweat from his face. "We need to get them to the castle."

He grabbed the arrow shaft in Androu's shoulder and strained to snap the wooden stick, careful to break it at least a hand's-width from his skin. Kendrick handed him the rods from Duncan's back, and Robert stuffed the four feathered-shafts into his tunic.

16

He gathered the young lad in his arms and glimpsed at Kendrick and Lachlan. "I'll carry Androu. Can the two of ye manage Duncan?"

"Aye, Lachlan get on the other side of him," Kendrick said as he knelt.

The men lifted Duncan, and the old man cried out— the pitiful sound poignant. Robert clenched his jaw against the ache squeezing his chest. He cradled Androu in his arms and led the group back to the castle.

His stomach roiled.

Lord, please don't let them die.

When they entered the bailey, Nichola ran through the door and onto the landing. She pressed her hands to her mouth and shook her head. "Nay, oh nay." She hiked her gown and dashed down the stairs. "What happened? Are they alive?"

"Aye, barely," Robert shouted. "Get Aine."

Although the woman was up in years, she was all they had to treat ailments and mend broken bones. Nichola ran off as Robert carried Androu up the stone steps. He raced into the main hall where the clan had gathered for the evening meal.

Tessa placed a tray of leeks on the long trestle table and turned. "Oh Lord. What happened?" The old cook scurried behind Robert and his men.

"It was the MacDougalls," Kendrick yelled. "They attacked and shot them in the back."

The clan gathered. Women hugged their children close, their eyes wide.

"The whoresons," a man yelled.

"I knew they couldnae be trusted," another chimed in.

Others roared in agreement. Fists shaking, they followed Robert down the hall. As he disappeared into a chamber, Michael faced the concerned group and held up a hand. "Wait here while Aine treats them. I'll let ye know how they fare."

He shut the door as Robert placed Androu on a table face down in order to extract the arrows. Michael hurried

17

across the room and dragged another table next to them. "Lay Duncan here."

Kendrick and Lachlan eased the old man down. Duncan cried out and groaned as they settled him on the hard surface.

Robert was anxious to begin the arduous task of removing the arrows. He grasped his dagger and took a deep breath. Jaw clenched, he slit Androu's shirt and tore open the fabric, revealing the implanted barb.

Aine shuffled into the room and peered over Robert's shoulder. "Ye'll have to push the arrow through. The jagged edges will do more harm if they're jerked out."

Duncan and Androu had lost a lot of blood. Their faces were pale, their breathing shallow. Robert stared at the embedded rod. What if the damn thing splinters and causes worse damage? How would they extract the fragments?

He exhaled loudly. He didn't have a choice. The barbs had to come out. Aine handed a mallet to him. His gut churned as he tugged his brother toward him until his small arm dangled over the side of the table. "Ye will need to support him while I shove the arrow through his shoulder."

Lachlan nodded and grasped Androu's bicep.

Sweat slid down the middle of Robert's back. Taking a deep breath, he channeled his anger and slammed the mallet on the shaft. The arrow shot through Androu's thin shoulder and clattered to the floor.

Androu screamed and struggled against Lachlan's grip. Blood flowed from the wound and dripped on Lachlan's boot.

Aine stroked the lad's head. "Shh, 'twill be all right."

Whack! Duncan hollered. Robert's stomach churned. He tried to ignore the agonizing sounds from behind him and concentrate on his brother, but the man's wails reverberated through his head.

He drew his mouth into a tight line, focused on extracting the second arrow and dragged Androu's leg over the edge of the table.

"Nay, nay, please nay!" Androu cried and thrashed against Lachlan's grip.

18

"Hold him still." Robert's voice sounded harsh even to his own ears.

"It has to be done, lad," Aine said, cradling Androu's head. "Take a deep breath. He's almost finished."

Sweat peppered Robert's forehead and upper lip. He hit the rod with all his might, his brother's screams echoing in Robert's ears. The sharp arrow penetrated the other side of Androu's leg, but Robert had to hit it again. "Damn it!"

Androu howled. His arms flailed, but Lachlan grabbed them and pinned his upper torso down. "Shite," Lachlan cursed and tightened his grip.

"Hold on, lad. Hold on." Robert slammed the shaft once more, and the arrow shot out the other side of Androu's wee leg.

Androu sobbed, the gut-wrenching sound piercing Robert's core. He pressed a cloth over his brother's shoulder and wrapped his arms around the lad. His small frame hung limp, his chest heaving from his wails.

Robert smoothed Androu's hair. "Shhh, ye'll be all right, brother."

Alastair MacDougall will pay for this, if it's the last thing I do.

Kendrick wiped his brow with his forearm. "We got the arrow out of Duncan's shoulder, but we can't remove the one in his back."

Robert jerked his head toward Aine. "Can't ye get the barb out? He'll die if we leave it in."

Aine shook her head. "Nay, Laird, not where it's lodged. I've never done that afore, and I fear he'll die if I start probing around. We should see how he fares afore we put 'im through that."

Robert knew Aine thought Duncan would die, and she didn't want to torture him more. Instead, she bandaged the wounded areas the best she could.

"Carry Duncan to his chamber," Robert told Lachlan and Kendrick. He glanced down at his brother. "They'll rest more comfortably in their own beds."

When he picked up Androu, the lad moaned. His head rolled against Robert's shoulder as he carried him to his room. He laid him down and stood over him.

"Ye've done all ye can," Aine whispered.

No, I have not done all I can.

But, I will.

~~~

MacDougall Castle
May 1297

Cameron threw off her blankets and slid from bed. A chill in the air sent a shiver slithering across her shoulders, and she rubbed her arms before reaching for her wrap and shoes. She pushed aside the heavy russet draperies covering her window. Sunlight streamed into the room. From her vantage point high in the keep's tower, she could see forever. To the left, her chamber overlooked a dense forest bordering pastures full of her father's cattle. Several large birds gracefully landed on a small lake at the back of the field.

To the right, she had a direct view of the inner bailey. A lad with bright red hair chased a young lass around the well. Her dark curls bounced as she weaved between several women carrying baskets of laundry. One of them swatted at the boy, but he sidestepped her and laughed before he turned and ran off.

Cameron's younger sister, Lindsey, dressed in lad's clothing, led a chestnut mare through the yard. Like their older sister Heather, Lindsey had their mother's beautiful blue eyes, but she clearly didn't give a fig about her appearance. She'd stuffed her thick auburn hair into a cap, and her shirt and trews would most likely be wrinkled and stained. Her sister was passionate about animals, horses in particular. Cameron remembered their father's rants of inappropriateness while Mum encouraged Lindsey's desire to work with the beloved animals. As her mother had said on many occasions, Lindsey does *run* the stables.

20

Anxious to get out-of-doors, Cameron tugged her tawny woolen gown over her head and thrust her arms in the sleeves. She longed for a breath of fresh air as yester eve she had cared for numerous sore throats and runny noses, tended a woman's burned hand, and helped bring a bairn into the world.

She grabbed her healing basket and searched the contents. Little ground ivy and yarrow remained in her clay jars, but she knew the spot to find more. Once she collected the special herbs, she would visit Mum. She ran a comb through her hair, picked up her basket and small knife off her bedside table, and headed for the door.

Cameron trotted down the stairs and into the great hall. The room bustled with activity as her youngest sister, Elsbeth, cleaned dust from the wall hangings and replaced stale rushes on the floor.

She held a cushion against her waist. "Ye're off to visit Mum?"

Cameron stepped beside her. "I am. I need to replenish my herbs as well. Fergus is improving, but he goes through my brews quickly."

"How's he doing?" Elsbeth asked.

Cameron sighed. "The wound is healing, but his spirit is low. He fears he won't regain the use of his arm."

Elsbeth's violet eyes softened. "I'll sit with him later this morning."

"Thank ye." Cameron hugged her dear sister. "Well, I'm off. I'll see ye this afternoon."

Cameron slipped through the heavy oak door and rushed down the long flight of stone steps leading into the inner bailey. Hurrying along the gravel path, she tilted her face to the sun. The warm rays peeked through puffy grey clouds, and she hoped the rain stayed at bay until she returned.

A woman carrying a basket of vegetables strolled past. "Pleasant morn to ye, mistress."

"Thank ye, Betsy. I hope ye enjoy the lovely day." Cameron smiled and tugged her wrap tightly around her shoulders. Hunger pains rumbled, reminding her of Rena's sweet buns. Mouth watering, she ducked into the dim, stone kitchen. The aroma of fresh baked scones greeted her, causing her stomach to growl in anticipation of tasting one of the treats.

Rena bustled around a worktable, waving her hands as she instructed two serving girls rolling dough. "Spread it even. Not too thick, but not too thin."

"Good morning," Cameron greeted the women.

Rena glanced over her shoulder. "Ahh, mistress. 'Tis a fine morn indeed. May I prepare ye a meal to break yer fast?"

"I want one of yer scones, but a bit of goat's milk would taste good first."

"The lads brought it in a few moments ago and stored it in the back room. Yer sister is in there now."

Cameron skirted around the busy kitchen staff stoking the large fire in the hearth, slipped down the narrow hall, and into a side room. Crates and boxes of kitchen supplies lined the walls, and trays of Rena's sweet buns set next to the milk urns on a long worktable.

"Get away from me," Heather shrieked and backed into the room, shoving Symon and struggling against his meaty embrace.

"Symon Fraser, what are ye doing?" Cameron shouted and marched over to them. "Leave her alone."

Her cousin jerked his head around, his dark evil eyes glowering.

Heather broke from his strong hold and backed away from him, wiping his slobber from her neck. Her upper lip curled, and her face grimaced. "Ye stay away from me."

He faced the women, and Cameron glared. "I wonder what Da would think of ye attacking his daughter? Yer time here would come to an abrupt halt. He would beat ye within an inch of yer miserable life and toss ye out on yer ear."

Symon advanced on Cameron.

She held her ground while her hand slid into her basket, feeling for her knife.

His greasy blond hair, shorn to his ears, lay stuck to his sweaty head. "Ye will not tell yer Da, or ye'll answer to me."

His hot smelly breath assailed her nostrils. He'd been drinking. The stench permeated the air around his dirty disheveled frame.

Cameron narrowed her eyes. "Ye stay away."

He smirked while leaning into her. "Or what, healer lady? Or what?"

She pushed her knife against his stomach. "Or I'll skewer yer fat belly with my wee blade."

Symon's eyes widened.

"Mistress?" Rena called down the hall. "Did ye find the milk?"

Symon backed away. He glared at Cameron, then turned his shifty eyes to Heather and back to her again.

"Aye, Rena," Cameron answered the cook. "Thank ye."

Symon gave them a malicious grimace. "This is not over between us. Ye'll both be sorry."

He leered at Heather before he turned and stormed out of the room.

Heather released a long breath, and Cameron embraced her older sister's shoulders. "Are ye all right?"

She nodded. "Aye, he caught me off guard without my dagger."

Cameron shook her head. "He makes my stomach turn."

"Please don't tell Da..."

"Why not? He would put a stop to this. Why do ye withhold things from him?"

"I don't. I do not want him to worry over this. He's verra busy, his hands are full..."

"Do not tell me he can't handle his own nephew."

Heather's mouth drew into a tight line, and her back straightened. With her blonde hair secured on top of her head, she resembled their mum when she became cross and irritated. "Just let me handle it."

Why do I even bother to voice my opinion? Heather shields Da nay matter what the circumstances. Ever since Mum passed away, she had protected him. She stepped in where

23

Mum left off, and like Mum, she took his side on every issue. Even over the feud with the Grahams.

Cameron searched Heather's blue eyes, then reached for the jug of goats milk beside her sister. "I'll not mention it, but ye need to make sure ye're not alone with Symon. Promise ye'll watch out for him."

"I will."

She poured the milk into a jug and took a sip. When she moved to leave, her sister grasped her arm.

"Cammie...thank ye."

Her shoulders relaxed, and she nodded. She placed the mug on the table. "Remember yer promise."

Cameron held Heather's gaze, then slipped back down the hall. She grabbed a scone off the worktable and bit into the warm bread lightly sweetened with honey. "This is heavenly, Rena."

The cook beamed as Cameron waved and padded into the bailey. The light meal satisfied her complaining stomach, and she picked up her pace, passed through the interior wooden gate and strolled into the outer bailey.

To her right, several men hammered a wagon wheel, their loud clanging reverberating against the bailey walls. To her left, Blake stacked cartons next to the barn. His hands, wrapped with leather strips, grabbed a barrel and set it on top of another. Sweat stained the underarms of his tan tunic and damp, blonde hair stuck to his forehead.

"Hello, Blake."

The stable hand looked up and grinned. "Mistress Cameron." His forearm brushed a lock of hair from his eyes. "Are ye off somewhere?"

"Aye, to Mum's gravesite."

Blake stepped toward her and placed his hands on his lean hips. He glanced at the main bridge leading from the castle and back at her. "Ye shouldn't go alone."

Cameron waved in dismissal. "Och, nonsense. I visit her every day."

He tilted his head, his eyes squinting. "Ye're sure?"

24

"Do not concern yerself." Cameron turned and rushed through the outer gate, calling over her shoulder, "I'll be fine."

She strolled down the dusty road past the village at the base of the castle, along the narrow dirt path winding beside several cottages, and into the woods. The sun filtered through the trees, casting its light on green ferns and budding flowers.

She inhaled a deep breath. A brown-streaked skylark sailed to a great height. She shaded her eyes from the sun as the bird hovered while thrusting its melodious whistle across the sky's vast expanse. A spotted song thrush announced its presence and fluttered about the trees as squirrels jumped from branch to branch. Although it was early May, with the warm sun, the morning felt like summer.

Cameron made her way through the thick forest recalling the manuscripts she had read the night before. Her uncle often brought the precious books to her from his travels. She cherished Ian's gifts. However, months had passed after Mum's death before she gathered the courage to open them again. After she had failed Mum, she questioned herself, her methods, whether she should continue to practice the healing arts. But once she opened the binder, fascination with discovering different curing methods took over. She had poured over the documents until the wee hours of the morning, reading about advancements made in treating the sick and injured.

For many years, she studied under Muire, the clan's healer, and coveted any literature that furthered her learning. Cameron had dreamed someday of becoming a well-known healer, but when Mum's death shook her confidence, she had a hard time treating patients again. It had taken many months to pull herself out of her self-pitying despair and find the fortitude to pick up her healing basket again.

With time, belief in herself grew, and she immersed herself in learning all she could absorb. At least Da left her to pursue her education. More like, he relished her attention away from him and his silly feud with the Grahams. However, since Da and Robert Graham sealed a truce, the past few days had been relatively calm—no more late night raids, no more pranks played on each other. Indeed, she could get used to this peacefulness.

Robert Graham.

Remembering how he had held her in his arms, his hard body pressed into hers as his earthy scent enveloped her, the corners of her mouth tugged up. She closed her eyes, and her insides tightened in an excited dither. Secretly, she relived those short moments with him over and over again. But those thoughts were only fanciful daydreams.

Her eyes fluttered open. With her quest to become a healer, she had discouraged suitors, swearing never to submit to a man. Too often, she had witnessed her mum's pain over Da's liaisons. No, that was not a life she intended to lead. Nevertheless, she cherished the stirring memories of being in Robert's strong embrace.

She continued down the worn trail to a damp, shady area where ground ivy grew. The plant reduced pain and swelling around bruises and was useful when treating coughs and sore throats. Kneeling beside the vines, she cut the soft, hairy leaves and placed them in her basket.

She stood and made her way deeper into the forest, stopping along the way to collect cuttings. A patch of feathery-leaved yarrow to staunch the flow of blood from wounds, sprouted in the sunshine. She snipped the soft, dark green leaves, and then discovered a cluster of comfrey. The ointment made from crushing the large leaves and mixing them with water soothed and healed cuts and bruises. She clipped several plants and placed them alongside the others in her basket.

A twig snapped.

Her head jerked toward the noise.

Robert Graham leaned against a tree, holding broken sticks in his hands. Her heart slammed against her chest at seeing him again. He didn't utter a word, but instead he stared at her with solemn intensity.

She stood and faced him. Why was he here? What did he want?

26

He dropped the sticks on the ground and pushed away from the trunk. Dark hair hung past his broad shoulders. His cream-colored shirt lay open at the neck, exposing suntanned skin and black curls. Grey woolen trews hugged his long muscular legs as he stalked toward her. His eyes no longer held the twinkle that so easily caused flitters in her stomach. In fact, his thick brows drew together, and his dark eyes narrowed.

She clutched her basket in front of her and stepped back, trying to calm her body's trembling.

He stopped within a few feet of her. Unlike their earlier encounter, his large muscular frame loomed over her, his wide chest and broad shoulders crowded her.

He pushed the sleeves of his shirt up revealing thick forearms. His cold, dark eyes seared her with, what? Hatred? What had she done?

She drew herself up and took another step back. "What do ye want?"

"I want *ye*, lass."

Chapter Two

Two stocky men sporting scruffy beards—the same men Robert had with him two days before—drifted out of the depths of the woods.

Cameron's gaze shot from man to man and back at Robert. Her heart raced. Clenching her basket, she raised her chin slightly. "What do ye want with me?"

"Ye'll know soon enough."

"Ye're on MacDougall land, and I *order* ye to leave," her voice rose.

The men scoffed, but Robert's stony face remained impassive. His dark countenance spoke volumes. He closed in on her. "Aye, we'll be leaving. Ye're coming with us."

One of the men grabbed her basket, but she held tight. He jerked it from her hands, stinging her fingers. Her small blade tumbled to the ground. Robert's lip curled as he grabbed her around the waist and threw her over his shoulder.

Air whooshed from her lungs. She kicked and screamed, fighting with everything she had. Her fists and legs hit solid muscle, but her blows had little effect on his powerful body. She had ventured too deep into the forest. No one would hear her cries for help.

She pounded his back. "Let me down! Who do ye think ye are?"

He reached his horse and with her still struggling on his shoulder, he effortlessly climbed onto the animal. He lowered her before him and shook her. "I'll bind and gag ye, m'lady, if ye prefer. I will not have ye screaming and hollering the whole way home. 'Tis yer choice."

She stared over her shoulder at him. His dark glare brooked no argument. "Why? Why are ye doing this?"

"I'm extracting payment from yer da."

"Payment?"

"The subject's not open for discussion." He signaled to his men and spurred his horse. They sprang forward. Frantic,

28

she grasped the saddle to keep from falling as they galloped through the woods toward Graham Castle.

The ride was long. Determined not to lean against the beastly man that snatched her from her home, her muscles ached from sitting rigid. She settled between his muscular thighs, his thick arm wrapped around her waist. The big, black warhorse easily carried the weight of them as he raced through woods, across fields, and onto the Graham's land.

Graham Castle stood at the top of a hill overlooking pastures of grazing cattle and dense forests. Large torches blazed bright into the darkening sky. Solid battlements, secured behind grey stone, ran across outer gates surrounding the fortress. Guards patrolled the ramparts, ready to drop the portcullis and defend at a moment's notice.

Robert spurred his horse up the hill. Cameron grabbed a hank of the animal's mane as they galloped onto the dirt path winding through the village at the base of the castle. Small thatched huts lined the road with candlelight slipping through the wooden window slats. Dogs barked in greeting and chased them into the bailey.

A gate closed behind the incoming party with a resounding bang. Robert guided his mount into the yard. Several women paused from their chores and stared at her. Men laid down their tools and started toward them.

"Traitor," one yelled.

"Whore!" another added.

Cameron swiveled her neck to see who called the hateful names. The crowd sneered and shook their fists. They followed, shouting in anger.

Her heart pounded. While she held her head high and tried to ignore their insults, she trembled with fear. What did they want? Why did they loathe her?

Robert swung off his horse. He reached up, plucked her off the saddle, and set her before him. Her weak legs wobbled, but he grabbed her wrist and dragged her up the stone staircase.

Cameron had to run to keep up with his long strides. Her toe caught the step, and she pitched forward slamming her

29

knee onto the hard rock. Pain shot up her leg, and she grimaced.

Robert grabbed her upper arm and steadied her as she rubbed her shin.

He tugged on her arm. "M'lady?"

His eyes softened a mere second before he reached behind her knees and lifted her. She grasped his thick neck as he carried her up the remaining stairs and into the castle.

Servants stopped their duties and gaped as he stormed across the massive great room. Cameron's chest heaved with fear. What would he do to her? Everything had happened so fast. Was this his plan all along? For Da to let his guard down under false pretenses of a truce so Robert could kidnap her? Did he intend to hold her for ransom? Was that his *payment*?

Robert marched down a long dark corridor into a room at the end of the hall. He let her legs drop, but held her against his chest. Her toes touched the floor, and he eased away, his gaze holding hers. "Ye will remain here until I send for ye."

He turned abruptly, stormed from the room, and slammed the door. A bolt scraped against its brackets.

The room fell silent. Cameron shivered and wrapped her arms around herself. She peered around the sparsely furnished chamber. A small bed hugged the wall. A table with a pitcher and basin was next to it. She sat on a bench positioned in front of a cold fireplace. Her shoulders slumped, and she trembled.

No one at home knew where she was.

~~~

Robert strode down the hall. Nichola waited, wringing her hands. "Androu and Duncan are feverish. We bathed them with cool water, but Aine doesn't know anything else to do for them." She rubbed her forehead. "I pray they pull through."

They needed more than prayers.

He brushed past her, marched down the hall and into Androu's room. His young brother lay on his stomach, his hair

30

wet from the bathing Nichola had administered. He moaned. His face flushed pink, his skin hot.

"Shite!"

Androu needed attention.

Nichola slipped her arm around Robert's waist.

He stared at Androu's still form. "I should have gone with them. This would not have happened if I had been there."

Nichola rubbed his back. "Nonsense. Those men would have attacked ye, too."

He glanced at his sister. "Let me know if his condition changes."

She turned her tear-filled eyes to him. "I will."

He squeezed her arm, then left the room and headed into Duncan's chamber. Aine sat in a chair next to his bedside. She stood when Robert entered the room.

"Keep yer seat." He marched to Duncan. The old man appeared to have aged ten years. Fever caused red splotches on his captain's cheeks and highlighted his pale, drawn face.

Aine wrung her gnarled hands. "All we can do is pray he pulls through this."

"Damnation, woman! That is *not* good enough," Robert yelled, and stormed from the room. He trod down the stairs and into the solar, poured a mug of mead, and downed the drink in a gulp. After slamming the mug on the table, he dropped on the chair before the fire and put his head in his hands.

Could he risk the MacDougall healer treating Duncan and Androu? What if she tried to finish what her father had started? Could he trust Cameron given her father's treachery?

Did he have any choice?

He poured more mead. Swirling the amber liquid in his mug, he considered his foolish belief the Grahams could ever band together with the MacDougalls, fighting side by side instead of against each other. He shook his head and drained the contents of his mug. The fiery liquid burned a path down his throat and into the pit of his gut.

Da's swordbreaker—now *his own*—leaned against his chair. When Robert was a wee lad, Da had the unique design

31

made with serrated edges like the teeth of a comb on one side. Da used it to capture an opponent's blade, and with a quick twist, it snapped the attacker's weapon from their hand. Robert grabbed the sword and held it to the light of the flames. Wire bands encircled the blade, outlining notched segments. He rotated it back and forth, the reflecting glow mesmerizing.

His thoughts rolled back to the night Da died. Robert had been off at war for some time and little of his emotions remained after witnessing the brutality of his friends and family falling beneath their enemies' blades. Death had become a part of everyday life. Upon his father's passing, he was surprised at the strong ache in his chest, believing his emotions were damaged beyond repair. While he had not always agreed with Da, he had loved him.

He shook his head remembering the many MacDougall raids he took part in with his father over the years. Carefree days before the English stormed onto their soil demanding Scot's allegiance—carefree days before the mass carnage, the butchery and massacre of their people. His heart hardened upon witnessing the bloodbath. Those carefree days were now in the past.

He fingered the edges of the blade. He had never understood the feud with the MacDougalls, just that there had always been one. His father, consumed with Alastair MacDougall, neglected his family, and his somber mum had given up fighting for Da's attention. Robert would never forgive her for abandoning her bairns. He loathed the hurt she inflicted on his siblings, leaving without a care to their welfare.

Nichola, only ten-and-three years at the time, had stepped in to mother their young siblings, Androu and Isobel. Now she sat by their brother's bed, praying he didn't die from Alastair MacDougall's heinous act.

Time passed with Robert growing angrier. He had no choice but to force the MacDougall healer to treat Androu and Duncan, even if he had to hold a knife to her pretty throat.

He got up, strode to the door, and yelled for Lachlan. "Bring the MacDougall wench."

32

Cameron

~~~

"Get up."

Cameron opened her eyes and tried to focus in the dim light. Robert's man who had snatched her basket stood over her. He held a candle, the shadows outlining his stony expression.

"Move. *Now*," he ground out.

Cameron glowered at him and slid off the bed.

He shoved her shoulder, steering her toward the door.

She whipped around. "Ye need not push me."

She stormed ahead of him, and once again, he prodded her, this time toward the stairs. They reached the bottom floor, and he shoved her down a dark hall. Torches secured in brackets lined the damp passage, their flames flickering in a cold draft. The chill intensified shudders of fear racking her body, and she tugged her wrap tighter around her shoulders while praying for the strength and courage to confront her abductor.

Finally, they stood before a worn oak door. The man opened it and thrust her inside.

Cameron glared over her shoulder at him. *Boorish pig.*

"She's here." He sneered at her before closing the door behind him.

The glow of firelight swathed the dark quiet room, sending eerie shadows dancing across the walls. The aroma of smoky peat pervaded the intimate space. Robert leaned back in a large chair before the hearth, his elbows on the arms of the furniture, hands folded.

Her pulse raced, and she attempted to steady her trembling. What did he intend? Would he mistreat her while holding her for ransom?

Stilted moments strung tight without him acknowledging her presence. Finally, he turned and fixed his steely glower on her.

"How dare ye," Cameron shouted and stomped before him. "Ye steal me from my home, mishandle me, and throw me into a room without so much as a word as to why I'm here or

33

what ye want. How dare ye treat me this way! Did ye forget ye joined hands with Da, sealing a truce between our clans?" She shook her head. "Yer word is obviously not worth much, *Laird* Graham."

Robert shot from his chair. She gasped and stumbled backward. He grabbed her by the front of her gown and jerked her within an inch of his face. "If ye were a man, I'd beat ye to death for yer remark."

He shoved her from him and stalked across the room. "Yer da is the one who has *no* honor." He turned back and crossed his massive arms over his chest. "And I promise I'll deal with him accordingly."

She advanced, her fists balled at her sides. "What are ye talking about? *Ye* were the one that stole onto our land like the thief ye are and kidnapped me behind my father's back."

In two strides, Robert was upon her again. He grabbed her upper arm and jerked her against him. "Aye? At least I didn't shoot ye in yer back."

"What are ye talking about?"

He yanked her through the solar door, down the long narrow corridor and up the stairs before marching her into a chamber off the main hall.

Cameron ran to keep up with his long strides, his grip strong.

A young woman with blonde hair and sad blue eyes sat beside a lad's bed. As she watched Robert storm into the room, dragging Cameron behind him, her back straightened.

He hauled Cameron to the bed and pointed. "*This* is what yer trustworthy da did. He shot my brother in the back and leg while he ran from yer merciless father. Now he lies here fighting for his verra life!"

Cameron recoiled from his every word. Da would never shoot a lad.

He spun her around and dragged her back through the door and into another dark room. A man lay face down on the bed with a broken arrow shaft jutting from his back. Blood soaked grey bandages surrounding the protruding rod.

34

An older plump woman with white hair sat next to the bed. Her head jerked toward them, her dark eyes wide.

Robert shoved Cameron to the foot of the bed. His eyes blazed fury, and his broad chest heaved, his breathing hard and loud through his nose. "This shaft is another example of yer father's handiwork."

Cameron reeled at the thought. "There has to be some mistake. My father would never do this."

Robert snatched four arrow shafts from his tunic and thrust them at her. "I removed two from my brother, and my men extracted one from Duncan's shoulder." His voice raised and eyes glowered. "We had to break off the one still lodged in his back."

No! She stared at the MacDougall red and black feathered arrow shafts with horror. Heart pounding, her mind raced.

"Aye, I see ye recognize yer da's markers," Robert stated flatly. With a low menacing tone, he continued. "Ye will tend them. Ye had best hope ye cure them, and they do not die. For if they do, I promise I will strike the MacDougalls as ye have never imagined. Ye will have nothing to return home to, lass. Do ye hear me?"

His dark, demanding gaze bore into hers.

She seethed at her father for taking part in the feud and at Robert for abducting her, throwing her into the middle of this now deadly fight. Cameron returned his glare. "I need my basket."

Tense seconds passed with Robert staring at her. "Aine, fetch the lady's basket." When he finally spoke, his tone was laced with venom.

"Aye, m'laird." The old woman shuffled from the room.

Cameron broke Robert's stare and turned to Duncan, but Robert grabbed her, his grip tight on her upper arm. "I'm warning ye, lass."

She narrowed her eyes, and her chin rose in confidence she did not feel. "I'm a healer. I would never intentionally hurt anyone." She paused, piercing him with her glare. "Not even my enemy."

She jerked her arm from his grasp and stepped to the bed. As she lowered the blanket to examine Duncan's back, Aine hurried into the room carrying Cameron's basket. The woman placed it on the table beside the bed. Duncan burned with fever. Upon exposing his injury, Cameron saw the arrowhead lodged near his spine. The shaft disappeared into a swollen mound of flesh and infection. The red and irritated wound oozed pus around the protruding stick. Could she extract the barb safely? Cold fingers of diffidence crept into the pit of her stomach.

She swallowed hard. "This will have to come out. We can't leave the arrow embedded."

Robert's nostrils flared, expelling a deep breath. His jaw clenched, and he held his mouth in a tight line. Finally, he curtly nodded.

She rummaged through her basket, withdrew a needle, and held it to the dim candlelight to thread it. "I'll need yer knife."

When he didn't respond, she raised her brow and extended her hand, palm up. "I have to cut it out."

The old woman advanced. "Cut it out? But that might kill him."

Cameron's gaze shot to the woman, then back to Robert. "I have no choice."

He scrutinized her. His eyes narrowed with suspicion. Silence stretched between them. Finally, he extended his dagger. When she closed her hand around the handle, he held onto the blade for a moment before relinquishing it.

Cameron had no time to waste. Her hands trembled. She dabbed the wound with a cloth and wrinkled her nose. The putrid smell of decaying flesh gagged her, and she swallowed the bile rising in her throat.

She pushed an errant lock from her brow with her forearm. "This will hurt, and ye must keep him as still as possible. The arrowhead is lodged in a bad location."

36

"Get on the other side," Robert addressed Aine while positioning himself next to Duncan.

"I donnae like it," she mumbled. "'Tis risky jamming a blade in his back."

Cameron tried to ignore Aine and took a deep breath to calm her nerves.

She could do this.

She *had* to.

While supporting the arrow shaft with her fingers, she slit Duncan's inflamed skin. The blade eased into the rotten tissue. The dead skin sloughed off and she cringed, the stench overpowering.

Duncan hollered and struggled against Robert's grasp. "Hold still, man."

"She's killing him," Aine wailed.

"No, I'm not," Cameron replied. "'Tis necessary."

She made another incision. A yellowish liquid mixed with blood, oozed from the gash and down his back. The more she cut, the more pus seeped out. Although deeply embedded, the arrowhead became visible. Her fingertips grasped the slippery barb. She probed with her blade and finally, wiggled it free.

Blood now coursed down Duncan's back. She grabbed her needle and began stitching the gash. "Blot that for me."

Robert snatched her cloth and wiped off the excretion while Cameron drew the needle and thread through Duncan's skin. When she tied off the last stitch, the blood flow stopped. She mixed a poultice of comfrey and smeared some on and around the infected area.

"I have to drain the wound on his shoulder." When Robert didn't object, she opened the incision and squeezed around the edges to expel more yellowish-white sticky fluid.

Robert grabbed his blade and wiped it on his trews before thrusting it into the sheath at his side.

"I need a bowl of water," Cameron said.

The older woman hobbled from the room.

Cameron selected shaved willow bark from her basket. "I'll make a brew to help his fever and pain."

Robert remained silent. His ominous stare fixed on her every move, and her body trembled under his scrutiny.

Aine returned a few moments later, and Cameron crushed the shredded bark into the water. "Please steep this over the fire. We have to get some down his throat."

Cameron ignored Robert's glowering dark looks and concentrated on her patient. He would not intimidate her, or so she tried to convince herself. She dipped a cloth into a small pitcher and wrung out the excess water. Leaning over Duncan, she ran the cool rag over his hot skin. Evidence of a serious malady had set in with red marks streaking across his back, splaying from the fetid wound. She prayed he would fight this off, not only for his sake, but for her clan's as well.

Aine handed the warm brew to Cameron. The old woman glared, her back stiff as Cameron stirred the concoction and addressed Robert. "I need ye to turn him so he can drink this."

Robert rolled Duncan over and propped up his shoulders. The old man groaned, his head resting against Robert's arm. "Come on. Have a wee sip."

Cameron held the bowl to Duncan's dry cracked lips, and dribbled the contents into his mouth. A small amount trickled down his chin, but he managed to swallow a portion of the brew.

"That's good," Robert said, before he lowered the elderly man. He stood back and crossed his thick arms.

Cameron wiped her hands on a cloth. That was all she could do for the moment. At least, Duncan quieted and appeared somewhat comfortable. "All right, I'm ready to move on to yer brother's room."

Robert motioned to the door with his head. "After ye."

Cameron picked up her basket and marched from the room. The hulking beast that had bullied her earlier followed them down the hall.

38

When she entered the lad's room, she heard his moans. She stepped to the bedside, set her basket down and leaned over him to feel his brow. Like Duncan, his skin burned with fever. His face flushed red, and sweat drenched his bedclothes.

The young blonde woman who sat next to the lad jumped up, shoving the bench back with her legs. Her gaze swung to Robert. "Are ye daft? Ye would have the enemy tend our brother?"

"We have no other option," he snarled. "She will heal him or suffer the consequences."

The other man grasped the woman's shoulder. His ominous gaze swung to Cameron, and his lip curled in a sneer. "She knows what will happen to her clan if she fails."

The woman's blue eyes blazed hatred. Her nostrils flared, and she crossed her arms over her chest.

Cameron's pulse hammered in her ears. Belief in her healing abilities waned, and her insides churned with fear rooted deep within her stomach, but she forced the negative thoughts away.

"Will ye boil water?" She eased onto the edge of the bed, and stroked the lad's hair, her hand trembling.

Robert's sister jerked past the bench and over to the hearth.

"What's his name?"

"Androu," Robert answered.

"Ye're going to be all right, Androu. I'm here to help ye." She took a cool wet cloth from a basin on the side table and wiped his hot face. His head rolled from side to side. "Easy, lad."

He quieted somewhat at her ministrations. "Help me roll him so I can examine his wound."

Robert lifted Androu and laid him on his stomach. The lad's pitiful whimper wrenched her heart.

She tugged the bandage off and recoiled from the rank smell emanating from his red, puckered injury. Oh, Lord. She swallowed past the lump in her throat. "Do ye have soap?"

39

The woman fumbled through a drawer in the bedside table and handed a slice of fatty wood ash to Cameron.

She ran the soap over Androu's gash. The hot mound was full of pus. Why would someone harm this lad? Da would not have done this. The Grahams were mistaken. "I need that hot water for a poultice and a cloth to bandage the wounds."

The woman handed a bowl to her and tossed a cloth on the bed. Cameron dropped several leaves into the water and smashed the herbs with a wooden pestle until they made a sticky substance. She wiped her hands and threaded another needle while addressing Robert. "I have to lance this, and I need yer knife again."

This time, he didn't hesitate to hand her his blade.

"This will hurt, Androu. But 'tis necessary to make ye feel better." She slit the stitches on his little shoulder and a yellowish secretion oozed out.

He groaned and thrashed, his upper body rising off the table.

Robert patted Androu's head. "Easy, lad."

She applied pressure around the cut to drain the liquid before packing the cavity with a mixture of herbs. Wrapping a cloth around the injury, she asked, "What about his leg?"

The woman pulled the blankets down. A bloodied bandage wrapped the lad's thigh. Cameron slit the dirty fabric and peeled the crusty edges apart. She sighed in relief. This injury was not as bad as the one on his shoulder, but she treated the wound much the same. Afterward, she wrapped a long cloth around his leg and tied the ends.

"He must take some of my herbs." She mixed another concoction and pushed her hair from her eyes with the back of her forearm. "Will ye turn him again?"

When Robert propped his brother up, Androu sobbed, his body shaking. "I know, lad. I know. Drink this brew, and we will leave ye be."

Cameron dribbled the concoction into Androu's small mouth. He swallowed and coughed. With his eyes scrunched tight, a tear slid down his pale drawn face.

She stroked his baby soft skin. Her chest squeezed.

"That's good, Androu. Ye got most of the brew down." Robert shook his head. "No more, he's had enough."

Cameron covered the lad with a blanket while the woman picked up several discarded bandages.

Robert ran his palm over Androu's head. "Sister, I expect ye to watch her." His deep voice filled with vehemence. "Do not let her finish what her da started."

"Nay, I'll not let her harm him further."

Cameron drew herself up. Harm him? She would never hurt a child. On the contrary, she did everything she could to help them or anyone in need.

As Robert marched across the room, he addressed the brute that had snatched her basket. "Guard her. Don't let her leave unless ye're with her."

The beast stared at her. His steely grey eyes emanated disgust. He followed Robert into the hall and shut the door.

With the exception of the fire popping in the hearth, the room fell silent.

Cameron could feel the woman's glare on her, smoldering contempt oozing from her eyes. She didn't blame her. If one of her sisters lay wounded by the Grahams, she would feel the same.

How could this have happened? There had to be some other explanation, but...the feathers. She would recognize them anywhere. Da prided himself on intertwining the red and black colors. They *were* MacDougall markers.

She ran her sweaty palms over her gown before she faced the woman she knew stared at her back.

Robert's sister tilted her head and raised her left eyebrow. Her arms crossed, her piercing blue eyes unwavering.

"I am terribly sorry for what has happened," Cameron said.

She narrowed her eyes. "Are ye?"

Cameron's head bobbed, her eyes beseeching. "I understand ye feel my da did this, but he would never do such a thing."

41

Robert's sister was quiet for a moment. "All my life ye MacDougalls have been a thorn in my side. My mum left because she couldn't stomach the fighting with yer clan any longer."

Cameron stiffened. How sad the ridiculous feud had been a tragedy to both families.

"I had such high hopes when my brother requested a truce with yer da." She looked down at Androu, and back at Cameron. Her eyes scrunched together, her brow furrowed. "Why, Mistress MacDougall? Why did he shoot my little brother in the back?"

Cameron stepped toward her. "I do not believe Da did this. He shook hands with yer brother and gave his word on a truce." She paused. "Regardless of how the circumstances may appear, he's an honorable man."

Androu cried out, and Cameron turned to him. He thrashed from side to side, kicking and fighting an invisible enemy. She sat at his side and ran her hand over his dark hair. "Calm down, lad, or ye'll pull yer stitches. Try to lie still and rest."

She wrung excess water from a rag and gently dabbed the cloth over his hot face.

Androu's glassy eyes tried to focus on Cameron. "Mum? Is it ye?"

His sister stooped next to him and kissed his head. "Shhh, Androu." A fat tear rolled down her cheek, but she wiped it away.

"The potion I gave him should help him rest. The fever makes him a bit delirious."

Androu quieted, and his sister sat in a chair next to the bed. She lowered her head and brought his fingers to her mouth. Her eyes closed, and she whispered a prayer against his hand.

Cameron's throat clogged with emotion. The medicine *had* to work. She didn't want the lad to die, and she surely did not want her family destroyed.

42

Chapter Three

Robert climbed the stairs to his bedchamber and collapsed in the chair before the fire. He leaned over and put his face in his hands. Duncan and Androu were pale and weak. Neither was a strong warrior who could withstand such horrific wounds. He would not forgive himself if they died. He should have been with them, protected them from the MacDougall's treachery.

His thoughts turned to Cameron, and he scowled. She appeared to have a genuine desire to help people. Not that it mattered. She was his enemy, a means to an end, and he would be damned if his feelings toward her would soften. He would ensure she healed Androu and Duncan, and use her to avenge the attack. Alastair MacDougall would experience the ache in his chest, the churning of his stomach, the agonizing pain of believing he had lost a loved one.

He stared into the flames.

Alastair MacDougall.

The churl had shaken Robert's hand—sealed a truce. The old laird made a mockery of his offer. How dare he attack his clan.

Fury washed over him.

He would get even with the MacDougalls. They would pay for their heinous act. Aye, Alastair MacDougall may have begun the confrontation, but Robert would end it.

Closing his eyes, he saw Cameron tending Androu, her gentle voice comforting his brother. She acted as if she cared that he lived. Mayhap because she feared his retribution upon her clan. As she damn well should.

What was it about her that stirred him, had him eager to be near her? Hell, he almost lost his mind on their ride back to the castle. Her breasts had grazed his arm repeatedly, and her soft bottom nestled snugly between his legs. His cock rose and strained against his trews. Aye, he wanted to bed her, and by God, he should. He had every right to use her body to settle the score.

The door opened and closed behind him. Rosalind's spicy scent preceded her muted footsteps as she traipsed across the floor. The servant ran her fingers across his shoulders and leaned into him, her breasts brushing the back of his head. She bent and nuzzled his neck. Her hands slid down his chest, and her fingers trailed to his abdomen. "I'm here ta pleasure ye, laird," she purred.

She slipped around to the front of his chair and knelt. While glancing at him from beneath dark lashes, she pushed between his legs. Rosalind had come to his bed many times before he left for the rebellion, but her blonde hair and large breasts no longer held his interest.

When she reached for his belt, he grabbed her hand and shook his head. "Nay, it's late, and I'm going to bed. Ye need to leave."

Her eyes widened. "Leave? Ye want me ta leave?"

"Aye."

Rosalind's fingers walked up his chest, and she crushed her generous bosom against his stomach. "Ye'll miss me in the night." She eased her hand between his legs and cupped his manhood. "When ye become hard with wantin' me, ye'll wish I was here."

Robert held her hands and stood. "Goodnight, Rosalind."

She pursed her lips and pouted. "Well, donnae say I dinnae warn ye."

Several hours later, Robert awoke to the sound of a log rolling in the hearth. He opened his eyes and realized he had fallen asleep in his chair. Leaning forward, he put his elbows on his knees. He rubbed the back of his neck before he rose, walked to the basin and splashed water on his face.

Grabbing a cloth off the table, his thoughts turned to the MacDougall lass and his concerns over Duncan and Androu. He tossed the rag aside, strode across the room, and out the door.

The keep was quiet when he made his way down the stairs to his brother's room. Cameron and Nichola sat side by

44

side next to the bed. His sister turned to him as he strode across the room. Androu's cheeks flushed red. He wore no shirt, and Cameron bathed his arms and face. She spoke quietly, comforting him even as he slept.

"I want to speak to ye," Robert said.

Cameron glanced up, and her green eyes narrowed. She dropped the cloth in a bowl and followed him into the hall.

He crossed his arms. "Will he live?"

"I believe he will, but only time will tell." She hugged her waist. "I gave him more draught, and that will help alleviate his pain and bring down his fever."

"And Duncan? How does he fare?"

Cameron exhaled. "Duncan's injury is more serious. The arrowhead lodged close to his backbone did a good deal of damage. I did the best I could in removing the barb, but…"

Robert grabbed her upper arm and loomed over her. "What, Mistress MacDougall? Do ye pretend to care for yer hated enemy? Save yer false performance for someone who believes MacDougall lies. Ye'd best produce some magic out of yer wee basket to heal him, or yer clan will cease to exist."

Robert released her and yelled down the corridor, "Kendrick, escort Mistress MacDougall to Duncan. She's not to leave until he's much improved. Let me know if he worsens."

Kendrick advanced, but he stopped short when she stood unmoving, glaring at Robert. Her defiant, green eyes flashed anger. After a moment, she spun around and stalked off to Duncan's chamber.

By God, she would do what he said, or she would suffer the consequences.

~~~

Another day passed. Cameron sat at Duncan's bedside bathing his face and arms. Last night he battled a raging fever, but in the wee hours of the morning, his high temperature finally broke, and he appeared to rest easier.

45

Now confident he would survive his injury, Cameron sighed with relief. She never doubted the severe retribution Robert would have taken against her father and family, and she thanked the Lord Duncan appeared to recover.

Gretchen, one of the women from the kitchen who had helped tend Duncan throughout the night, had left hours ago for much-needed rest. The room was quiet with the exception of an occasional snore from Kendrick. When he was not glaring at her or watching her every move, he spent the night sleeping in a chair, which was propped against the wall, balanced on two legs.

Lachlan stepped into the room and nudged Kendrick's shoulder. "I'm here to relieve ye."

The chair legs banged on the floor. "Huh? Oh, aye."

Kendrick stood, stretched, and left the room.

"I need ye to turn Duncan so I can change his dressing," Cameron ordered.

Lachlan didn't reply, but he did as asked.

She unwound the bandages. Yesterday ragged edges of dead skin lined the injury, but today the swelling had gone down and the angry, red irritation had lightened. Indeed, the area appeared much healthier, and although Duncan was far from recovered, his progress encouraged her.

When Lachlan flipped him back over, the old captain groaned.

"Careful! Ye'll tear his wounds open," Cameron admonished as she heated another medicinal brew in the hearth. Sitting back on her heels while the tea steeped, she pushed fallen tendrils of hair from her face. The muscles in her back and neck ached. Exhausted and dirty, she longed for a bath and soft bed.

After Duncan swallowed the concoction, she picked up her healing basket and stepped toward the door.

Lachlan blocked her path. "Where do ye think ye're going?"

The ornery beast. "I need to check on Androu, if ye don't mind."

46

Lachlan paused. Finally, he grunted in agreement. She swept past him, and he followed her down the hall and into the lad's bedchamber.

"Androu's awake," Nichola exclaimed. She sat on the edge of the bed, a smile spread across her face. Her blue eyes sparkled as she motioned to Cameron. "He's no longer warm with fever."

"Och, lad, ye gave us a scare," Lachlan announced and clasped Nichola's shoulder.

Dark circles marred the skin under Androu's eyes, his cheeks a bit pale. He blinked several times as he struggled to stay awake.

Cameron set her basket on a bedside table. "Well, lad, I'm happy to meet ye. How do ye feel?"

She placed her hand on his forehead, relieved to feel his cool skin.

Androu eyed her suspiciously. "I'm thirsty and hungry," he responded, his voice scratchy.

Lachlan chuckled. "That is indeed a good sign."

Cameron poured a mug of cool water. "I imagine ye are. Let's start him with a light broth."

"I'll fetch it straight away." Nichola beamed, patted her little brother's hand, and hurried from the room.

Androu's large, brown eyes were full of questions.

"My name is Cameron, and I'm trying to heal yer wounds. Why don't we get ye into a clean nightshirt?" She reached into a chest at the foot of the bed and extracted a fresh tan tunic.

"Yer brother will be happy to see ye." Lachlan patted Androu's uninjured leg. "Ye've had us all mighty worried."

Cameron stepped beside Androu and held out the tunic, her brow arched in question.

Androu's eyes studied her, but he let her slip the shirt over his head.

Nichola entered the room carrying a bowl of broth. "Here ye are." She sat on the edge of the bed and spoon-fed

47

him. "Yer coloring is coming back, and I see ye didn't lose yer healthy appetite."

Cameron gathered the soiled linens from Androu's bed and stacked them on the side table. After he finished the soup, she smoothed the bed covers over his legs. "I'd like to tend yer shoulder."

"All right." Androu eased over, wincing and scrunching his eyes tight.

The once inflamed red skin now tinged pink. "Yer wound looks much better."

When she tugged the blanket down to examine his thigh, he jerked the cover over his bare bottom and glared. She couldn't help but grin. "Ye needn't show off yer rear end. I'll hold the blankets to yer backside."

With that injury still a bit red and irritated, Cameron covered it with her poultice and applied a fresh bandage. She straightened and wiped her hands on a cloth. "Ye're healing nicely."

Androu turned over, and Nichola tucked the blankets around him.

"Well, look at ye," Robert called out.

Cameron instantly grew alert, her back stiffened.

Robert stepped to the other side of his brother's bed. "How do ye feel?"

"I'm tired, and my shoulder and leg hurt."

"Aye, yer wounds will pain ye for some time, but I'm pleased ye're awake."

He turned to Cameron, and all tenderness vanished. "Ye didn't see fit to inform me of his improvement?"

Her mouth fell open. "I'm only just now learning of his progress myself."

His eyebrow quirked. "Indeed? And why are ye only now learning of it?"

Taken aback with his unreasonable questioning, Cameron drew herself up. "I've been in Duncan's chambers, treating his wounds as ye demanded."

48

Robert's dark eyes bore into her. "Exactly where ye should be now. Nichola can tend Androu." He crossed his arms over his chest. "Ye had best get back to Duncan's side, lest he takes a turn for the worse."

"I cannot believe ye treat me with such little respect. I've been at Duncan's side for two days without rest."

"And ye'll *not* rest until he improves."

Her heart pounded, and her breathing became erratic. She clenched her jaw. Did he challenge her to rebuff his unfair comments? She snatched her basket and hurried from the room.

"See she stays with Duncan until I say otherwise," Robert shouted, ensuring she heard his orders.

"Don't worry," Lachlan yelled as he followed her down the hall. "She's not going anywhere."

~~~

Another day passed, but Duncan had yet to awaken. Cameron had not slept, and she was exhausted. With her stomach unsettled, her heavy lids closed of their own accord. Her head bobbed, and she jerked awake.

Nichola placed her arm around Cameron's shoulders. "I thank ye for saving my little brother, and for working tirelessly to heal Duncan's wounds. But ye need yer rest, or we'll have to heal *ye*. Let Gretchen and me sit with Duncan while ye get some sleep. I'll come for ye if we need ye."

"I am tired and would love a wee nap." Cameron straightened, and her aching legs and back screamed in protest. She definitely needed rest. When she moved toward the door, Lachlan stepped in front of her. Taken aback, she stopped abruptly.

His dark eyes glared, his muscular body intimidating. "The laird hasn't given permission for ye to leave. Sit down."

She started around him. His bullying would not frighten her. "I don't care. I'll not sit here any longer."

The fiend stepped to the side and once again prevented her from leaving the room.

"Lachlan," Nichola implored. "Let her pass."

49

Leveling the worst scowl she could muster, Cameron threatened, "Ye had best get out of my way."

Robert marched into room and around Lachlan. "Ye're in no position to deliver orders, Mistress MacDougall."

She turned her glare on Robert, and Nichola rushed between them. "She needs food and rest, brother. She has not had either for days. I suggested she go to her room right before ye came in."

Robert stared at Cameron for a moment. "Ye may take her to her chamber, but she's not to leave unless she's needed by Androu or Duncan."

Tired of him and his guards telling her what to do and when to do it, she stormed from the room. Nichola caught up to her, and they continued the short distance with Lachlan close behind.

She welcomed the cold dark chamber. Back stiff and shoulders aching, she trod into the room.

"I'll bring ye something to eat," Nichola said, before Lachlan tugged her out of the room and slammed the oak door.

Cameron heard the unmistakable slide of the bolt locking her inside. She sank on the bed. Exhausted and utterly miserable, she worried over thoughts of her father and sisters. Her family would fret over her disappearance. They would wonder what happened to her and believe the worst.

Tears trickled down her cheeks. Would she ever get home? She curled up and cried herself to sleep.

~~~

"Cameron?"

She opened her eyes to find Nichola standing beside her. Several lads hurried into the room bringing a wooden bathing tub and buckets of hot water.

"Would ye like to freshen up a wee bit?" Nichola stepped to the hearth and threw in a log. "I'll light a fire to take the chill out of the air."

An old woman stomped in carrying a tray of meat, cheese, bread and cider. She plunked the food on the table and

50

turned to Cameron, raised her nose, and promptly left the room.

Nichola shoed the lads out, and shut the door behind them. "Don't mind old Tessa. She's suffered years of feuding with yer clan, and she's a mite resentful."

"I understand." Steam rose off the water in the tub, and Cameron longed to plunge into the warmth. "Nichola, ye did this for me?"

"Aye." Nichola crossed the room while shaking out a gown. "What happened was not yer fault. I'm sure ye were in the same situation as me. I've had little say about the feud with yer clan." She paused. "Ye saved my little brother and Duncan, and I appreciate yer healing ways and yer gentle touch. I no longer want to be considered yer enemy."

Cameron slid off the bed and embraced Nichola. "Ye've been verra kind, and I thank ye for understanding." She glanced at the bath. "The water looks delightful. I can't wait to climb in."

"I left soap on the table and here's a drying cloth." She dropped the fabric on the back of a chair. "And I brought ye a chemise and one of my gowns. The dress may be a wee bit long, but it's clean."

Cameron shed her dirty clothes and eased into the tub.

Nichola padded across the room to the door. "I'll let ye have some time to yerself. If ye need anything, knock and tell Lachlan."

"Nichola?"

With her hand on the door, she turned back.

"Thank ye."

She smiled and closed the door behind her.

The warmth soothed Cameron's aching muscles. She sank further into the steaming water and washed away the dirt and grime collected over the past few days. She dunked her head and lathered her hair. After ridding herself of the filth, she lay against the tub and closed her eyes.

Before long, the water turned chilly. Sighing, she stepped from the bath and wrapped herself in the drying cloth. A comb lay next to the gown. "Nichola thought of everything."

The fire popped and hissed. The familiar homey smell of peat was comforting. Sitting in front of the hearth, she dried her hair as she had done so many times before. Her heart ached with thoughts of home. Shaking her head, she slipped into the clean chemise and curled up on the bed.

With Duncan and Androu well on their way to recovery, Robert would send her home, and her ordeal would be over. He had no other reason to hold her prisoner.

~~~

The next morning, Cameron tugged Nichola's borrowed gown over her head and brushed her hair. Unbraided, the tresses hung in curls down her back. After having slept through the night, she was ready to face the Grahams. She knocked on the locked door and attempted to gain her guard's attention. "Hello? Is anyone there?"

Several moments passed before she heard the bolt scrape across the brackets. Kendrick opened the worn oak door and peered at her. "What do ye want?"

"I need to check on Androu and Duncan."

The man continued to glare. Finally, he stepped back and dramatically swept his arm in the direction of the bedchambers.

Cameron marched to Androu's room. When she entered, he was sitting in bed talking to Nichola.

Cameron placed her basket on a chest at the foot of his bed. "Good morn."

"It is a good morning. Did ye get some rest?" Nichola asked.

"I slept well, thank ye." Cameron placed her hand on Nichola's shoulder and smiled at Androu. "And how are *ye* feeling today?"

Androu knit his brow. "I'm better, and I want to get out of bed."

52

"Ye had a serious injury. If ye're doing well tomorrow, ye can get out a wee bit. Now, turn over so I can tend ye."

The young lad muttered and reluctantly eased onto his side. He resembled his older brother. They had the same coloring and the same dark scowl.

The puckered skin no longer appeared red and irritated. She pulled the covers over him. "Healing nicely. Now, rest in bed one more day so ye don't aggravate those areas. I'll come by to check on ye later."

"But I feel fine. Why do I have to stay in bed?" Androu grumbled.

"And I'm glad ye do, but ye need one more day of rest."

Androu stuck out his bottom lip and crossed his arms over his chest while Cameron gathered her supplies.

Nichola patted his leg. "I'll make sure he stays in bed."

Cameron picked up her basket and padded across the room toward the door.

"I'm off to tend Duncan," she called over her shoulder before heading to the older man's room with Kendrick trailing behind.

When they approached his chamber, Cameron overheard Duncan talking to Robert. "Aye, I saw Symon Fraser."

Both men looked up when she entered the room. Robert's dark eyes caused butterflies to flit through her insides. She inwardly scolded herself as she set her basket at the foot of the bed. Why did his presence cause such irrational fluttering in her stomach? "How are ye feeling?"

Duncan rubbed his shoulder. His hazel, red-rimmed eyes appeared weak. "Well, I'm sore and tired, but I'm alive. I have ye to thank. And I do thank ye, lass."

"I'd like to treat yer wounds. Can ye turn over?"

Robert helped the older man roll onto his stomach. Cameron gently removed the bandages, and for the second time this morning, she was pleased to find healthy, healing skin.

"Ye're mending nicely." Robert helped him settle back into bed, and she patted Duncan's old wrinkled hand. "Ye'll feel good as new before ye know it."

She straightened and turned to Robert. "Now that yer brother and Duncan are well on their way to recovery, I'd like to go home."

"No."

She drew herself up as if his answer slapped her. "What do ye mean *no*? Ye have to let me go."

Robert looked at her long and hard. "I do not have to do anything I don't want to do."

He turned to leave, but Cameron dashed in front of him, placing her hand on his broad chest. "Ye cannot keep me prisoner. I saved yer brother and Duncan, and this is how ye repay me, by having me guarded and locked up?"

Robert regarded her for several long, silent moments. Her fury increased when his gaze traveled across her breasts before returning to her face.

"Verra well, m'lady. We won't guard ye *if* I have yer word ye won't attempt to leave."

"How verra generous of ye." Cameron sneered. "Why are ye so unreasonable? Why must I stay here against my will?"

Robert leaned within an inch of her face. "Ye are staying here until I say different. Yer da will feel the pain of believing he has lost his loved one. *He* will experience sitting by helpless to do anything about it."

Suddenly, Cameron realized how she fit into his scheme. He was using her to hurt her father. "Da didn't do this," she said, shaking her head.

"So ye say. But ye can't deny yer clan's arrows were lodged in their backs, can ye? Duncan saw yer cousin leading the attack. He's yer father's bloody captain. Do not tell me yer da did not know about this."

Cameron didn't have answers. She couldn't explain what happened, but she did know her da had not been involved.

"Yer silence is deafening, lass," Robert said quietly. "Ye should thank me for not marching on yer father and taking retribution against yer clan." He continued in a low and menacing tone. "I'm waiting for yer word ye'll not attempt to leave."

Cameron's mind raced. *Not attempt to leave?* Why, he must be mad. She had to get home to stop this senseless brutality between their clans.

Seconds passed with Robert glaring at her, his dark eyes searing.

She tried to steady her voice. "All right."

He raised his eyebrow. "All right?" His eyes narrowed. "All right what? I would hear yer vow."

"I won't attempt to leave." *At least not at the moment, but as soon as I have a chance...*

"Verra well, ye are free to roam the grounds, but if ye so much as step outside the perimeter of this castle, I promise ye'll regret doing so," Robert warned. "Do I make myself clear?"

"Aye, ye have made yourself quite clear." Despair closed in around her. She numbly picked up her basket and left Duncan's chamber. When she reached her room, she closed the door, leaned back against it, and slid to the floor.

He planned to hold her prisoner. Indefinitely. Her father and her sisters would be frantic with worry.

Duncan identified Symon as the one leading the attack. She was not surprised. Her cousin would act without Da's knowledge. Indeed, he could be planning another attack right now. If he struck, the Grahams would most certainly even the score.

What am I to do? Only one word came to mind. *Escape.*

Chapter Four

Cameron lay on her side, staring at the flames flickering around clumps of moss in the hearth. Peat smoke wafted on the chilly air, and the fire crackled and popped, the orange glow mesmerizing. Sleep eluded her as Laird Graham's words of how she fit into his scheme of revenge echoed through her mind. Perhaps she would check on Androu. After her confrontation with Robert, she had retreated to her bedchamber and failed to visit the lad. Although he was well on the way to recovery, she wanted to see how he fared.

She tossed aside the blankets, padded across the room and retrieved her wrap. Tugging it around her shoulders, she strolled out the door and down the hall. This late, the keep was quiet. Only the guards patrolling the ramparts would be awake.

Cold air swirled around her bare feet, as she hurried into Androu's chamber. Someone must have recently stoked the fire in his hearth. The dark room was aglow, sending shadows dancing across his still form. She crept to his bedside. He laid face down, his little hand tucked beneath his chin. What a precious lad. How could anyone harm him? Symon's smirk loomed before her. Her cousin would feel no remorse over attacking innocents. Of that, she was sure.

She leaned over and touched Androu's brow. It was cool, and she sighed with relief. "Ye had a close call, lad."

The back of her finger stroked his soft skin. A dark lock had fallen over his eye. She brushed it off his forehead and ran her hand over his silky hair.

The door creaked, and her head whipped around. Robert leaned against the doorjamb, arms crossing his chest. His black hair appeared as if he had recently raked his fingers through it. His shirt lay open to mid chest, with the sleeves rolled up revealing strong forearms. Brown trews hugged his powerful thighs.

Her mouth went dry, and her heart hammered in her ears. Why was he up so late? Had he been watching over his brother?

He pushed away from the door and started toward her. "Good evening, mistress."

His low voice sent chills over her body. Nervous tremors caused her to shiver, and she smoothed the front of her gown, willing herself to remain calm. "Laird Graham."

"Androu is well?"

"Aye. I only wished to check on him, but he sleeps peacefully, so I'll return to my chamber." As she reached to tug the blanket over Androu, Robert's arm collided with hers.

He chuckled, the sound stirring. Candlelight cast shadows over his rugged face. He stood so close she could see the stubble lining his strong jaw. His eyes darkened with an intensity she couldn't explain. Realizing she stared, prickly heat crept up her neck and spread across her face. She turned back to Androu and tugged the covers over his shoulder.

Robert clutched her arm, and she stilled. His warm touch was comforting. "Thank ye, Cameron."

She studied his brown eyes. He thanked her? Was he trying to apologize for their heated exchanges?

When she straightened, his hand slid to hers, and his thumb rubbed slow circles on her skin. "I've pushed ye hard, lass. My anger at yer Da blinded me to yer kindness."

Mere inches away, she absorbed the heat of his body. He tilted his head to the side and brushed an errant strand of hair behind her ear. The simple gesture jolted her. His calloused fingertips caressed the side of her face, and she longed to lean into him. Arousing memories of him holding her against his hard body triggered a traitorous reaction. She stepped closer, and he lowered his head.

His lips brushed hers in a whisper of a touch. Mead on his breath and his musky scent wafted past her nose. He slipped his hand to the nape of her neck and tugged her closer still, his lips easing over hers. She placed her palms on his chest, itching to explore the sculpted mounds of his muscle. When his tongue slid into her mouth, her senses reeled. His other hand roamed down her back to cup her bottom, molding her against his hard body.

What was she doing? She must gain control of herself, but her body screamed for more of his caresses, more of his hot mouth on her skin. She should be ashamed. Stepping back, her chest heaved. She tugged her wrap tighter around her shoulders and tried to calm her breathing.

Robert dropped his hand to his side. "I should not have done that."

"No, ye shouldn't have. Not when ye hold me against my will."

He exhaled, his hands affixed to his lean hips. "Don't start."

"I know ye understand the importance of peace between our clans. It was ye, after all, that requested the truce." She hoped to play on his sense of righteousness.

He huffed. "A truce yer father made a mockery of."

"My da was pleased and hopeful over yer offer. He didn't do this. Ye must let me go."

"I can't."

Her hands balled into fists at her side. "Why not?"

"I'll not argue the point with ye. Yer da will suffer the consequences of his actions."

"How long do ye intend to hold me prisoner?"

"For as long as it takes yer da to regret his treachery."

She leveled the fiercest scowl she could muster on him. "Ye can't keep me here forever, Laird Graham. I'll leave at the earliest opportunity."

He shook his head, and a smile that didn't lighten his eyes spread over his stony face. "No, mistress. That's where ye're wrong."

Determination to thwart his plans billowed through her. She would show him who was wrong.

~~~

The next morning, Robert gathered his troops on a grassy field south of the castle as the early morning fog dissipated with the sun's warming rays. A group totaling not quite one hundred farmers and sheepherders stood before him,

58

men with little experience of war devices. With the help of his seasoned warriors, he intended to rectify that weakness. Given the continued hostilities, their training was crucial.

He draped his arm around a wooden edifice. "Complete with a melon head, he *does* resemble an English knight."

His men chuckled, and he stepped away from the figure.

"The axe is light enough to use with one hand." He gripped the handle and thrust it high over his head, then slashed down to the left and to the right. "It's small and easy to maneuver, but heavy enough to split open armor and slice through chain-mail."

He held the sharp blade up and jabbed at an invisible enemy. Dropping the axe on the ground, he bent and picked up a mace. "But ye won't find a more useful weapon than the club. Little power is needed to wield it, but the blow it delivers is devastating."

He swung at the wooden knight, and the cudgel slammed into the melon. Rind and fruit spewed in all directions. The men roared. Robert grinned and stepped back while brushing off fragments of pulp stuck to his shirt. "It will require unrelenting practice to become adept with these weapons. Let's get to work."

Robert clutched his swordbreaker and strode down the line of sparring men. Michael clashed blades with Kendrick in an even match. For a moment, Michael appeared to get the best of Kendrick, but at the last minute, Kendrick closed in and ended the competition.

Michael bent over, hands on his knees.

Lachlan slapped him on the back. "Ye almost had 'im."

"Nay, I was only playing with 'im," Kendrick boasted and wiped his face. "He didn't have a chance."

Michael straightened and threw his head back with a howl. "Ye wait until next time. I'll show ye who's playing."

The men laughed.

Robert crossed his arms. Their techniques had definitely improved since they arrived from the rebellion. They would be prepared when called to fight. "Good job."

Movement on the road caught his eye, and he shaded his face from the midday sun. A lad ran from the woods, stumbling and falling in the dirt while looking behind him. He struggled to pick himself up, and with obvious determination, he limped toward Graham Castle.

"What the hell?" Robert breathed out. "That's Davie, from the MacCarthy clan."

"Laird Graham, Laird Graham," the boy screamed.

Robert ran to him, several of his men following. He dreaded what he would hear. He could think of only one reason the lad would come for him.

Sassenachs.

Robert stooped next to the boy of no more than ten years and grasped his shoulders. "What happened, lad?"

Davie's dark eyes were wide, his frantic face grimy and bruised. "The...the English. They attacked us in the night. We need yer help. Ye've got to hurry."

Robert's chest tightened. "Tell me how many soldiers. What of yer clan?"

"I don't know. There were hordes of Sassenachs." Tears streamed down his dirty face. "My mum and sister were raped and killed."

Oh, God, no. Robert lowered his head and briefly closed his eyes. He swallowed the anger surging into his chest. This is why he insisted his men be trained.

The boy whimpered, then broke into sobs while relaying the tale of devastation and destruction wrought by the English marauders.

Barely controlled murderous rage billowed inside Robert. "Ye need to tell me about the soldiers. What do ye remember?"

Davie sniffled. "It was dark. I was asleep upstairs when they broke down our door. I heard my mum scream and then my sister. When I peeked between slats in the wall, I saw

60

soldiers. Everywhere." He put his hands over his face and cried. "I hid. I was scared, and I hid."

Robert held him against his side. "I'm sorry, lad. There was nothing ye could've done."

More tears trickled down Davie's dirty cheeks, but he wiped them away. "I climbed out the window and crawled across the roof. I saw them beating people when they ran, fires were all over the place, and everyone was screaming." He grabbed Robert's arm. "They got the Laird. I saw the soldiers storming up the stairs, and I jumped down and ran here. Laird MacCarthy always told us to go to the Grahams if we needed help."

"Ye did the right thing." Robert turned to his men. "Michael, prepare to move out. Lachlan and Kendrick, meet me in my solar."

Robert threw open the front doors and ran into the keep, ushering Davie into the hall along with him. "Prepare for attack," he shouted.

Nichola hurried across the room with Cameron trailing behind. "What's happened?"

Cameron knelt next to Davie and stroked his head.

"English soldiers marched upon the MacCarthys. We're riding to help, but ye need to prepare in case others are intent upon striking." He glared at Cameron. "Do I need to lock ye up?"

She stood and shook her head. "No, I can help."

"I don't have time to worry over ye, but ye *will not* leave these premises, or I *will* hunt ye down. Do ye understand?"

"Aye."

The thought of the murdering soldiers harming Cameron hit him in the gut. He blinked and shook his head. Nay, he only intended to ensure he had his prisoner secured.

Right?

He didn't have time to consider his reaction. He scaled the stairs to his bedchamber, grabbed his daggers and shield, and ran back to the solar. He dropped his weapons on a chair, leaned over the desk, and rummaged through a stack of papers.

Lachlan and Kendrick marched into the room and stepped to his side.

Robert unrolled a map of Graham Castle's borders and searched for a shortcut to MacCarthy lands. "We'll sneak in the back of the castle. I assume the English have control, and we need to surprise them. Kendrick, take Gilbert, David, and Brian to the northern entrance that sits high overlooking the bailey. Send up yer signal when ye're in position, and pick off as many of the bastards as ye can."

Kendrick studied the drawing. "Aye, we'll take care of 'em."

Robert pointed to the map again and addressed Lachlan. "We'll wait until they're in place. When we see their signal, we storm in."

"Aye, I'm with ye," Lachlan agreed.

Robert folded the map and stuffed it in his pocket. "Let's go."

He led the men down the stairs and into the great hall. Nichola issued orders to clear the room and bring in straw mattresses to hold the women and children gathered in the keep. Servants bustled to do her bidding. His gaze swung across the room as Cameron grabbed a blanket off a table and wrapped it around Davie's shoulders.

Robert turned and raced out the door and down the long flight of stairs, Kendrick and Lachlan following. He swung onto Eton's back. "Michael, I am counting on ye to defend the castle. Close and secure the gates, and do not let anyone in."

"Aye, m'laird, don't worry over us."

Robert and his men thundered out of the bailey heading south toward MacCarthy land. The immense gates banged shut, and heavy iron bars slammed across them.

~~~

Servants carrying linens hurried into the great room. They weaved around the bedding, depositing their bundles. An older man stoked the fire in the stone hearth and several lads scurried in, their arms laden with buckets of water.

Cameron eased her arm around Davie's back. Despair filled his brown eyes. Her chest constricted, and she embraced him. "Laird Graham will do all he can to help yer clan."

She brushed sweaty hair from his face. Dried blood and dirt smeared his cheeks. His clothes were torn, and a ragged cut crossed his shoulder.

A man shouted to bring the cauldrons into the kitchen and several boys ran through the room, dodging servants hurrying in with candles and supplies.

"Come with me." The boy let her guide him to a bench in the main hall. "Lie down, and I'll return shortly."

He stretched out and stared blankly. She draped the cover over him and hurried to the workroom. Her mind raced with possible injuries Robert and his men might suffer in battle. While grabbing stacks of rags for bandages, she uncovered wooden sticks to use for holding broken limbs in place.

Aine and one of the servants, Gretchen, hurried into the room. "What can we do to help?"

"Take these into the hall." Cameron stuffed the splints into their outstretched arms. "We may need them later. And please ask Tessa to begin boiling water," she called as they rushed away.

She grabbed her healing basket and rummaged through the soft wraps for bandages, string and twine. She shook her clay jars of ground ivy and yarrow. "I've still got plenty of my herbs. This should be more than enough."

Relieved, she collected her supplies and returned to her young patient. Several lasses raced past her, and she sidestepped two boys struggling with a barrel of water.

She veered around the servants and made her way back to Davie. "We need to clean ye up a wee bit, lad. Let me help ye out of yer tunic."

Davie sat, and she tugged the shirt over his head. He had several scratches on his side and a long thin cut across his chest. A faint odor of smoke mixed with sweat clung to his weak frame. Bruises marred his thin arms, his skin grimy with soot and ash.

Gretchen returned with a pail of water.

"Thank ye." Cameron handed a container to her. "I need some in this bowl."

The maid poured the water, set the bucket at Cameron's feet, and shuffled back to the kitchen calling over her shoulder, "I'll bring ye more."

Davie lay down, and Cameron stooped beside him. She ran a soft rag over his face and chest, managing to wipe away most of the dirt. Her heart broke at his empty, faraway look. When he closed his eyes, Cameron swallowed hard and prayed the Lord would be with him and all the MacCarthys.

~~~

MacCarthy Castle

Flames curled around charred wooden remains. Homes at the base of MacCarthy Castle were gutted and blackened from smoke, and a few old men and women shuffled through the rubbish and debris.

Robert's gut tightened. He would see the murdering Sassenachs dead. He peered past dense foliage. Enemy soldiers tossed aside charred ruins, hunting for valuables, anything of worth they could steal.

With the horses left a distance away, Robert and his men had sneaked up on the enemy. He held up a hand, signaling his men to get in position. Kendrick and several others disappeared into the thick woods surrounding the castle.

With the setting sun, the afternoon light accented heavy acrid smoke. The drizzle of earlier rains caused steam to rise in the air, and a pungent smell of death hovered over the grounds. Angry shouts came from inside the bailey.

Robert motioned his men toward the castle. They crept forward, waiting and watching for Kendrick's signal. A few minutes later, a single blazing arrow shot high into the sky. Barbs whistled into the bailey.

Men screamed and shouted as Robert and his men stormed into the yard. The English stumbled over lifeless bodies and discarded rubbish, frantically grabbing for their weapons.

A soldier attacked Robert. The two circled each other before Robert lunged and thrust his blade into the man's gut. Shouts behind him and the clanging of clashing steel resonated through the bailey.

Another of the enemy rushed in. Robert parried blow for blow with the burly warrior, forcing the man backward. His swordbreaker grabbed the attacker's weapon, and with a twist, snapped the metal. The soldier backed, tripped over rubble, and Robert plunged the sharp sword into the man's chest.

From behind, a man roared and charged. Robert spun and raised his shield. Vibrations from the strike rippled down his arm. Muscles straining, he shoved the man away. He twisted, darted to the right, and clubbed the back of the soldier's head.

He pivoted to the left. Lachlan struggled to fend off two assailants, blood soaking his shirt. Robert jumped over a dead body and rammed his elbow into the face of one of the men battling Lachlan. The whoreson went down with a satisfying thud, and Robert slammed his shield over the soldier's head.

Robert spun as Lachlan finished off the other soldier. "Are ye all right, man?" he yelled over the noise.

Lachlan held his injured shoulder. "Aye."

Breathing hard, Robert scanned the bailey. The fighting ended as quickly as it started. Though he saw many of his men injured, all remained on their feet. He turned to find Kendrick at the top of the keep steps, his sword held high, signaling they controlled the castle.

Robert took a deep breath. His tense muscles eased, but the carnage around him made his stomach roil. The senseless brutality pierced his heart.

Injured and dying men moaned. Dead bodies lay scattered through the inner bailey. Children wandered aimlessly amongst them, their lost faces smeared with dirt and soot. Adding to the confusion, dogs barked while running around the muddy yard. A crumpled wagon frame smoldered, flames flickering around the burnt ruins. Fire from the stables leapt into the sky, and the thick acrid stench clogged his nose and burned his eyes.

Several nude women lay splayed in the dirt, their stares frozen. Blood coagulated around them, beginning with their slit throats and running down their mutilated torsos. Bile rose in his throat, and he turned from the sight. While he and his men may have dispatched the English, the soldiers had nonetheless inflicted immense damage to the MacCarthy people.

Robert ran up the stairs and into the keep. Broken and overturned furniture, fragments of busted crockery, and debris covered the floor. He marched into the hall, his boots crushing rubbish.

"MacCarthy?" he shouted, searching for Buford.

Kendrick ran into the room and skidded to a halt. "They're in the bowels of the dungeon."

Robert prayed his old friend lived. He dashed down the narrow, steep flight of stairs and descended into the cold recesses of the castle. A dank, musty odor assailed him. Frigid water pooled around his boots, but he sloshed his way through the passage.

"MacCarthy? Where are ye?"

"We're here!" Men's voices and shouts drifted from the darkness. "They locked us in."

"It's the Grahams. We came to help," Robert yelled and turned the corner to see Buford peering out a small window set in a solid oak door. Robert raised the heavy iron bar from the brackets, and freed a room full of battered men. They stumbled into the dank corridor.

"Thank ye, man," Buford gasped, and grabbed Robert's hand, pulled him to his chest, and patted him on the back. "Thank ye."

The old laird's thinning grey hair lay plastered against his head. An irritated, red cut traversed his cheek over purplish-

66

black bruises. His left eye was swollen half shut. Though beaten, he appeared to be stable.

Kendrick and Brian wrenched open another cell door, and scores of wounded and battered men joined those in the already crowded hallway.

"We arrived as fast as we could," Robert said.

"Those murdering bastards attacked in the dead of night. We were caught off guard. That'll never happen again." Buford wiped his face and paused. "How did ye know we needed ye?"

"Young Davie ran to us for help."

The old laird smiled. "He's a good lad." He grabbed Robert's arm and shook his hand again. "If ever I can repay ye..."

More men rushed from the dark, forbidding cells. "Let's get out of here," one yelled, and the group hurried for the narrow steps.

The wall sconces barely lit the narrow corridor as Robert helped Buford up the long flight of stairs.

When they stepped into the main hall, the laird gasped. "Lock these bastards up," he ordered, and kicked a soldier lying on the ground.

His men rushed the injured, forcefully grabbing and shoving them toward the dungeon. Dragging those unable to walk, the MacCarthys ignored the enemy soldiers' screams and threw them headfirst down the long flight of stairs.

Robert left the MacCarthys securing the men and stepped out-of-doors. Lachlan leaned against a wall, holding his arm to his side. Robert made his way over to him. "Let me see."

Blood soaked his friend's sleeve from a ragged hole that gaped open.

Robert tugged off his belt and looped it around the top of the injured arm. "He got ye pretty good." He searched Lachlan's pale face. "Can ye ride?"

"Aye."

"Kendrick?"

67

His friend stooped over one of the dead soldiers, searching the man's pockets. He raised his head. "What?"

"Help Lachlan to his horse and have the men mount up."

"I don't need help," Lachlan complained.

"Don't argue," Robert commanded.

Lachlan hesitated, then stalked off, his gait unsteady. David half-carried one of the McCarthy men through the bailey, as Brian held a small lass in his arms and climbed the stairs. Others brought the Grahams' horses into the clearing.

With the immediate needs of battling the enemy taken care of, Robert and his men were ready to return to Graham Castle. He stepped beside Buford. "Ye've got everything under control?"

The man placed his hand on Robert's shoulder. "Thanks to ye." He paused. "Ye're welcome to stay the night with us. I'll have our healer tend yer men."

Robert thought about *his* healer. Dark hair framing her soft face, her luscious lips begging for his kiss. He shook his traitorous thoughts away and glanced over Buford's shoulder at the destruction. "Nay, we've only a short ride home. I've got a small crew manning the gates so we'd best head out."

Buford grasped Robert's hand. "Thank ye again for all ye did."

~~~

Upon hearing the men returning, Cameron raced from the main hall and into the bailey.

Robert jumped from his horse, shouting orders to get the wounded inside. Her heart leapt into her throat. He was safe. Why did relief pour through her at seeing his face? She composed herself and hurried into the yard.

Blood smeared Tavish's cheek, and Iohne leaned on Kendrick, hobbling on one leg. Brian helped Gilbert off his horse. The man's arm hung limp against his side.

She motioned to the men. "Come this way. Place them on the tables and straw pallets set about the hall."

68

Robert helped Lachlan off his horse. Blood soaked Lachlan's tunic, and his eyes were weak and heavy.

"Get him inside," Cameron said, as she led the way up the stairs. She weaved around the straw mattresses to an empty pallet.

Robert half carried his friend, helping him shuffle into the room.

She shook out a blanket. "Lay him down here."

Robert eased Lachlan down, and Cameron draped the cover over the injured man's legs. Robert paused, studying her. "I've got to see to the others."

A ragged cut crisscrossed his forehead. Her fingers rose to his face, and dark stubble brushed her palm. "Ye're hurt."

His eyes softened so briefly she wondered if she imagined it. He pulled back. "'Tis nothing."

Her hand dropped to her side as he turned and rushed from the room.

Kendrick helped Iohne ease onto one of the beds. The man yelled. Grasping his leg, his face contorted.

"Bring water for pain draught," Cameron yelled.

A servant dropped a bucket and water splashed across the floor. "Watch what ye're about," a woman hollered.

Cameron's head jerked toward the shrill sound. A buxom servant with blonde hair, hands firmly affixed to curvaceous hips, reprimanded the girl. She turned a glare on Cameron, and her lip curled in a sneer. A chill ran down Cameron's spine at the venomous look.

"Here's more water." A lad placed a bucket on the floor between several pallets.

A graveled bellow pulled Cameron's gaze to Aine as she led Gilbert toward a pallet against the far wall. He dropped to his knees while clutching his arm, his face and clothes bathed in sweat.

"I will clean the wounds and ready the men for ye, mistress," the old healer called and filled a bowl.

"Rip the cloth into strips we can use to bandage them," Cameron instructed a servant.

Nichola stepped up behind Lachlan, her hand over her chest. Her frantic eyes searched his body. "Oh, no," she whispered, and stooped next to him.

His eyes fluttered shut, and he fought to remain awake. "I'll be fine, lass."

Cameron rummaged through her clay jars and extracted several valerian roots. "He needs pain draught. Crush these in warm water, and get him to drink it."

Nichola grasped a bowl off the table and hurried to the hearth.

Cameron withdrew the knife from her basket.

"Now ye've got yer chance to be rid of me," he said smiling, but his eyes spoke his mind. He did not trust her.

"Don't be absurd. Lie still." She cut the tunic from his shoulder and peeled the blood-crusted fabric off. Dirt stuck to the edges of a large dark hole in his bicep.

Nichola stopped short, her eyes wide. "Here's the pain mixture."

Cameron held the bowl to Lachlan's mouth. "Ye need to drink this."

Sitting at Lachlan's head, Nichola whispered to him, caressing and comforting. "Please. The brew will help ye."

Was there something between them?

His eyes narrowed, but he opened his mouth and let Cameron dribble the contents in while watching her closely.

She placed the bowl on a side table. Her forearm pushed a stray lock from her forehead, and she gazed across the room, hoping to find Robert. He invaded her thoughts. She found herself constantly searching for him, wanting to be near him.

Shaking her head, she turned to Lachlan and inspected the injury. A lump stuck in her throat. The stab wound was deep. While it missed the major muscles of his arm, the injury could be devastating for a warrior.

Twenty stitches later, she sat back on her heels and wiped her brow. "Spread this salve across the gash. And then he needs to rest."

70

Nichola's brow knitted, distress lining her forehead. "Will he be all right?"

Cameron stared at Lachlan's pale face. He had tormented her—gave her no consideration. "Aye, he's too ornery to die."

~~~

Hours passed with Robert watching Cameron flit from man to man, administering concoctions and salves. Sitting before the hearth, he stretched his legs toward the fire and settled in for the remainder of the night. He would keep an eye on her and ensure she did not attempt to escape in the confusion. At least he tried to convince himself that was the reason his gaze constantly returned to the woman.

By morning, she finally finished stitching, bandaging, and setting broken bones. From outward appearances, she genuinely seemed to care about his men. She even comforted his toughest warriors, while gently working to heal them.

"Thank ye, lovely miss," Philip said, holding Cameron's hand.

"Don't ye sweet talk me. I saw how ye gave Nichola a hard time over yer draught," Cameron teased and moved to the next man.

Robert shook his head, stepped to a table and poured a mug of mead. He drained the contents, the liquid soothing his parched throat. Wiping his mouth on the back of his sleeve, his gaze once again sought the object of his dreams, the reason for his sleepless nights.

She worked her way toward him. Wisps of dark hair had slipped from the strip of fabric holding her locks, and framed her face. His gaze traveled to her gown's bodice covering treasures he longed to explore, curves his fingers yearned to touch.

"Ye're next, Laird Graham."

His gaze lifted to her face. "I'm fine," he answered sternly.

71

"No, ye've got a gash across yer forehead that needs tending." She rinsed her fingers in a bowl of water on the table before him and motioned with her elbow. "Sit."

He dropped onto the stool in front of her. She had the most beautiful green eyes filled with hazel shards streaking into deep onyx centers. Her breasts were level with his face. All he had to do was lean forward... She bent over him, and his cock twitched.

Dabbing the cloth on his face, she wiped away dried blood. Her hands trembled. Did his closeness affect her the way it did him? He couldn't take his mind off her luscious curves. He could still feel her tight rear snuggled in his lap when he'd spirited her away from MacDougall Castle. His manhood swelled with the arousing memories.

Cameron smeared a salve on his forehead. "I don't think I need to bandage the cut."

She wiped her hands on the rag and peered down at him as she dropped the cloth in a bowl. A jar slipped from her other hand and fell over in her basket. She fumbled with the supplies while replacing the vials. She licked her lips, then turned away from him toward the room filled with injured men.

"Will they survive?" he asked.

"I believe so. Some suffered cuts and broken bones, but fortunately, other than Lachlan, none were too serious. As long as we can ward off any threat of fever, they should be all right."

"Mistress Cameron." Aine hurried toward them from across the room. Her white hair stuck out at odd angles around her head, and she wrung her wrinkled hands. "Ralph has torn his stitches loose."

"I'll be right there."

"Thank ye." The woman turned and shuffled off.

Robert slid his hand down her silky hair and brushed the side of her face with his knuckle. Her plump lips parted. His thumb rubbed her soft cheek, then traced the edges of her luscious mouth.

72

"I...I must tend yer man," she whispered, her mouth closing over the tip of his finger.

He sucked in air at the innocent gesture.

Her eyes widened, the firelight flickering in the green depths.

He held her gaze. God's blood, she was beautiful, and he wanted her.

She ran her hands down the front of her gown, then turned and hurried away. With every sway of her hips, his cock pulsed in agony.

His gaze rested on her as she tended Ralph and gave instructions to the servants on the needs of the injured men. Nichola sat at Lachlan's side, holding his hand while he slept.

"Ye need yer rest," Cameron insisted.

"I'll go up shortly."

Cameron mesmerized Robert. She had helped his clan again, but he scowled at his softening feelings toward her. She was a MacDougall, here because of what her father did to his family.

But, he couldn't deny the lass mystified him. He stole her from her home, pushed her to her limits to treat his kin, and still she offered her healing ways. She displayed steely determination to mend and patch up his men with limitless patience and kindness.

Robert frowned. His thoughts punched his gut. He would need to stay away from her, steel his emotions *and* his body against her. She would not tunnel her way into his soul and foil his plans to make Alastair pay. The old laird had not suffered enough.

Determined to punish her clan, he longed to plunge his sword into Alastair for the actions he took against his people. His resolve hardened.

Alastair *would* pay.

~~~

Cameron entered her chamber and set her basket on the table beside the bed. With her hands on her lower back, she leaned over, stretching aching muscles. She gingerly shuffled to the washbasin and shed her gown. Clad in her thin chemise, goose bumps rose on her arms, and she quickly splashed water on her face. Stopping only long enough to throw another bunch of peat on the fire, she slipped under the soft, warm blankets.

She stared into the flames, her thoughts on Robert Graham. She wanted to hate him. She *should* hate him. Why did he affect her so? His nearness had her pulse beating fast, her insides tied in knots. She stammered, fumbled, and shook around him. To her horror, she admired him.

Guilt washed over her.

How could she have these feelings toward her captor? Toward the man who snatched her from her home as revenge against Da?

But...he was strong and passionate about the Scottish rebellion, fighting for their freedom. She saw his honorable character, going to the aid of the MacCarthys and the gentle manner in which he treated Davie.

Scrunching her eyes tight, she willed her pulse to stop racing, her hands to stop trembling. Her feelings were not rational. She turned over, smashed her pillow, and jerked the blankets over her shoulder.

She was merely overwrought and exhausted. With adequate rest, she would think clearly and eliminate her delusional thoughts. Robert and his men watched her every move, but in several days, they would leave for a hunt.

When they left, she would escape.

Chapter Five

Early morning mist swirled around Robert's feet. Pink and red streaked the sky, the sun not yet cresting the horizon. Men and women wandered through the bailey performing chores. He nodded in greeting, wrapped his cloak tighter around his neck and strode into the barn.

Kendrick threw a saddle on his horse. "We'll be ready to head out shortly."

"Good, we'll have an early start." Robert patted Eton's rump as he stepped around him.

"Aye, the men are anxious for a little playtime," Kendrick called over his mount's back.

"We'll see who's playin' when I bag the largest buck," Philip teased.

"Ye'd best get going now if ye plan to beat me," Kendrick shot back. "I seem to remember the last puny thing ye brought in."

Robert chuckled as he cinched the girth on the saddle. He led Eton from the barn and into the bailey with several men following, anxious to get underway.

Nichola and Lachlan strolled across the yard while Robert secured his bow and arrows to Eton's saddle. Cameron stepped beside his sister. Why was she in the bailey? He would wager she was not here to wish him well and see them off.

"I packed some bread, cheese and dried beef jerky for ye." Nichola handed him a worn sack. "How long will ye be gone?"

"We'll be back within a day or so."

Cameron's eyes darted from man to man, watching them pack, readying for the hunt. Why was she so interested?

She was truly a beautiful lass. Her dark hair blew around her face, and he longed to reach out and feel its silky softness, to embrace her and…

Shite!

"I expect ye to be here when I return," he snapped at her, before addressing Lachlan. "Make sure she's watched. I

75

don't cherish the thought of chasing after her." He took in her flashing, green eyes. "If ye need to lock her up, then do so."

Cameron glared at him. "There's no need to lock me up. If I were of a mind to leave, I would whether ye have me guarded or not," she added defiantly.

Robert adjusted Eton's reins while listening to her challenging words. He stepped around the horse and towered over her. She stood her ground and tilted her head back to glare at him.

He looped his finger into the neck of her gown and hauled her face within inches of his. "I will have yer word ye will not leave this castle, or I'll hog-tie ye and throw ye in the dungeon until I return."

He pierced her with his stare, pausing to let his words sink in. He would ensure she was here when he returned, even if he had to play the brute to do so. "Do ye understand, mistress? Do I make myself clear?"

Cameron's chin rose, and she frowned.

"It's yer choice. What'll it be?"

Robert's men quietly shuffled about as though uneasy with his rough treatment of the beautiful woman who healed with a soft touch. He didn't care. He would not let her comment go unanswered.

Seconds went by with Cameron continuing to glare at him.

Brazen wench.

"Kendrick, toss me yer rope."

His friend grimaced, his eyes squinting. For a moment, Robert thought he would disobey. Finally, Kendrick untied the cord on his saddle and threw it to him.

Robert grabbed her wrist and looped the rope around it. "I won't be worrying about ye fleeing while I'm away."

He turned her around and jerked her other hand behind her back.

"Wait." Cameron wrenched against his grip. "I won't try to leave."

He continued. He would not put up with her insolence.

76

"Please."

"What's that, Mistress MacDougall? I didn't hear ye."

She twisted to face him. "I said I will not try to leave."

Her voice rose with strength, but nonetheless, her chin quivered. Her eyes filled with tears, and a twinge of guilt bubbled up, but he dismissed his weakness. He would admit she had helped his clan and saved Androu and Duncan. But she was still the enemy.

He stared down at her. "See that ye don't, or ye'll regret yer actions."

~~~

Cameron sat before the fire in her chamber's hearth attempting to read a book. But try as she might, she could not concentrate on the pages before her. After this morning's episode with Robert, Lachlan had whisked her to her chambers and barred the door. He would not take a chance she'd break her word and attempt to leave while Robert was away.

What possessed her to challenge him? She had virtually eliminated any chance she might have to escape. Cameron slammed the book closed. She could have at least gained freedom within the confines of the bailey where she'd have had the opportunity to study her options. She rebelled at being held prisoner and fumed at Robert's threat to keep her *hog-tied* in the cesspool of the dungeon. How dare he treat her this way.

A light tap on her door interrupted her thoughts. "Come in," she barked.

Nichola stuck her head in before sheepishly slipping into the room.

Cameron's shoulders drooped. "I'm sorry I snapped at ye."

Nichola knelt beside her chair. "I understand how ye feel. I'm sorry ye're in this situation. I wish I could do something for ye."

"Ye can. Ye can help me get home."

Nichola shook her head. "Ye know I can't do that."

"It's not right." Cameron rubbed her forehead. "Yer brother has no reason to hold me prisoner."

"I cannot…"

Cameron exhaled and paused. "I know." She placed her hand on Nichola's. "Ye didn't come in to talk about that."

"Nay. I hate to ask, but Glenda's husband, Walter, is feeling poorly. Would ye mind tending him? Glenda is mighty worried."

Cameron stood and grabbed her woolen wrap. "Where is Lachlan? He might not allow me to leave with ye."

"Oh, no, he would want ye to treat Walter."

Cameron sighed. "Let me get my basket, and ye can take me to him."

The women strolled down the main stairs and into the bailey, arm in arm, making their way to a small cottage set back from the entrance to the castle. Nichola rapped on the door, and an old woman with white hair peeked out. Her tense expression eased, and she opened the door wider. "Oh, Mistress Nichola, thank ye for comin'."

"We came as soon as we heard about Walter." Nichola placed her arm around Cameron. "Glenda, this is Cameron MacDougall."

The frail woman stiffened, and her eyes widened.

Nichola grasped Glenda's arm. "She's a *healer* and is here to have a look at yer Walter."

The woman studied her weak husband lying in bed and wrung her hands. "Well, I…that is, I don't know."

"Glenda, Walter is sick, and he *needs* attention."

Glenda's shoulders slumped. "Aye, we need yer help, mistress."

Cameron patted Glenda's hand before hanging her wrap on the back of a chair. "What seems to be the problem?"

"I don't rightly know. He was fine early this mornin' but by mid-day, he was complaining of 'is belly hurting."

Placing her basket next to the bed, Cameron stepped to Walter's side. She touched his forehead. His skin was too warm. "Did he have anything to eat?"

78

"Jes his usual. I gave him a thick slice of bread with a little honey."

That should not have caused his illness. "Walter, do ye have any pain?"

He groaned, nodded and held his torso.

Cameron touched his abdomen and was surprised at the tautness of his skin. Pulling the blanket down, her eyes widened at his distended abdomen.

Nichola inhaled sharply and put a hand to her mouth.

Images of Mum's extended belly flashed before Cameron's mind. Familiar tentacles of doubt spread through her gut and wrapped around her heart. Her fingers trembled. A sword injury, broken bone or burn was one thing. Something growing inside the body was another.

Cameron swallowed hard, and her mind raced. It could be many things, but unlike Mum's illness, it was something that came on rather suddenly. She rummaged through her basket and addressed Glenda. "Has he been vomiting?"

"Nay, he jes lies in bed groanin'."

"What can I do?" Nichola asked.

"Hand me a bowl and start boiling water."

Glenda pointed at the hearth. "I've got some over the cook fire."

"Do ye also have cold water? It will help to bring his fever down."

Glenda shuffled into a makeshift kitchen and dipped a bowl in a bucket.

Cameron extracted a jar of dried rhubarb roots and crushed them on the bedside table.

The old woman handed the bowl to Cameron. "Here, mistress."

"Thank ye." Cameron soaked a cloth in the cool water and gently ran it across Walter's face.

Glenda sat at her husband's head, and stroked his hair, her eyes wide.

"And here's the hot water," Nichola said, holding a pot. She poured the water into another bowl, and Cameron stirred in the roots. The liquid immediately turned brown and put off an odd odor. As she mixed the brew, she blew into the cup and cooled the concoction.

A knock sounded on the door, and Nichola hurried to answer it.

"Ye have Mistress MacDougall with ye?" a man asked.

"Aye, Michael. Walter isn't feeling well, and she's tending him."

"Ye see that she does not leave without ye. I'll have a man waiting outside to escort ye back to the keep."

Nichola closed the door and turned.

Cameron's gaze locked onto her friend's.

Nichola's blue eyes softened, and her shoulders shrugged as she mouthed, "I'm sorry."

Cameron nodded and turned to Walter. "Ye've got to drink this. It doesn't smell verra good, so gulp it as fast as ye can. I know 'tis awfully tart, but take it down."

Glenda scooted onto the bed at his head and pushed on his shoulders. "Sit up, Walter. Ye must do as she says."

He leaned forward, and his wife helped hold him up. Wrinkling his old nose, he sputtered, drinking the foul concoction.

After he lay back, Cameron clutched Glenda's arm. "The potion will cause him to empty his stomach, and he'll have to use the chamber pot. I'm sorry, but we need to purge his system. I'm afraid he has food poisoning."

The old woman gasped, her eyes wide. "Food poisoning?"

"Aye, he has the symptoms of it." She prayed her diagnosis was correct. Memories of Mum vomiting and wasting away flashed through her mind.

"Here is the chamber pot." Nichola handed the container to Cameron.

Within minutes, the concoction took effect. Cameron held a cold cloth over his brow. "Ye're going to be all right, Walter. Let it out."

The women tended him through the night while he battled his illness. Once he settled down, Cameron sat back in the chair and watched over him.

Nichola offered a mug of ale. "I think ye can use this."

Cameron's shoulders relaxed. "Aye, I can."

Glenda dozed in the chair next to her husband.

"Do ye think he'll be all right?" Nichola whispered.

"He's weak, but I think he'll recover." Cameron looked past her and around the cottage. "What could've caused it?" She got up and walked through the makeshift kitchen, fingering the items on a worn wooden table. "Glenda said he only had bread," she whispered. "But I wonder…"

"What? What is it?"

"I don't know. He must have eaten *something* that made him sick." Sighing, she turned and walked back to Walter's side. He rested comfortably. She lifted the blanket and pressed his stomach. "His belly is no longer tight."

Tension eased from her sore muscles, and her body relaxed. Her diagnosis had proven correct. A spark of hope flickered in the pit of her belly. She had saved Walter.

After placing the cover around him, she stepped to Glenda and gently shook her shoulder. "Let me help ye to bed so ye can rest."

The old woman's tired eyes blinked several times. "Will my Walter be all right?"

"I believe he will. Try to sleep."

Glenda curled up next to her husband and soon was lightly snoring.

Cameron sat on a bench next to the bed, and patted Nichola's leg. "Why don't ye go to the keep and get some rest? I'll stay with them for a while until I know Walter is over the worst of his illness."

Nichola sat a bit straighter. Her eyes grew wide. "Uh, I'll wait here and keep ye company."

Cameron studied her new friend. Michael had forbidden Nichola from leaving Cameron alone while they were away from the keep. She also knew he had the cottage door guarded.

Her chance of escape would have to wait.

A few hours later, dawn broke with Walter still resting comfortably. Nichola and Cameron slipped from the hut and strolled to the keep. The residents had filled the main hall to break their fast.

Nichola tugged on Cameron's arm. "Come have a sweet bun with me before ye retire."

Lachlan marched toward them. His dark scowl spoke volumes.

"No, thank ye. I think I'll go up to my chamber. I'm a bit tired." She patted Nichola's arm and stepped around Lachlan, then started up the stairs.

"Where have ye been?" Lachlan demanded.

Cameron's ears perked up as she reached the next floor. She slipped around the side of the landing and peeked down at Lachlan and Nichola.

"We were with Walter and Glenda. Walter was verra sick, but Cameron healed him." Lachlan pushed a strand of hair from Nichola's face as she continued. "I feel so badly for her. She's a loving lass."

He dropped his hand, and shook his head. "Don't forget, she's yer enemy."

Nichola squared her shoulders and exhaled loudly. "Ye don't know her, Lachlan. She's not like ye think."

"She's a MacDougall. That's all I need to know." He turned and strode through the front door.

~~~

"Mistress?"

The fog of sleep surrounded Cameron, but someone shook her shoulder.

"Mistress MacDougall?"

Cameron squinted, trying to focus on the young lass wringing her hands. She rose on her elbow and rubbed her scratchy eyes. "Aye? What is it?"

"We have a problem. A number of people have come down with a bellyache, and they're verra sick."

82

That immediately caught her attention, and she listened in earnest to the young girl.

"Mistress Nichola is asleep, and I didn't know what to do."

Cameron threw back the blankets and swung her legs over the side of the bed. "Give me a few minutes, and I'll be right down."

"Oh, thank ye, mistress. Thank ye," the girl said, and ran from the room.

Cameron padded across the floor and stopped in front of the basin. She yawned and splashed cold water on her face. She couldn't have been in bed more than a few hours, and she was exhausted.

The room was cold with the fire burning low in the hearth. Rubbing her arms, she grabbed her gown, slipped the borrowed dress over her head, and grasped her warm wrap. She shivered, drawing the cloth tight around her shoulders.

"A bellyache," she muttered, before she picked up her healing basket and headed down the stairs.

When she reached the bottom floor, Dara, one of the serving girls, ran over to her. "Thank ye for coming."

"What's wrong?"

Dara shook her head. "I donnae know. Robin came in a while ago asking for somethin' to settle her stomach. Then, Hume and Tavish sat on the bench complaining their bellies hurt."

Bonnie entered the hall, holding her middle and groaning. "Mistress, I don't feel well."

Her mind whirled. She stepped to Bonnie, and placed her hand on her forehead. She was warm and pale.

Cameron turned to Dara. "Where are the others?"

"In the kitchen."

"Is there a place I can use to examine them?"

The maid pointed to a door across the hall. "I will have some lads bring mattresses into that room."

Cameron took Bonnie by the elbow and guided her across the hall. "Please get someone to help the others into the room and boil water."

A short time later, several lads placed straw pallets in the small space. "Would ye start a fire in the hearth? It is freezing in here." She shivered and helped Bonnie lie down. "Tell me what ails ye."

The woman groaned and held her stomach. "It hurts."

"May I have a look?"

Bonnie tugged the blanket down and lifted her gown. Upon seeing her extended belly, Cameron again suspected food poisoning.

Nichola hurried into the room, tugging a blue woolen wrap around her. "Ye should've called for me." She helped Robin settle on the pallet. Hume and Tavish dropped next to her. Nichola's blonde brows scrunched together, her blue eyes filled with worry. "What's happened?"

"I don't know, but I suspect it's something they've all eaten." Cameron searched her basket. "Ye need to stop the kitchen from serving anything until we find out what's causing this."

"I will. What else can I do?"

"I need the same things I used last night for Walter, several bowls and a bucket of hot water." Cameron's gaze skimmed the mattresses. "And I'm afraid we'll need a number of chamber pots."

Nichola rushed from the room calling for Aine and Gretchen, while Cameron examined the men and women. Each one had the same symptoms so she extracted the container of dried rhubarb roots.

Dara ushered several lads carrying heavy buckets into the room. "Here's the hot water."

"And here are the bowls ye requested," Nichola said as she stepped beside Cameron and placed the wooden containers on a table beside the hearth.

Aine shuffled in while tugging a wrap around her shoulders. "I'm here to help, mistress."

Rosalind, the bossy, buxom blonde servant, sauntered in behind them. She glared at Cameron, her arms crossing her chest.

Gretchen motioned to Rosalind. "Will ye hurry?"

"We need to make a tonic to purge their systems." Cameron clutched a rhubarb root. "That's the only way to get the poison out."

"Oh, dear." Aine raised her eyebrows. "We may need more chamber pots."

"Take some of these roots and crush them in a bowl." Cameron did so as they watched. "Add a small amount of hot water, and stir the contents well. The brew doesn't smell or taste good, but if they can drink it, they'll feel better."

Nichola grabbed several bowls and passed them out to the women. Rosalind's upper lip curled into a sneer. She roughly mashed the rhubarb, slinging bits and pieces of fleshy stems and leaves onto the table.

Only a worktable away, Cameron picked up a bowl and strained to hear her conversation.

"What's wrong with ye?" Aine questioned.

"I donnae want ta help her." Rosalind waved her arm in Cameron's direction. "She thinks she's so high and mighty, like *she's* the Lady of Graham Castle. Robert...I mean *Laird Graham...*" She grinned when Aine raised her eyebrow. "Shouldnae have brought her here."

"Ye have nothing to say about what Laird Graham does."

"Ye donnae know anything. He takes *me* ta 'is bed and makes love ta *me*." Rosalind broke off another root, threw it in the bowl, then pointed at Aine. "And ye'd best watch the way ye treat me. *I* will be Lady of this castle afore long."

Cameron's stomach roiled. Robert bedded Rosalind? Somehow, the thought greatly disturbed her. She glanced at the servant. No doubt, he enjoyed her voluptuous curves.

"Psh, that'll be the day. Either ye're daydreaming or ye're completely mad." Aine scoffed before continuing to crush the dried rhubarbs.

85

The woman glared at Aine. Hatred radiated from her eyes. "When I get with child, he'll have nay choice but ta marry me. I'll have power over ye and all the servants. Ye'll be waiting on my every need."

She'd had about enough of Rosalind and her *plans.* Cameron weaved around the table and stood before her. "How are ye getting along? About finished?"

Rosalind roughly plunked her bowl on the table, spilling the smashed roots and stalked from the room.

"Do not worry over her." Aine handed her bowl to Cameron. "Do ye want me to start passing the brew out?"

"Aye, we need to get each one to drink a full cup."

Gretchen, Aine and Nichola helped administer the brew. Before long, the patients gagged and retched.

"I need help." A woman frantically called out, and entered the room carrying a small child. "My Marie is sick."

Cameron rushed to the woman and took the child.

The mother's dark eyes filled with worry. "She was fine this morning."

And so the day went, but by early evening, the flow of people subsided. Straw pallets filled with patients lined the walls in the great hall, while others lay on blankets placed on the hard floor.

Cameron pushed a lock of hair from her eyes and stepped to Gretchen who was helping Silas. "How's he doing?"

"Well, he's been vomiting, and he can't stay off of the chamber pot," Gretchen said, shaking her head.

Cameron patted the woman's shoulder. "That's what he needs to be doing."

Her gaze slid across the resting clan members. What could have caused the illness? She motioned to Nichola. "Come with me. We need to find out what they all ate this morning."

They strolled into the kitchen. The servants had cleared away the dishes, and the worktables were clean.

"What was served at the morning meal?" Cameron asked.

86

"The usual mutton and thick bread," Nichola replied.

Cameron picked through containers, peering inside and sniffing the contents. Nothing appeared out of the ordinary.

"Here's some of the leftover bread." Nichola handed a piece to Cameron.

She pinched the crust and tasted the crumbs. Her shoulders shrugged, and she shook her head. "I don't taste anything unusual."

Cameron continued searching the kitchen and spotted a large container on the floor. "What's in that?"

"Oh, that's where we pour the milk. Lads milk the goats every morning, and we collect it in that barrel."

Cameron took the lid off the empty container and leaned over it. A sour stench buffeted her face. She jerked away, her hand covering her nose. "Oh my, this smells awful."

She heaved the large jug into the middle of the floor and grabbed the torch off the wall. Peering into the urn, she understood the problem.

"Nichola, green chunks are lining the barrel." She wrinkled her nose while examining the slimy substance. "If they drank the milk stored in here, they would become verra sick."

"Oh nay, Tessa would never have…" She gasped and put her hand to her mouth.

Cameron straightened. "What is it?"

"I just remembered Tessa hasn't been here. She's with her daughter who lives at the MacCarthy's. After the attack, she asked to stay with her for a few days." Nichola looked back at the rancid milk curds and shook her head. "She left in such a hurry, I'd wager she failed to mention she washes this barrel out after each meal."

Cameron sighed with relief and stuck the lid back on the container. "Well, at least we know what caused the poisoning."

"I'll ask someone to take this out-of-doors and clean it straight away."

With the mystery solved, Cameron slipped back to the main hall. Flames from the large hearth sent shadows dancing across the high ceiling. Candlelight flickered in candelabras positioned throughout the room casting a glow over her recovering patients. She stooped beside a young lad and ran her hand across his head, then tucked a blanket around his shoulders.

With the exception of an occasional cough or snore, the hall was quiet. Cameron eased into a chair next to the hearth and soaked up the warmth of the fire. It felt good to sit. Her back ached, her muscles tender.

Nichola touched Cameron's shoulder. "Ye're so verra tired. Why don't ye go on to yer bed?"

Cameron patted Nichola's hand. "I'll rest here in case someone needs me."

Nichola placed a soft wrap around Cameron's shoulders. "Verra well. Goodnight."

Her retreating footsteps faded. Wood creaked as Cameron relaxed against the back of the chair. She tugged the wrap tight, and her gaze skimmed the room. Men, women and children, slept on pallets scattered throughout the hall. She had helped them through a serious illness. Food poisoning, if not caught soon enough, could easily kill. Hope soared through her body with another successful treatment.

She shook her head. The Grahams had wheedled their way into her soul. All the more reason to leave and stop further attacks Symon might have planned. What if he lay in wait? With Robert gone, he could storm the castle and take over. She had to get home. Da surely did not know of her cousin's actions.

A cough interrupted Cameron's thoughts. Aggie kissed Marie's little head and wrapped a blanket around her wee shoulders. Cameron's heart tugged at the sweet scene. She longed to have her own children someday, but she would not tolerate a husband's infidelity.

All men do it. Although Mum voiced the excuse, her eyes held the pain of Da's affairs. No, Cameron yearned for a faithful man who would treat her as his partner and not quell her study of the healing arts. However, that vision dissipated with each passing year. With her desire to become a healer, she had discouraged suitors. Her focus had always been on learning, and now she worried her age of four-and-twenty years would soon become an issue for having children.

She heard the whispers in her clan. Their comments of 'spinster' and 'past her prime' had hurt, but they were true. She had let her dream consume her, and now she questioned her conviction. Did she truly desire to live her life alone? Never marrying, never experiencing the love of a man or giving birth to their children?

Faint morning light seeped through the windows of the great hall when Aine and Gretchen slipped in from the kitchen. Aine watched the sleeping patients. "Everyone seems to be well."

"Aye, they've been resting peacefully for a while." Cameron stood and draped her wrap across her shoulders. "I think they'll be fine," she said, yawning. "And, now that ye're both here, I'll go to bed, too."

Aine patted Cameron's hand. "Thank ye, mistress. I don't know what we would've done without ye."

"Ye're welcome. Let me know if ye need me." She picked her basket up and headed toward the stairs.

"She's a sweet lass," Gretchen said.

"Aye, we're lucky she was here."

While their comments touched her, thoughts of escape were never far. She would gain their trust, and when they least expected it, she would flee.

Chapter Six

A bright orange ball of sunlight rose over the trees. Robert and his men trotted down the dusty road to the dense forest. He looked forward to the hunt. What better way to get the MacDougall lass from his mind?

The men quietly made their way off the road and down a worn path. Light filtered through the trees, and a gentle breeze blew around them. Deer and wild boar thrived here, and Robert hoped to spear the large hog he had battled a couple of years ago. On several occasions, he had gotten close enough to wound the male boar, but he always came shy of bagging the beast.

They had ridden for several hours when Robert spotted a herd of large bucks grazing at a tree line. He pointed to the deer, and he and his men silently dismounted. They crept through the tall grass, slinking low and hurrying to take cover behind several large boulders lining the roadside.

Thom signaled Robert when he and Philip settled into place. Robert notched an arrow in his bow and drew the string tight. He aimed at a buck, the wood creaking, and let the missile fly. The big deer crumpled to the ground. Kendrick, Thom, and Philip followed suit with each man spearing one of the animals.

Robert beamed. "We'll eat well tonight."

The men laughed and clapped each other on the back, while making their way to their horses.

Robert nodded at a clearing adjacent to a large pond. "Make camp there."

"Aye, m'laird." Young Alane untied the sack of food from his saddle and hurried off to find wood for a fire.

It was late in the day before they finished preparing the venison. Robert stood and stretched his tired muscles. He wiped his brow with his forearm and studied the gutted deer. The meat would be a welcome sight to the Graham clan.

Sticky and reeking of blood, he grabbed his satchel off Eton and made his way to the campsite. Two boulders wedged together created a welcoming gurgling noise of water before the flow emptied into a deep pool. Robert looked forward to taking a swim to rid himself of the stench. Dropping his bags next to a large rock, he jerked his tunic over his head and stepped out of his trews. His men's laughs and shouts drifted from camp as he waded into the refreshing water and plunged into the depths.

The freezing current rushed past his face. He glided to the middle of the pool, grabbed a handful of sand and scrubbed his skin until it tinged pink.

His thoughts turned to Graham Castle. And Cameron. He remembered the proud stance she took before him yester morn, standing with her head held high, her squared shoulders, and her angry green eyes. He had wanted to grab her and pull her against him—teach her a lesson. He shook his head. The intention of the hunt was not only to stock their stores, but to get away from Cameron. He needed to clear his mind. She had become a distraction.

His stomach rumbled. It was well past time for the evening meal. He emerged from the pond and threw on his clothes before grabbing a flask off his saddle. Taking a large gulp, he closed his eyes and let the ale slide down his parched throat.

He stepped to the fire, listening to the banter of his men.

"Not only is she beautiful, but she's a sweet lass," David said.

"Och, man, she doesn't want ye slobbering all over 'er. She's a lady," Philip teased.

"I cannae help myself." David closed his eyes and inhaled. "She smells so good, and her hand is so verra gentle."

The men laughed, and David opened his eyes, grinning.

Kendrick stabbed his dagger into the dirt at his feet, sparks flashing in his eyes. "Ye're full of shite. She's a MacDougall. Do ye forget what her clan has done to us?" He gawked at the men milling around camp. "Ye can't let a pretty face make ye a fool."

Robert listened with interest and took Kendrick's words to heart. He would do good to remember that advice.

~~~

Fog rolled in and covered the ground as the men broke camp the next morning. Robert secured his belongings onto Eton's back. Patting the large black horse, he ran his hand over his withers and grabbed the reins.

Philip, carrying his saddle, slipped in the mud. "Damn this weather."

"What's wrong? A lil' rain will make the hunt more interesting," Thom said, chuckling.

Philip grumbled, and the men around him laughed.

"Mount up." Robert swung onto his saddle. The men finished loading the venison. "We'll ride to the northern border where I hope to meet my friend, the elusive boar."

He nudged Eton ahead. Atop their horses, he and his men trotted out of the woods and onto the dirt road heading north. The day progressed with cold drizzle. Droplets of freezing water slid inside Robert's tunic, and he shivered. What a miserable day for hunting, but the Graham larders needed replenishing, and he was determined to bring home the large pig.

Late in the afternoon, Robert held up a hand. "We're close." He dropped to the ground and examined hoof prints in the mud. "The ole laddie has been through here recently."

He stood and walked a few paces toward the dense woods, following the path of the boar. Slapping his reins in his hands, he faced the men. "We'll leave the horses here. I don't want to risk them getting injured." He spotted a large stone overhang covered in vines and ivy and guided Eton underneath the sheltered outcropping. "We'll camp here tonight."

"Aye, this looks to be a good place," Philip agreed.

Robert tugged the saddle off Eton. He slung his bow and arrows across his back, and strapped a dagger to his belt. Peering through the undergrowth, he pointed at a clump of disturbed earth. The pig had rooted around, broken stems highlighting his path. "He went this way."

Kendrick secured his satchel across his shoulders as he stepped next to Robert. "We'll get him this time."

"Let's go, lads." Robert grabbed his spear and led the men down the tattered path and into the thick dense foliage. Water dripped off the trees as they made their way into the forest. They crept forward, listening for sounds of the immense beast.

Before long, Robert heard a deep grunt. He held up a hand, and everyone froze. Hogs had an excellent sense of hearing, but did not see well. He counted on remaining downwind and sneaking up on the animal.

His old nemesis was dangerous. It had only been two years since the hog gored a horse as the rider tried to impale the great beast.

Robert inched forward and peered around the foliage. He saw the animal and signaled his men. Sidling closer, he raised his lance over his right shoulder and sent it sailing through the air.

The boar spotted the men and sprinted to the left. The blade grazed the hog's shoulder. The animal tore through the bushes, squealing. Robert grabbed his dagger off his belt and raced after him.

Blood-lined leaves indicated he had wounded the beast. Robert dashed through the shrubs. Thorns and branches tore at his clothes, scratching his face and arms. He jumped over fallen debris and limbs, and ducked under low hanging branches. Ignoring the nicks and cuts, he concentrated on the boar.

Shouts from his men steered the great beast toward a clearing. The pig screeched and grunted, thrashing through the brush. A large boulder blocked his path, and the massive hog turned and faced his attackers.

Robert crouched, his dagger in his right fist. His men ran up behind him as the wounded boar pawed the ground, sizing up his opponents. Robert held out his left arm. "He's mine."

The beast snorted and watched Robert inch closer. The large, dark head sported formidable tusks. Remnants of roots and dead leaves hung from the fangs.

"Be careful," Philip warned. "He's a mean one."

The men fanned out at Robert's back, issuing words of warning and encouragement.

However, there was no warning when the immense beast charged. All 200-pounds barreled straight for Robert. Grappling with the pig, Robert wrapped his left arm around the ferocious animal.

Stiff bristles scratched his arm as he drove his blade into the beast's powerful chest. Warm blood gushed from the wound. The furious and mortally wounded animal thrust his powerful head, and speared Robert's right thigh.

A burning pain shot through his leg before the large animal quivered, and his dead weight sagged. Robert straightened and rolled the creature onto the ground.

"Ye got him!"

"Ye did it, man!"

"Good job, Laird." The men slapped him on the back, each offering congratulations.

"We *will* eat good for weeks," Kendrick called out.

Robert's heart pounded. He wiped sweat from his face with his forearm. Hands on hips, he calmed his heavy breathing. A scorching pain seared his thigh, causing his eyes to water. The hog's blood, mixed with his own, covered his trews.

Shite! He took a deep breath and put his weight on his uninjured leg.

"He's a big one, 'e is," Philip said.

"Get him to camp before it gets dark." Robert grimaced with pain as he helped the men secure the boar to a large branch. Several men hoisted the hog onto their shoulders, and the celebratory group laughed and joked, while making their way back.

94

It was late in the night by the time Robert limped to the lake. He dropped his saddlebag and clean clothes on a large boulder, and eased down. He fished out a swath of leather and jerked his dagger through it to cut a thong. When he stripped off his braies, blood mixed with drizzling rain ran down his leg. The wound gaped open and pulsed hot. He wrapped the strip of leather around his thigh and secured the ends.

Grunting, he stood and hobbled into the frigid pool. His leg ached. When water seeped into the wound, a fiery pain coursed through his thigh. He pinched the gash and squeezed out blood. Small fragments of wood protruded. His jaw clenched, and he stuck his finger into the wound, fishing out particles of mud and muck.

Kendrick stepped to the side of the pond. "Och, mon. What happened? Did he get ye?"

"Aye, the bastard gave me a partin' gift."

"Ye'd best get Mistress MacDougall to tend it when we return."

Robert jerked his head up. "No. I do not want her fussing over me."

Kendrick rubbed the back of his neck. "Well, to hear the men talk, ye're the only one who doesn't want her fussing over him."

"I do not want her to know about the wound. I mean it, man. I don't want her help."

Kendrick straightened. His brow furrowed, and he shook his head. "A boar wound is dirty and can turn into something serious. Ye can't ignore the pain and the obvious signs. Ye need to seek the help of the MacDougall healer." He paused. "I understand how ye feel about her clan. Hell, I feel the same way, but I'm not stupid. Cameron's a talented healer, enemy or not."

Robert turned his back on his friend, waded farther into the water and dove into the depths of the pool. The last thing he needed was for Cameron to tend him and run her hands over his thigh. Even in his pain-filled state, his imagination caused his cock to swell. No, he would treat the wound himself.

95

When he grew tired, Robert emerged from the freezing pool and grabbed his clean trews and tunic. He wiped his face and shook his head, sending water flying around him. He glanced at his injury. The cold appeared to have reduced the inflammation.

He gingerly put his weight on his injured leg and hobbled to his saddlebag. He extracted his flask of mead, leaned against a boulder and held the wound open. Bracing for the assault, he sucked in a breath and poured the searing liquid into the gaping hole.

A scorching pain forced him to his knees. The fiery liquid would cleanse the area. He had used the technique on many blade wounds. He would treat his injury and keep the lovely healer at bay. He refused to have her tend him and work on his sympathies.

~~~

Exhausted from a restless night, Robert opened his scratchy eyes. His leg throbbed. Surely, the gash would get better as the day wore on. He eased off his pallet and unwound the dirty bandage. The raw, irritated edges of his skin gaped open, and the gash pulsed with every heartbeat. He hobbled to the stream and submerged his leg. Cold water rushed over the hot lesion.

Sweat trickled down his temple as he ripped a strip of cloth and wrapped it tight around his thigh. His head swam as he grabbed his trews off a rock and gingerly eased them on. He leaned against a boulder and gritted his teeth while tugging on his boots. Carefully putting weight on his injured leg, he hobbled to Eton and threw the saddle on the horse's back.

"We're ready to head out," Thom called. "We stored the meat, and we're breaking camp."

"Good, we'll be on our way then." Robert tightened the girth under Eton's solid belly and cinched the strap. "Mount up," he bellowed.

"Laird?" Kendrick sat atop his large chestnut horse. His dark brows drew together. "Ye're all right?"

96

"Aye." Robert secured his belongings, clenched his jaw and swung onto the saddle. "Let's head out."

He nudged Eton toward Graham Castle with his men following. Blood seeped through the bandage and onto his breeks. "Damn bastard."

Searing hot pain shot through his leg. His thigh had been no match for the hog's sharp tusk. He shifted, easing his weight off his right side. The horse's head jerked up, and his ears lay back. Robert patted the animal's neck. "Easy boy, it's only my blasted leg."

The men rode for hours before finally stopping to rest and eat. The wind picked up, raining leaves from swaying trees. Robert studied the horizon. Thunder rumbled, and dark clouds gathered. "We don't have much farther to go. If we hurry, we might beat the storm."

"It'd be good to get back before the downpour," Kendrick agreed.

The men galloped down the road. Large raindrops soon turned to sleet with stinging ice-like needles. The wind intensified, and Robert hunched low over Eton. The miles blurred. It was late at night when the rain subsided, and they thundered into the bailey.

Lachlan grabbed Eton's bridle. "Welcome back."

Duncan shuffled up behind him. His weight loss emphasized the bones in his face, his hollow cheeks and sunken eyes. He stood hunched over, his lean frame gaunt.

"It's good to see ye out of bed. Ye're doing well?" Robert asked.

"I'm still mighty sore, but feeling stronger."

Androu ran down the stairs and excitedly splashed through the puddles. "How'd ye do? Did ye get him?"

"Aye, we got him." Robert swung off Eton, and while putting his weight on his left leg, he ruffled Androu's hair.

"He was a mean one," Alane exclaimed and wiped the water from his face. "The hog charged the laird, but yer brother stabbed him!" He made an exaggerated gesture demonstrating the dagger thrust for Androu.

Robert laughed. "Get inside. Michael, have the men store the meat."

His captain slapped Robert on the back. "Aye. Congratulations."

"Come in, come in and warm up." Nichola ushered the men into the hall. Several lads rushed to take their cloaks. She put her arm around Robert. "Congratulations on bagging the beast. The meat will be wonderful."

Even with the pulsating fire in his thigh, Robert's gaze searched the great hall for signs of Cameron. He kissed his sister's forehead while murmuring, "So, how's our prisoner?"

Why did she haunt his thoughts? The pain in his leg alone should clear his mind of her, but all he could think about was her beautiful smile.

Nichola drew back from him and knit her brows. "She's fine."

"What is it? Why the look?"

"I don't think Cameron should be a *prisoner*. She should be allowed to return home."

Robert turned his back on his sister and walked away calling over his shoulder, "Don't start, Nichola. I don't want to hear it."

"Let me help ye with a hot bath, m'laird," Rosalind purred, and ran up the stairs behind him.

Robert scowled when she followed him down the hall to his bedchamber. He opened the door, and placed a hand on the doorjamb, blocking her entrance.

"I'm tired and going to bed." His leg throbbed, his wound on fire.

"But Robert, yer bath...don't ye want me ta help ye relax?" She ran her hand over his back to rest on his rear-end. When her fingers slipped around to the front of his trews, he grabbed her wrist.

"No, Rosalind." An excruciating pain shot down his leg. "Goodnight."

Robert dropped her arm and shut the door behind him. He hobbled across the room, pulled his tunic over his head, and

98

threw it on the chair. Cringing, he leaned over and yanked his boots off. Sweat dotted his brow, and his head swam. He tugged his trews. A fingernail scraped the aggravated wound. Pain seared him, and he gasped.

Once he stripped to his braies, an unpleasant odor wafted from his leg. He untied the band around his thigh. Yellow pus mixed with blood oozed from the burning wound. "Damn it!"

Perspiration trickled down the middle of his back as he limped to the washbowl. He held a wet cloth on his leg, the fiery pulsating throb almost unbearable. Tilting his head back, he exhaled loudly. Why didn't he get out of the way of the animal? He knew better. It was not as if he was an inexperienced lad on his first hunt.

He grabbed a flask off the side table and took a large gulp. His eyes watered from the intense liquid sliding down his throat. After catching his breath, he guzzled more, then emptied the container on his wound. Pain seared through his leg. He sucked in a breath and hissed.

His hand shot out and grabbed his satchel. He rummaged through it and found another flask, then guzzled a mouthful. The pain would lessen, and his wound would be better on the morrow. He would treat it as he had other injuries. There was no need for Cameron to tend him.

The night wore on with him swigging the numbing alcohol.

~~~

Curled up in a chair before her bedchamber's hearth, Cameron turned the last thick papyrus sheet of *La Vita Nuova*. She closed Nichola's precious book of poems and sighed. Dante had adored Beatrice. He held her on a pedestal, respected and admired her. How would it be to have a special man love her the way Dante loved Beatrice?

A loud knock interrupted her thoughts. "Aye, come in."

The door swung open, and Kendrick stormed across the room. Prominent frown lines traversed his pale face, his blue eyes intense. "I need yer help."

"What's wrong?"

"It's Robert. When he didn't show up for training, I checked on him. He's burning up." Kendrick ran a hand through his wavy brown hair. "The hog gored him during the hunt."

Cameron's heart sank. "Gored?"

She bounded from her chair and reached for her wrap and healing basket on the bedside table.

"The damn beast got 'im in the thigh."

Her pulse hammered through her ears, and her chest squeezed. Kendrick dashed down the hall with her close behind. "Why did he not tell me this when he arrived last night?"

"He thought it would heal with his own methods. He treated it as he has other injuries, but it didn't work this time."

"What? A wound from a blade is not the same as being gored. He should know better."

"I know. I should have made him seek yer help."

He rushed into Robert's room with her behind him.

"Please stoke the fire. It's cold in here." She placed her basket on a table and stepped to the bed. "Laird Graham, can ye hear me?" When he didn't answer, she spoke louder and shook his shoulder. "Laird Graham?"

He groaned.

She touched his flushed face with the back of her fingers. His skin burned. She removed her wrap and lowered Robert's blanket. Sweat glistened on his bare chest. His linen braies covered his lap and ran to the middle of his thigh where blood soaked the material. She worked the undergarment higher and gasped, her eyes widening. The hog had torn a massive hole in his thigh.

"Oh, my Lord." Kendrick exhaled loudly.

"Aye, we certainly need His help." The skin around the wound had receded, leaving a gaping cavity. Creamy pus and

100

coagulated blood filled the crater. "Quickly, Kendrick, I need cold water to bring down his fever, but I also need ye to boil some in the hearth."

"I'll get some directly."

"And bring some cloths for bandages as well," she called as he ran from the room.

When she grabbed the basin off the side table, her hands shook. She fumbled with the bowl as she placed it next to him. Even in his weakened state, his masculine body made her body quiver.

Kendrick marched back into the room carrying a bucket in each hand and linens under his arm. He set the containers next to the bed. "Here's yer water."

She ladled some out of the bucket, took a slice of soap from the bedside table and scrubbed her hands. "I'll need yer knife."

Kendrick turned his head slightly at her request. A moment passed before he dropped several rags on the chair and pierced her with his glare. "I'll have yer word ye won't use my blade against my friend."

She squared her shoulders and returned his glower. "I give ye my word."

He handed her his knife. She dipped a cloth in the cold water and leaned over Robert. When she wiped his face, he turned into her hand. She stilled. She knew the cold felt good to his hot skin, but she was briefly surprised at his reaction to her touch. Determined to focus on her task, she banished thoughts of Robert Graham, the man, and turned her attention to her patient.

The cloth turned warm, and she rinsed it in the icy water. He sighed when she stroked his face and arms, letting the water dribble over his chest. "It's all right, rest easy," she whispered.

Kendrick stood over her. She soaked another cloth in the hot water. "He must be held down while I clean his wound. It will hurt, but 'tis necessary."

Kendrick stepped to the door and shouted down the hall, "Philip, bring a couple of men to the laird's chambers."

Cameron mixed herbs needed for Robert's pain. Her hand slid under his sweaty hair and cradled his head. His eyes fluttered as she dribbled the contents into his mouth. His throat worked the brew down. He turned his face into her chest. Satisfied he had swallowed most of the concoction, she eased him back.

A few minutes later, Philip and two other men raced into the room.

"I need ye to help me hold the laird down while the mistress treats him," Kendrick instructed.

Philip and the others gathered around the bed. "What happened?"

Kendrick rubbed the back of his neck. "The hog gored him."

"I had no idea the beast got 'im. He never said a word." Philip's greying brows knit, his eyes wide with concern.

"Two of ye hold his left side." Kendrick turned to the third man. "And ye hold his right shoulder while I hold his knee."

"Are ye ready?" Cameron asked.

When Kendrick nodded, she took the hot cloth out of the bowl and laid it across the wound.

Robert roared, his body bucking against the men struggling to hold him.

"The hot rag will loosen the skin around the sides of the gash so I can clean the wound better," she shouted over Robert's profanity.

After a moment, the cloth cooled, and she removed it from his leg. She touched the ragged puncture wound and a thick, yellowish substance oozed out.

Again, Robert thrashed and fought against the men.

"Hold him tighter!" Kendrick scowled.

"He's too strong," Philip exclaimed, throwing his body over Robert's torso.

102

Cameron's fingers trembled, but she applied pressure to the area and expelled much of the thick substance. She drew the frayed sides apart and cringed as she probed around the opening with her finger. Oh, Lord. The revolting smell emanating from the hole gagged her. She choked back bile rising in her throat and concentrated on her exploring fingers.

"Aaah," Robert yelled, his face contorting.

"Ye're killing him," Kendrick growled as though he suspected her of purposefully inflicting pain.

"*No*, I'm not. There are bits of material in the cavity that will continue to cause decay if I don't remove them." Ignoring his scowl, she delved into the bloody and putrid tissue where she extracted sharp pieces of wood and fragments of the forest floor.

She discarded the debris and once again explored the cavity. A solid shard the size of her fingertip was wedged tight. "Och, there is a much larger piece."

"Hurry! Be done with it. Ye're torturing him," Kendrick ground out.

Carefully, Cameron pulled the wound open.

Robert yelled and flailed against the men. Blood ran down his knee and dripped on the bed.

She made a small incision and, probing with the tip of Kendrick's knife, slid the blade under the sliver of wood and flipped it out. She quickly dabbed a fresh gush of blood off his leg. "I think that's the last of it." She applied a cloth to his injury. "Put pressure on this while I fetch my needle."

Kendrick held the rag to Robert's leg while she washed sticky blood and pus from her fingers. She grabbed a needle from her basket on the side table and stepped back to Robert. Kendrick moved to the side, and she deftly began sewing the jagged edges together. Robert perspired profusely, and his head rolled from side to side.

Sweat trickled down the middle of her back as tense minutes passed with the men's eyes on her every move.

"Will he live?" Kendrick asked.

Cameron finished the stitches and tied off the ends. "I don't know." She picked up a cloth off the table and wiped her hands, while pointing to red streaks creeping from the wound. "That's not a good sign. He's a sick man. I'll not fool ye by telling ye he'll be well."

Kendrick stared at Robert. "That's all, lads. Ye can return to what ye were doing."

Uncertainty and concern filled their eyes as the men cast a last look at their laird and left the room.

Cameron eased next to Robert and gently dabbed the wound with a clean cloth. She applied a thick poultice over the puckered gash and studied his pale face. He stilled, and his breathing calmed.

"I gave him something for pain that should help him rest. He'll need his strength to fight this." She leaned back in the chair. "Ye know a wild boar's tusk is extremely dirty. They root in the ground for grubs, using their tusks to do their digging. When that animal gored him, not only did it jam slivers of wood against yer laird's thigh bone, but all of the filth on the tusk went straight into his leg."

Kendrick rubbed the back of his neck. "Damn it."

Cameron reached for a new cloth. Dipping it into the cold water on the table, she once again bathed Robert's hot skin, tenderly running the fabric over his face. The water dribbled down his neck, and she followed the drops, dabbing and soothing his burning flesh.

After retrieving his knife from the edge of the table, Kendrick stepped to the door. "Lachlan?" he yelled.

A few seconds later, Lachlan appeared. "What is it?"

Kendrick motioned him inside.

Lachlan rushed to Robert's side, his eyes growing wide. "What the hell happened?"

"The ole boar gored him in the thigh before he went down."

"Will he be all right?"

"I don't know, but I need to get back to the training, and I don't want to leave him alone."

104

Lachlan settled on a bench beside the bed and stretched his legs in front of him. "Aye, I'll watch her."

"Let me know if he worsens," Kendrick called over his shoulder as he strode from the room.

Cameron clenched her teeth and turned her back on Lachlan. She felt his eyes on her as she continued to run the cool water over Robert's hot skin.

A few minutes later, Nichola raced into the room. "Is it true?" She ran to Robert's bed and started weeping. "Oh no, no."

Lachlan rushed over and gathered her into a comforting embrace.

Cameron stood and rubbed Nichola's back. "He's not gone yet. He is truly ill, but I'm doing everything I can to help him."

Nichola grasped Cameron's hand. "I know ye are."

"He's a strong man, and that will help him recover," Lachlan added. With his arm around Nichola's shoulders, he steered her to a bench next to the bed.

She leaned forward and took her brother's hand, and then glanced at Cameron. "He is lucky ye are here to treat him."

Cameron tried to smile. At least Nichola did not regard her as the enemy.

The day wore on with Cameron trying to bring down Robert's fever. He tossed and turned, mumbling unintelligibly. Cameron dribbled cold water into his dry mouth and dabbed the drops off his chin.

Late in the evening, Lachlan murmured to Nichola. She had fallen asleep with her head on his shoulder. "Let me take ye to yer chambers."

Nichola sat up and rubbed her eyes. "How's he doing? Any change?"

"Nay, he still sleeps," Cameron answered.

Nichola took her brother's hand. "He's so hot. Is there nothing else ye can do?"

The familiar pain of self-doubt crept into Cameron's gut. How many times had she asked herself the same question about Mum? "I'm doing everything I know. Fever is a serious thing, and I'm afraid only time will tell how he does."

"Ye need rest, Nichola," Lachlan said, stroking her arm.

She looked at Cameron through tear-filled eyes. "Ye will call me if he worsens?"

"I will."

Lachlan escorted Nichola out of the room and shut the door behind them.

The chamber fell quiet. The fire crackled and popped, casting shadows across Robert's face. Cameron dipped another cloth into the cool water and ran it across his arm and over his broad chest. Water slid down the contours of his sculpted abdomen. With trembling hands, she reached down to catch the errant droplets, and his fevered skin scorched her fingers. She opened her hand and ran her palm across his large, muscular torso. Dark hair covered his chest, stopping just shy of the brown around his nipples.

She had seen men with little clothing hiding their manly parts, but Robert was different. Normally, she paid little attention to her patient's physical *attributes*. But Robert's body beckoned her to touch him, caress him.

She searched his face and continued to slide her hand across his chest. Her stomach clenched at her brazen inspection. Soft hair created a narrowing line down his torso, across taut ridges of muscle and disappeared in his braies. The flap in the material lay open, and a dark nest of curls peeked through.

He sighed, and she jerked her hand back. Relieved he had not caught her admiring his form, she let out a breath. She would be horrified if he awoke to her fondling him.

In sleep, his features were relaxed. His brow no longer stern, his dark scowling eyes did not sear into her. Indeed, he appeared restful. She dipped the cloth back into the bucket and dabbed his hot face. Once again, he turned his head into her

106

touch. Pushing a dark curl off his brow, she marveled at its softness.

Shaking her head, she dropped the rag into the bucket and stepped to the fire. She stared into the flames and wrapped her arms around herself. Surely, it was wrong to be attracted to him—to want his touch on her skin. When she closed her eyes, she could feel him holding her as he had at the elder tree. His hard body pressed into hers, and his strong arms surrounding her.

She opened her eyes and chastised herself. She should not have amorous feelings toward the man who kidnapped her and held her prisoner. She had never had such thoughts, had never reacted so strongly to any man. It frightened her.

Da must be beside himself with worry and her sisters distraught. They must fear her dead. And what of her cousin, Symon? Did he plan more attacks on the Grahams? She needed to stop him.

In desperation, she peered at the door and back at Robert. How far would she get if she were to open the door and just walk out? With their laird ill, now was her time to escape.

She stepped toward the door.

Robert groaned and thrashed about.

She paused and looked at him. He was ill—dangerously ill. Could she abandon him? Could she leave him to die? She took another step, and he called out in his delirium.

Her shoulders slumped. No matter how much she wished to return to her family, she could not desert him. She also knew she might make it to the stairs only to have one of his men drag her back. She shuddered over the punishment Robert's men would mete out for her attempt. No, she would wait for a better chance to escape. She would bide her time and be ready when the opportunity arose.

Cameron returned to his bedside and prepared another brew. She put her hand under his neck, raised his head, and tipped the bowl to his parched lips. "Ye need to drink this, Laird Graham."

His eyes fluttered. He shook his head and pushed the bowl away.

"Please, Robert," she urged and again, placed the bowl to his lips.

His confused, glazed eyes tried to focus on her. His hot fingertips touched her face and stroked her cheek. Under the effects of fever, she knew he was not aware of his actions. He opened his mouth and sipped, then dropped his hand to his side. His gaze traveled to her lips.

After he drained the contents of the bowl, she laid him back and wiped his mouth. In his delirium, he reached around her neck, pulled her to him and gently kissed her.

Heat radiated off his skin as his mouth sent exhilarating waves skittering through her body. He broke the kiss, and she straightened as he closed his eyes.

Her lips tingled. She leaned back in the chair and studied him. How she longed to feel his mouth on hers when he was fully aware of his actions.

No, she must harden her resolve toward him and steel her body against the effect he had on her. Escape would be nearly impossible if she let her emotions rule.

If she managed to heal his wound, she would request he send her home. He would be indebted to her for saving the lives of his brother, clan members and for his life as well. He would honor her wishes. Her heart ached at the thought of leaving him. She would miss him.

Once again, she wrung out the cloth and continued to bathe his sweltering skin until he rested easier.

~~~

Robert's leg throbbed. His dry mouth matched an acrid desert, his gritty eyes full of sand.

Cameron slept in the chair next to his bed. He tried to focus on her, the haze in his mind slowly dissipating. Firelight danced across her face. Her head rested against her shoulder, and her hands lay in her lap. His gaze traveled across her breasts. Her chest rose and fell steadily.

He scowled. Why was she in his chamber? His leg ached, and he was drenched in sweat. He moved slightly, and her eyes opened.

"Ye're awake." She gingerly sat up as if stiff from sleeping in the chair. Leaning over him, she touched his forehead. "How do ye feel?"

He jerked back. "What are ye doing here?"

She dropped her hand. "I'm here to help. Ye've been verra ill."

"I don't need yer help."

Cameron's small frame drew up. "Had I known that, I wouldn't have wasted hours tending yer wound and losing sleep over ye."

The door opened, and Kendrick stepped into the room. "Thank God ye're finally awake." He strode to the side of the bed. "Man, ye look terrible."

Robert rubbed his thigh, and winced. "That's because I *feel* like shite."

Cameron placed the herbs in her basket on the bedside table. She bent and picked up her wrap off the bench.

"Will he be all right now?" Kendrick asked.

"Aye." She stared down at Robert. "Ye need to stay in bed and off that leg. Ye owe me, Laird Graham. I didn't have to help ye. I kept ye alive, now I ask ye to release me."

Robert crossed his arms over his chest as he observed her proud stance. "I can't do that."

"What do ye mean? I saved yer life."

He gave Cameron the fiercest, darkest glower he could muster. "I appreciate yer help, but it does not change anything." He paused, letting his words sink in. "Yer da *will* pay for what he did."

Cameron narrowed her eyes before she spun and stormed from the room.

Robert pinned Kendrick with a threatening glare. "I told ye I didn't want her fussing over me."

"I didn't have any choice. Ye were close to death." Kendrick rubbed the back of his neck. "The lass brought ye back."

Robert frowned. "Aine could've treated me."

"Nay, Aine wouldn't have known what to do." Kendrick planted his hands on his hips. "While we were gone, the castle had an outbreak of a belly-ache. Seems it was food poisoning from the goats' milk. The MacDougall lass treated and cured dozens of Grahams. Aine didn't know what to do, but the lass did."

Lachlan stuck his head in the room. "Och, man, I'm relieved to see ye awake." He strolled to Robert's bed. "Ye're feeling better?"

"Aye," he answered, his voice curt.

"Ye gave us a scare."

Robert cast an annoyed glance at Lachlan.

Kendrick's arms crossed his chest. "He's not happy the McDougall lass tended him."

"I understand. I didn't want her kind tending me either." Lachlan rubbed his arm. "Well, I'm glad ye're awake. We had a visit from the MacDougalls."

Robert's eyes narrowed. "And?"

"They want ye to let them know if ye see Cameron. Seems she's gone missing, and the MacDougalls are scouring the area in search of her."

"They didn't suspect anything?"

"Nay, they weren't here long. They searched the bailey, but finding nothing amiss, they left." He turned and walked across the room. "I'll check on ye later. The men are training with Michael, and I need to get back."

Kendrick followed Lachlan to the door and paused. "I'll ask Aine to tend ye." He left the room and closed the door behind him.

Robert lay back and stared at the ceiling. He had witnessed Cameron's talent at healing. His thoughts turned to hazy memories of her bending over him, tending his wound, her gentle touch and soothing voice.

110

A growl of disgust erupted from his throat. He had grown accustomed to her being at Graham Castle. As if she were a mythological Siren, he was uncontrollably drawn to her. His eyes sought her when he entered a room—to get a glimpse of her smile, a whiff of her fresh scent, a snippet of what she was saying. But unlike the doomed sailors, he would toughen his heart toward her. No matter the allure, he would not let her break through his defensive shield.

While he battled his feelings for her, he could not deny Cameron was a perfect woman to have by his side, to mother his children, a Lady for his people. His stomach tied in knots. He swore no woman would ever get close to him again, a lesson his former betrothed taught him many years ago. *I only wanted ye for the title ye'll have someday.* The image of the older boy rolling off her and her lily-white legs drawing together carved into his mind.

After the humiliation and embarrassment diminished, his heart had hardened to the cruelties of women. Hell, his own mother deserted him and his siblings. However, it was difficult to treat Cameron like a prisoner when she was this willing to help his clan and family. But a prisoner she was, and Robert's desire for revenge against her father was fierce.

A niggling thought crept into the corner of his mind. Was it not his desire for *Cameron* that was so fierce?

Either way, she was not going anywhere.

Chapter Seven

Graham Castle
June 1297

A mug of hot cider warmed Cameron's hands as she sat before her chamber's hearth. Red and gold flames danced around the logs, the heat on her face comforting. She tugged a wrap around her shoulders. It had been a week since she last saw Laird Graham. Oh, she had nonchalantly inquired about him, but refused to tend his leg. Not that anyone asked.

After his unreasonable response to her tending his injury, she'd avoided him. She should have let him suffer, go untreated and risk losing his life. He was an ungrateful, perverse wretch.

But she missed him.

She rubbed her forehead. Her self-inflicted confinement to her chamber began to take a toll, not to mention she had to get out-of-doors if she held any hope of escape. She had organized and reorganized the herbs in her basket, read Nichola's one book until she could recite it, and continued to stare longingly out her small window.

"I've got to come up with a plan to get home," she whispered.

A knock on the door made her jump. "Aye, come in."

The door opened. "Good evening," a cheerful voice called out.

Cameron set her mug on the table. "Oh, Nichola, it's good to see ye."

Nichola wore her hair piled on her head. Blonde tendrils escaped and framed her face, and her soft blue dress matched her eyes. "I stopped by to see if ye'd come down for the evening meal. Will ye join me?"

Cameron *was* hungry, and she longed for company, but she didn't relish the thought of Robert's scrutiny, his searing eyes watching her every move. "I don't know."

"Ye haven't been downstairs the past few days, and everyone has asked about ye."

Cameron raised her eyebrow.

Nichola clutched Cameron's elbow. "They've grown accustomed to yer presence and want to thank ye for yer healing."

"Aye, I'd enjoy the company. Let me freshen up a wee bit." She stepped to the basin and splashed water on her face.

"Tessa's been cooking all day. They roasted the hog, and from the aroma in the kitchen, I'd say we're in for a treat."

Cameron dried her face and ran her hands over her hair. "I think I'm ready."

Nichola looped her arm through Cameron's, and they strolled down the stairs.

"Androu's wounds have healed nicely, and I'd like to take him out-of-doors on the morrow," Nichola mentioned. "The weather has been lovely, and it would be fun to spend time soaking up sunshine, instead of remaining cooped up in the keep."

Cameron patted Nichola's hand. "That does sound like fun."

"Will ye join us? I'll have Tessa prepare a basket of food for us to enjoy near the river."

A chance to be out-of-doors would afford her the opportunity she needed to formulate a plan of escape. "Aye, I would love to join ye."

They continued down the stairs, but when they stepped into the dining hall, Cameron froze, intimidated by the gathered Grahams—many of whom she knew harbored ill will toward her. Noisy conversations and the clanging of tankards and laughter filled the room. Crowds of men and women milled around, some sat at tables filling their plates, while children chased each other, weaving between the adults.

Robert sat at the dais positioned across the front of the room. Rosalind bent over him as she poured ale in his tankard. Her large breasts were crushed against his shoulder, her face inches from his.

"What is it?" Nichola asked, her brows drawn together.

"I didn't realize the *whole* clan would be here." Cameron bit her bottom lip. "Perhaps it would be best if I returned to my room."

She swiveled back to the stairs, but Nichola tugged her arm and steered her toward the dais. "Nay, please join me."

Once again, Cameron hesitated. Her pulse thumped rapidly. Robert's dark eyes were already fixed on her. She swallowed and ran a hand down the front of her grey, woolen gown. "I don't think yer brother will want me at yer table."

"Don't be silly. Ye're welcome to eat with us."

~~~

Robert waved Rosalind away and swigged a gulp of ale. He set his tankard on the table as Cameron walked across the hall. She no longer treated his wound, and he had not seen her for days. When he inquired, Nichola simply informed him Cameron remained in her bedchamber. He didn't want to admit he missed her, but she mesmerized him, constantly invading his thoughts. While his plan for retribution remained intact, his resolve to stay away from her melted. There was no reason to deny himself her company.

Cameron's eyes were wide as she sat at the table with Nichola. "Mistress MacDougall," he acknowledged.

"Laird Graham," she replied, and nodded slightly.

He pulled his gaze from her and glanced around the room. The atmosphere was light. Most of the inhabitants had begun to accept Cameron, and everyone celebrated the healing of the Graham residents.

"Ye've got to try Tessa's fresh bread." Nichola placed a hunk on Cameron's trencher and poured gravy over it. "It's heavenly."

Cameron took a bite. Her tongue darted out and licked her lips.

Robert almost choked. He stopped chewing, totally captivated by the innocent act. His shaft stirred. Shaking his head, he focused on his meal and resumed eating.

114

"Aye, it is delicious. I could make a meal of that alone," Cameron replied.

"Mistress, 'tis good to see ye again," Philip called down the table. He rubbed his right arm. "My wound ye treated has healed." Then, he placed his hand on his chest. "But my heart's been hurting for yer beautiful smile."

Robert scoffed at Philip's flirtatious comments, but Cameron's cheeks tinged pink. Did she enjoy his remarks?

She grinned at the man. "I'm relieved to hear yer arm's better. Perhaps I can find ye a wee tonic to cure yer heartburn, as well."

"Best watch out, lad. Some of 'er tonics'll put ye down," Walter interjected, obviously remembering the foul smelling rhubarb roots. The men around the table joined in the laughter, and it was Philip's turn to blush.

Robert picked up his tankard and leaned back in his chair. Cameron laughed at something one of his men said. Dark hair hung in ringlets down her back, and he longed to reach out and touch them, run his fingers through the silky softness. His thoughts turned to her small tongue innocently licking her lips and once again, his manhood swelled. Torturing himself further, his gaze traveled lower to the bodice of her gown straining against the weight of her breasts. How he longed to free them.

~~~

"Time for celebrating!" Travis stepped in front of Cameron holding his arms wide, and the room fell silent. "We thank ye, Mistress MacDougall, for yer caring ways."

He turned, indicating the clan gathered in the hall. Cameron's gaze skimmed the people standing around him and sitting at tables with their attention focused on her. Heat crept up her neck and spread across her cheeks.

When he faced her again, he continued, "Ye've helped many of us, some of whom would not be here tonight if it weren't for ye." He reached across the table and clasped her hand. "Come, dance and celebrate with us."

The residents stood, applauded and cheered. She had not expected this reception. Her heart swelled. Several men pushed tables out of the way, while musicians played the harp, lute and other melodious instruments.

Nichola nudged Cameron's arm. "Go on. Enjoy yerself."

Cameron glanced at her and back to Travis. Couples rushed from the crowd to the dance floor, clapping and shouting, eager to celebrate. Hume twirled Bonnie into his arms, and they skated across the floor. Walter hollered and grabbed Glenda, then spun her around in a circle.

The lively tunes lifted Cameron's spirits. What harm could come from one dance? She smiled and stood, letting Travis escort her around the table.

Cameron felt Robert's scrutiny. She tried to ignore him, but every time she glanced in his direction, he watched her. One dance turned into two, then three. Once a tune ended, the next man in line replaced her partner.

The music stopped and everyone clapped. "Mistress, may I have the honor?" Walter asked.

Cameron shook her head and held up a hand. "Oh nay, I'm worn out. Thank ye, but I'd best rest a bit."

He chuckled and returned to the dance floor.

She weaved between the merrymakers, skirting couples twirling to the lively tunes. A lad chased two lasses as they squealed and raced through the throng of dancers. Walter spun Glenda, bent her backward and planted a big kiss on her smiling mouth. The hall erupted in cheers. Cameron clapped at the man's antics. She veered to the side of the room and paused to watch the revelers, her gaze skimming the great hall in search of Robert.

He stood from the trestle table and patted Lachlan on the back. When he turned, his gaze captured hers, and her pulse thumped wildly. He started toward her. His broad shoulders and chest tapered to a lean waist and hips. His white shirt hung open exposing dark curls. Powerful legs, encased in brown trews, fit snugly in his black boots. He limped, favoring his injured leg.

She realized she was staring, but she couldn't seem to help herself. His shaggy hair hung to his shoulders. Dark stubble lined his cheeks and strong jaw. His smoldering eyes made her stomach flutter and her hands shake.

"M'lady." He stopped beside her and watched the revelers.

Stilted silence passed between them before she spoke. "Yer leg is doing well?"

"Aye, it is." He rubbed his thigh. "It's a wee bit sore, but it's better."

"That's good."

They turned back to the dancers. She searched for something to say, not sure where she stood with him. The last time she saw him, he had railed at her, making it clear he didn't want her near him.

"Would ye care for some fresh air?" His deep voice rumbled in his chest.

She searched his handsome face, his dark eyes.

"Aye, I would." The words tumbled out.

Robert offered his arm, and she accepted. He escorted her across the hall, out a side door, and into a garden.

A carpet of bluebells wove around a worn stone path. Foxglove, wild basil and garlic flourished on either side.

"Oh, my. How lovely."

"My mum started it years ago. Nichola tends it now."

They strolled the trail in amiable silence. Her skirt brushed several plants, and sweet scents of lavender and mint wafted up. She breathed in the delightful smells reminding her of home. How she missed tending her own garden full of herbs and colorful flowers.

The full moon cast its bright light on the pathway. A breeze blew in off the nearby river, chilling the night air. They reached the end of the path and paused. Trees swayed in the wind, throwing shadows across the courtyard.

Robert stood within inches of her. She yearned to lean into him, wrap herself in his strong arms, feel his lips on hers again. She should not have these thoughts about him, but she couldn't help herself. She longed to be with him. "I should be getting back. It's been a long day."

"Before ye go, I'd like to show ye something. It won't take long, and I think ye'll like it."

Her insides melted at his boyish grin, the dimples pressing into his stubbled cheeks.

"Verra well."

He clutched her hand, intertwining his strong warm fingers with hers, and shivers of excitement slithered through her body. He led her out a dark oak gate and through a corridor. A steep flight of stairs ascended to the right, and she followed him up and onto the battlements overlooking Graham Castle.

The dramatic sight stole her breath. Large torches positioned around the massive bailey threw blazing flames into the dark sky. Flags, of Scotland and the Graham family crest, vigorously waved and slapped their staffs. Armed men, with swords strapped to their backs, patrolled the gates.

She leaned over the waist-high grey stone enclosure and peered into the bailey. "It's beautiful up here."

"It's a favorite place of mine."

The wind whipped around her, and she rubbed her arms.

"Ye're cold?"

"A bit."

He slid his palms down her arms and back up. She closed her eyes, relishing the feel of his warm hands. "I like to come here to think."

Raised voices below caught their attention. Robert leaned over her shoulder to see the commotion, pressing himself fully against her back. He chuckled, and vibrations rumbled from his thick chest. She grew lightheaded from his proximity, or mayhap she'd consumed too much ale.

118

Regardless, she needed to get away from him. She couldn't trust herself not to turn in his arms and sink into his embrace.

"It really is getting late, and I must go in." When she moved to leave, Robert stepped in front of her and blocked her path.

"Wait." He hesitated. "I'd like to thank ye for yer care of my family and my people."

Cameron tilted her head. Did he try to make amends? "Ye're welcome."

The breeze blew a lock of hair onto her face. Robert brushed it away, his rough fingers tracing a line down her cheek. He slowly lowered his head, placing his mouth on hers in a sweet, gentle kiss. He straightened and briefly hesitated before capturing her lips in a more possessive, seductive manner. His tongue slid into her mouth, and he wrapped his arms around her, pulling her hard against his body.

She molded to him. Her hands eased up his chest and around his neck, her fingers entwining in his soft hair. She relished the feel of his strong embrace, his hands roaming across her back. She inhaled his male scent of leather mixed with ale, while his mouth played havoc on her senses. Her heart beat wildly, and her body trembled.

Robert's fingers slid lower to her bottom. His hard member pressed into her stomach, and a strange ache tugged at the juncture of her legs. When his hand cupped her breast, her breath hitched, and she brazenly leaned into him. At her encouragement, his thumb circled her hardening nipple.

Cameron's head reeled. She had never experienced anything like this, and while it was exciting, it frightened her. She regained her senses enough to push against his chest, breaking their kiss and his firm grip.

"Please," she whispered.

He hesitated, and when he dropped his hands, she slipped past him and hurried to her chamber.

She stepped into the room, leaned against the door, and closed her eyes. Her chest heaved. What had she done? She had allowed Robert to kiss and caress her, that's what she'd done. No, she had *encouraged* his advances. She groaned and pushed away from the door.

The fire in the hearth burned low. Cameron added a clump of peat and sank onto her chair, staring blindly into the flickering flames. She had to get out of Graham Castle and away from him before she did something to dishonor herself and her family. With more of his caresses, she would not be able to resist him. And the reception she received from the Grahams further strengthened her resolve to ensure Symon instigated no more attacks.

Nichola had invited Cameron on an outing with her and Androu on the morrow. Cameron jumped at the chance to be out-of-doors. Now more than ever, she had to take this opportunity to search for a means of escape.

Chapter Eight

Sunlight streamed through the small window, announcing the arrival of another beautiful morning. It was a perfect day for an outing. Cameron stretched and slid from bed, then stepped to the water basin, washed and dressed for the day. She grabbed her wrap off the back of a chair and strolled from her room.

When she reached the stairs, a muffled sound wafted from a room at the far end of the hall. She paused. Was someone crying? That chamber had always remained closed, but now the door stood ajar.

After glancing around, she continued down the hall. She eased the door open and peeked inside. A little lass with dark curls sat amidst a tangle of blankets in the middle of a bed. She hugged a pillow and wept into it.

"Hello, sweetling. Are ye all right?" Cameron stepped into the room. She hoped the child wouldn't be afraid of her. "My name is Cameron. Duncan and Androu were ill, and I was asked to tend them."

When the lass looked up, Cameron's breath caught. She had Robert's brown eyes and dark hair.

"What's yer name?"

"Isobel Graham," the little girl whispered and hiccupped. Her puffy red eyes blinked, and a tear dripped onto the pillow.

"Ahh, ye're Nichola's sister?"

Isobel nodded.

Cameron stroked the child's soft dark curls. "Why are ye so sad? Perhaps I can help."

Isobel studied Cameron. Her shoulders slumped. "I'm sick and can't get well. I don't get to go on outings." She fiddled with the cushion in her lap, and another fat tear slid down her cheek. "And I can't have any friends because they might make me sick."

Evidently, Isobel had heard she was not included in today's adventures. "Well, perhaps I can help. Can ye tell me more about yer illness?"

"I often times can't breathe well."

"No? Are ye usually sick with a sore throat and a runny nose before that happens? Or does that happen even when ye've not been sick?"

Isobel squeezed her pillow to her chest. "Oh, I don't need to be sick beforehand. It just happens."

"Would ye mind if I listened to yer back? I promise not to hurt ye. I'd like to hear how ye breathe."

Isobel nodded, and Cameron eased next to her on the bed. When Isobel leaned over, Cameron placed her ear against the child's back.

"Breathe in deep for me, and let it out slowly."

The lass did as she asked. The telltale rattling of discharge clogged her lungs.

She patted Isobel's back and stood. "Tell me more about yer illness."

Isobel straightened. "Nichola took me to the loch. She let me stick my toes in the water." Isobel's shoulders rose, and she held her little hands out, palms up. "I didn't get my whole body wet like the healer said."

Cameron tucked a dark errant lock behind Isobel's ear. "And did the healer think that caused yer illness?"

Isobel's head bobbed as she shook her finger. "If ye can't stay out of the water, no more out-of-doors for ye." Her hands dropped to the pillow. "I told him it happens even when Nichola doesn't take me to the water, but he wouldn't listen."

After learning her symptoms, hope flared. "I think I might be able to help ye."

Isobel's bottom lip poked out. "Da had more healers come in, but they couldn't do anything."

"Give me a chance. I have some ideas."

Cameron patted the lass's arm, then hurried down the stairs and around the corner to Robert's private chamber. Her hand stopped in midair. Recalling the last time she had seen

122

him, she swallowed hard. Her stomach clenched at the thought of him brazenly holding her against him. The warmth of his lips pressed against hers flashed before her eyes. Taking a deep breath, she knocked.

He called for her to enter.

She opened the door to find him sitting at his desk reviewing a stack of papers. He looked up, and his eyes widened.

"Laird Graham..."

"Robert. Call me Robert."

"All right, Robert. I'd like to talk to ye about Isobel."

His forehead wrinkled, and he stood. "Isobel?"

"I think I can help her. I've read about children who have her illness. A special blend of herbs may ward off her breathing attacks."

"Nay. We've had many healers treat Isobel, and not one could help her. I don't want to put her through anymore bloody *procedures.*"

She fumed. "Ye can't be serious. It is cruel to sequester her in a dark room for the rest of her life. I cannot believe *ye'd* want to live like that."

Robert leaned over the desk on his fists. "Tis what the healers recommended. What would ye have me do? Go against their training and have my baby sister gasping for air?"

Cameron let out a loud breath, and shook her head. "No. What I would have ye do is give me a chance." She searched his face and smoothed her palms down the front of her gown. "I'm asking for yer permission to treat her."

He crossed his arms and peered down at her with an intense look in his eyes. "What did ye have in mind to do for her?"

"I'll need some herbs that most likely grow in the woods north of here near the loch. When they're left to steep in hot water, they emit a vapor that soothes the breathing passages."

"Ye won't bleed her?"

"Oh nay, just a daily brew."

Robert hesitated, his eyes narrowing. "Verra well. Ye have my permission."

A smile broke across her face, and she clasped her hands at her chest. "I'll need to gather those herbs."

"We'll go this afternoon. I'll take ye to our north loch myself." He stepped around the front of his large oak desk. The closer he moved toward her, the more intimate and warm the room grew.

"I appreciate yer willingness to help Isobel."

"Ye...ye're welcome," Cameron stammered and stepped back. "I need to uh, to help Nichola with something."

She eased around him and hurried out the door.

~~~

Robert cinched the girth under Eton's belly. What was he thinking taking Cameron to the loch? He should send Kendrick, but the idea of being alone with her had him intrigued. To be near her, walk by her side and listen to her expound about her special herbs. He sighed. He could not resist her, and he knew where this would lead, but he saddled his horse anyway.

"What am I doing, lad?"

Eton shook his head side to side.

"Ye don't let a pretty filly turn yer head, do ye?"

The horse snorted, and Robert laughed. "Nay, I didn't think so."

He patted Eton's sleek neck and led him from the barn.

Cameron held her basket before her and hurried down the stairs and into the bailey. She had swept her long hair up and secured it with a ribbon, but dark wisps blew around her face. His sister's borrowed gown did little to hide Cameron's concealed treasures. What a beauty. Just thinking of spending time with her caused his pulse to increase.

He took her basket and tied it to his saddle, then turned back to her. "Are ye ready?"

124

"Aye, I told Nichola and Androu I'd join with them another day." She glanced around the bailey. "Which horse shall I ride?"

"Ye'll ride with me." Her eyes widened, and the corners of her mouth tugged up. Had he not been so close to her, he may have missed the subtle change. Did she like the idea of riding with him? He grasped her small waist, picked her up and placed her on Eton.

Robert swung up behind her. *Shite.* He closed his eyes and took a deep breath. Cameron's adorable backside nestled sweetly between his thighs. He nudged Eton into a trot, but that did nothing but cause her to bounce lightly in his lap. He couldn't utter a word for fear it would come out in a grunt.

Finally, she relaxed against him, and he enveloped her in his embrace. He tried not to think of how perfectly she fit between his legs, or how her breasts brushed his arm. Her soft hair grazed his chin, and he breathed in her clean lavender scent. His cock swelled. She must feel it straining against his trews, pressing into her luscious bottom. Inwardly he groaned—leave it to the fellow between his legs to rise up and let his presence be known.

They galloped down the dusty road and across the north pasture, riding for several miles before they came upon the loch. Robert slowed Eton to a walk, and they made their way to the shore. He slid to the ground and lifted Cameron off the saddle.

Her delicate fingers clutched his shoulders, and her green eyes locked onto his as he lowered her before him. His hands lingered at her waist. Her plump lips parted, and his manhood jerked. He longed to wrap his arms around her, bury his face in her hair and lose himself in her sweetness. She ran her palms down his arms as a gentle breeze blew strands of dark hair across her face. He brushed the tendrils away and cupped her cheek.

Ducks flew overhead, their loud squawks announcing their presence. The noise broke the spell Cameron had weaved over him. She leaned to look behind him and laughed. He turned to see several fowl had landed on the loch. A large male chased another. With his long neck stretched forward, he flapped his wings, spray flinging as he honked and propelled himself to run on the water's surface.

"What a beautiful place." Cameron shaded her face from the sun, and swept her gaze across the area. "I think I'll start with the edges of the forest to find what Isobel needs." She stepped away from him, picked up her basket and started toward the woods. "Do ye come here often?"

"Not often enough." Robert bent and grabbed a handful of pebbles. He tossed them in his hand as they continued around the water's edge. "Lachlan, Kendrick, and I swam here when we were lads."

He skimmed one of the stones across the loch's surface. It bounced several times before plunking in.

"Ye grew up with each other?"

He pitched another stone. "Aye, we've always been together. Lachlan's family was killed when he was a bairn, and Kendrick's father sent him to foster with my da. The three of us have been best of friends ever since."

Cameron smiled, and her eyes sparkled. His gaze slid over her pink cheeks and down to her plump lips...lips he would like to taste. She glanced toward the ground.

At a glimpse of her calf, his cock stirred again. What was it about her that caused his heart to drum when she was near? He longed to take her in his arms, nuzzle her neck and feel her soft body pressed against him. He shook his head and tried to clear his agonizing thoughts. Images of an old shriveled crone with baggy skin hanging of her bony frame and blackened teeth filling her mouth, kept the devilish friend between his legs at bay.

They strolled a good distance with Cameron stopping here and there to examine different plants. "Oh look, mullein. That will help ease Isobel's breathing."

He handed his knife to her, and she stooped and cut the large, hairy leaves. "In the summer, the stalks can grow to great heights, and it has beautiful yellow flowers."

126

She straightened and studied her basket full of herbs. "This should last a while."

"Is that all ye need?"

She bit her bottom lip while searching the surrounding area and then pointed to a sunny patch. "Just a bit of that sage."

After gathering her collection of herbs, they strolled around the water's edge. The setting sun highlighted different shades of red in her dark hair. A gentle breeze blew errant curls around her face, and her beauty once again struck him. His palms itched to touch her, caress her. He could not resist her and was through trying.

~~~

Cameron inhaled the refreshing air and marveled at the surrounding landscape. The afternoon sun sent shimmering rays across the loch and through the downy birch, their grayish-white trunks and limbs touting an abundance of green leaves rustling in the wind. To her left, alder trees stood tall lining the shore, their mirror image reflected in the water. Mossy ferns surrounded the roots and covered the ground, protecting nestlings and small creatures seeking shelter. Across the water, a mountain rose high with green and yellow leaved trees dotting the landscape. A breeze caused ripples to ride the surface and lap at the edge outlining the shore.

They arrived at a patch of low marshy ground and had to navigate over stones. Cameron stepped on a rock and slipped, her hand grasping air. "Aah!"

Robert's strong arm encircled her waist. "Careful, the moss can be slick."

Her shoe squished in the mud, and when she picked up her foot, muck plopped on the ground. "Oh, dear. I've ruined my slipper."

"Let me help ye."

Before she knew what he was about, he whisked her legs up and lifted her out of the swampy grasslands. Her heart skipped a beat, thrilled at his brazen embrace. She wrapped her arms around his thick neck, his soft hair curling against her fingers, her basket bobbing against his strong back. As he carried her to a dry area, she studied his handsome face. A thick growth of whiskers covered his cheeks and strong chin. His musky, mesmerizing scent drifted around her and for a moment, she wanted to throw caution to the wind and snuggle against him.

Too soon, he set her bottom on a boulder and knelt at her feet. Trying to compose herself, she placed her basket beside her and peered at him. With his dark head bent, he raised her skirt to mid-calf, slid her shoe off, then propped her foot on his thigh. His warm hands and touch stirred something deep within her. Head reeling, tingling sensations shot up her leg to her core. She longed to close her eyes and relish the feelings he invoked, to lose herself in his arms.

His dark eyes smoldered as he caressed her foot, then her ankle. "Ye didn't get hurt, did ye?"

"No...no, I'm fine," she whispered, her voice husky.

His strong hands massaged her skin, inching up her calf. She had heard lasses' whispers about this handsome laird and the pleasures he brought. What would it be like to lie with him, experience his caresses?

He knocked the mud off her shoe and helped her ease it back on. When he stood, he brushed a stray lock of hair from her brow. Sliding his hand around the back of her neck, he rubbed her skin with the rough pad of his thumb before he bent and gently kissed her. When she tentatively touched her tongue to his, he groaned and pulled her off the boulder to meld against his hard body.

She placed her trembling hands on his chest as he wrapped his arms around her. She gasped at the nervous tremors coursing through her. Her head spun. The feel of his strong arms and the play of his mouth awakened desire and stoked flames to life deep within her belly. Her arms inched around his neck, encouraging him. Her body yearned to feel his touch.

His hands roamed across her back and lower. He cupped her buttocks and lifted her into him. Her toes barely

128

touched the ground as his manhood pushed against her abdomen. She reveled in his caress, the feel of his lips on her skin. Her body screamed for more.

He broke their kiss and trailed his hot mouth down her neck while easing the top of her gown aside to bare her shoulders. A fog of desire overwhelmed her, and she moaned, melting under his ministrations, but when he ran his mouth across her collarbone and his scratchy whiskers brushed her skin, she abruptly came to her senses. Breathing erratically, she restrained her desire and newly awakened need. She was his captive, for heaven's sake.

Her body protested as she gently pushed away. "We need to get back," she whispered, her hand still on his chest.

He studied her lips and let his eyes travel across her bare shoulders, down to the tops of her breasts peeking out of her lowered bodice. His smoky eyes undressed her, left her exposed. Heat crept up her neck and spread across her face, and she tugged the gown back in place.

Robert entwined his fingers with hers. He raised her knuckles to his lips and kissed her hand. "As ye wish, m'lady," he whispered, but his eyes spoke of the pleasures awaiting her.

They walked in silence to Eton. He tied her basket to the saddle and lifted her onto the horse's back. He settled her in front of him and started toward the castle. Cameron couldn't think of anything except the sparks of pleasure Robert had ignited in her. She didn't understand why Robert kissed and caressed her. She thought he regarded her as the enemy. His actions were confusing, and her body screamed in protest of her rational mind. She craved his lips on her mouth, his hands on her body, caressing and loving. Her nerves stood on end. Every scrape of his arm against her breast was torment.

She shifted her weight, and he put his hand on her waist. "Don't do that."

Glancing over her shoulder, she turned slightly in his lap. "Do what?"

"Wiggle." He hissed. "Stop wiggling."

129

Suddenly understanding what the hard bulge against her bottom was, she sat straight and tried not to move, but he tugged her back against him. She closed her eyes and leaned her head on his chest. He kissed her temple, and her stomach churned.

Oh Lord, she was falling in love with him.

This can't be happening. But it was. She knew it. And she knew there was nothing she could do to stop it.

Before long they rode into the bailey and over to the stables. Robert swung down and reached up to help her dismount. He lifted her off the saddle and let her slide down his length, setting her on the ground before him. Their eyes met and held. One of the lads from the stables ran to take Eton.

Stepping back, she accepted her basket from the lad. After thanking the boy, she fled up the stairs.

Chapter Nine

"Come on, Issie," Androu yelled and ran ahead carrying the large basket of food, eager to locate the perfect spot next to the river. Cameron was thrilled with his continued progress. The way he took off with Isobel skipping along behind, ye'd never know of his recent injury just a month ago.

Tilting her head to the sun, she absorbed the warm rays. A light breeze blew puffy white clouds across the blue sky. "What a lovely day."

"Aye, it's perfect for a day out-of-doors. I just hope this is a good idea," Nichola muttered.

Isobel laughed and chased Androu down the grassy hill, weaving around boulders and trees dotting the countryside.

"We have to try," Cameron replied. "We won't know if the treatment works if we don't put it to the test."

"I worry it's too soon."

"What about here?" Androu stood under a large shade tree with a flat area underneath. The leaves rustled in the breeze filtering sunlight through the thick branches.

"Aye, this is a good spot." Nichola spread a blue woolen cloth at the base of the tree.

Androu set the food basket down. "Wanna go to the water, Issie?"

"May I?" Isobel asked, her brown eyes wide.

"Aye, but Androu watch out for her," Nichola yelled as they raced away.

The women settled on the cloth and watched the children play. The wind swayed tall grasses and white rippled waves frothed over boulders and rocks. Several ducks squawked and anxiously paddled from the shore as Androu and Isobel invaded their space.

Nichola turned to Cameron. When she didn't say anything, Cameron tilted her head to the side. "What is it? I can tell ye have something to say."

Nichola smiled. "I wanted to thank ye for all ye've done for Androu, Isobel and my clan. I know ye didn't come here of yer own accord and Robert holds ye against yer will." She paused. "I enjoy yer company, but I think ye should be able to return home. Robert has made yer da suffer long enough."

"I plan to talk to yer brother. He hasn't said how long he intends for me to stay."

Nichola picked a clover and twirled it between her forefinger and thumb. "What would ye be doing if ye were at yer home?" She glanced up, her eyes wide. "Are ye betrothed?"

Cameron shook her head and plucked a blade of grass. "Nay."

Nichola scrunched her forehead and touched Cameron's arm. "Did Robert bringing ye here ruin yer chances for marriage?"

Cameron considered her words and smoothed the grey, woolen skirt over her legs. "I don't know if I *want* to marry. I could not abide a husband's dalliances." She glanced at Nichola. "All men do it. Even my own da. I can't tell ye how many times I heard my mum cry over his infidelity."

"Well, I want to marry. I want lots of bairns." Nichola had a faraway look in her eyes. "Do ye not have dreams?"

"Aye, I have dreams." Cameron tossed the blade of grass and leaned back on her palms. "I dream of someday becoming a respected healer." The familiar twinge of doubt surfaced at her fantasy. "That's not likely to happen, but as long as we're talking dreams, that's mine."

"Do ye not wish for children of yer own?"

Androu pitched a pebble into the loch, and it skimmed across the surface. Isobel clapped and shouted, "Teach me! I want ta do it."

Cameron's chest tightened. A bairn? Her arms ached to hold a babe of her own. "That is not likely to happen. I will turn five-and-twenty in a few months. And it certainly won't come to pass as long as I remain captive."

Nichola touched Cameron's hand. "I wish ye'd stay with us."

Cameron sighed. "I miss my family, and I worry so for my da. I do not believe he attacked Androu and Duncan. I can't believe it."

Nichola's teeth raked her bottom lip, and her brows rose. "Ye might have a hard time convincing Robert."

Happy squeals caught their attention. Androu splashed Isobel and ran away with her fast on his heels. Isobel's little legs pumped, but her brother slowed and allowed her to catch him before he hoisted her onto his back and dropped in the grass. The children laughed and rolled down the hill to the water's edge.

"It's so good to see her running and playing," Nichola said. "My heart has been broken over her illness. She's never been able to act like a normal child nor have friends her own age."

"I'm hopeful the treatments will help her," Cameron said. "Staying in a dark room is no way to live."

"They're so dear to me. Mum left shortly after giving birth to Isobel. Androu was devastated." Nichola's voice caught with emotion. "He cried for weeks, asking for Mum. I worried he wouldn't get over her leaving, but one day his tears just dried up. He's not mentioned her since."

Cameron ran her hand down Nichola's arm. "I'm so verra sorry."

Her mouth drew together in a thin line. "When it was clear Mum wasn't returning, I stepped in to mother them, and we've developed a close bond."

"We don't want to overdo Isobel's first outing. Perhaps we should call them over to rest a wee bit."

Androu and Isobel squatted at the water's edge. The sun's rays streaked through dark clouds with a storm brewing in the distance.

"What are they looking at?" Nichola shaded the sun from her eyes. "Androu, Isobel, come up for lunch."

Isobel screeched when Androu jumped up holding something in his hands. She ran around him, jumping up and down when he darted toward the blanket.

133

Nichola squinted at him while he sprinted toward her. "What's he got?"

"Look what I found," Androu exclaimed excitedly.

When he got closer, Nichola screamed and leapt up. "Androu Graham, ye get rid of that right now!"

He clutched a slimy creature dripping mud as he raced behind Nichola. "Come on, sister. Ye know ye want to hold it."

"Get rid of it," Nichola screeched.

Cameron burst out laughing. She rolled on the blanket holding her sides at the sight of Androu chasing Nichola around the field with a slimy frog in his hands.

The lad finally took pity on his sister and carried the creature back to the water.

Isobel plopped next to Cameron and giggled. "That was funny."

Strolling back to the blanket, Nichola placed one hand on her chest and the other on her hip.

"I'm impressed. I didn't know ye could run so fast," Cameron teased.

"Oh, I'll have to think of some way to pay him back for causing me to lose years off my life." Nichola shivered. "He knows I've always been afraid of those creepy things."

Androu returned, fell to his knees on the blanket, and goaded his sister. "It was only a *wee* creepy thing."

Cameron shook her head and sighed. The Grahams had definitely wormed their way into her heart. Her thoughts turned to her own family. Here she sat having a meal out-of-doors in the glorious sunshine, while they most likely grieved for her. A wave of guilt washed over her, and her chest tightened.

Isobel and Androu peered over Nichola's shoulder as she rummaged through the basket. They were precious innocent children. If Symon attacked again, they could they be hurt or killed. She swallowed hard and studied the tree line. She would have to make her way through the dense forest to return home. She remembered the route Robert took, and she could retrace their steps.

"Here's a flask of milk, Issie." Nichola passed the container over her shoulder to Isobel. "And there's cider for the rest of us." She extended a jug with several cups to Cameron. "If ye'll pour, I'll get the chicken."

A dirt path snaked around several huts and into the woods. How would she manage to slip away unnoticed?

"Cameron, are ye dreaming?"

Startled out of her guilty thoughts, Cameron jumped. "Oh, no, just enjoying the day."

She grasped the container, and dropped the cups on the blanket. She would not let her plight interfere with the children's fun. Pulling herself together, she set aside her thoughts of escape...for now.

"Robbie!" Isobel shouted and jumped up.

Robert? Cameron's head turned toward the castle as he strode toward them, his sword dangling at his side. He grasped his young sister around the waist and hoisted her to his hip. She wrapped her arms around his neck, and he kissed her cheek while making a loud production out of the smack.

Isobel squealed with delight and patted his face with her little hands. "Ye just missed Nichola running around the field. Androu had a frog, but Nichola didn't want to see it."

Robert's deep laugh caused Cameron to smile. "I suspect not. Ye know Nichola is a wee bit of a bairn."

"Not like me. I'm not a bairn. I wanted to see it," Isobel exclaimed.

"Och, those things should stay in the water where they belong," Nichola shouted.

Robert chuckled as he continued toward them. When they reached the blanket, he set Isobel down, and she scurried next to Androu and fished an apple from the basket.

"I hope ye don't mind if I join ye. I'm famished." He unbuckled his sword and laid it at the edge of the blanket as he dropped next to Cameron, his dark eyes sparkling.

She held out the jug to him. "Would ye care for some cider?"

His head bobbed. "That sounds good."

135

When she handed him a cup, his fingers brushed hers, and a jolt shot up her arm. Trying to gain control, she turned to Androu. "And how about ye?"

"Aye." He bit into a chicken leg and handed a mug to her.

Clanging steel rang out, and a shout roared from the castle. Androu's head whipped toward the noise, and then back to Robert, his brows scrunching. "Didn't ye finish training?"

Robert leaned back on his left elbow and stretched his muscular legs before him. "I did." He glanced at Cameron. "I left Kendrick in charge so I could join ye."

She searched his face. He left training…to be with them? With her?

"But ye never do that," Androu protested.

Robert tilted his face to the sun. "Well, I made an exception. It's a beautiful day, and I needed a rest."

"We're pleased ye did," Nichola said, and handed a piece of chicken to Cameron. "Would ye care for a leg, Robert?"

Cameron licked her fingers. "Tessa outdid herself. Ye should try it. This is wonderful."

He sipped his cider and watched Cameron over the rim of his cup. "I'll start with an apple."

Nichola tossed the fruit to him, and he bit into it. Juice dribbled down his mouth. His tongue sneaked out and licked the drops.

Cameron's stomach tightened, and remembering his hot mouth on her skin, she swallowed hard. When her eyes lifted to his, he was staring at her. The corners of his mouth tugged up. Her heart slammed against her chest.

"I want to catch a fish," Androu announced, then plopped a sweet cake in his mouth.

Isobel clapped. "Me, too! Me, too!"

Robert balanced his mug on his thigh. "Bring me two long sticks."

Androu jumped up and raced off with Isobel fast behind him. The children scurried from one place to the next, bending

136

and picking up small branches. Androu threw one to the side and found another.

Isobel held up a twig. "What about this one?"

Androu laughed. "Nay, that one is too puny."

Robert pitched his apple core down the hill. "She's doing well?"

"Aye, she is, but we won't let her overdo it," Cameron reassured him.

The two ran back to the blanket, Androu thrusting two sticks toward Robert. "I found some."

Robert removed his dagger from his belt. With his dark head bent over the task, his thick fingers worked the blade over the wood, and he whittled the end of both sticks into sharp points. What a dear brother. "Take these, and see what ye can spear."

Androu grabbed one and handed the other to Isobel, then raced away. The little lass's legs scurried to keep up.

Nichola straightened, and shading her eyes from the afternoon sun, she watched them run down the hill toward the water's edge. "I'm not sure she should be playing with that sharp stick." She stood and brushed off her skirt. "I think I'll make sure she doesn't spear *herself* instead of a fish."

She hurried away leaving Cameron alone with Robert.

Nervous energy welled. She gathered the remnants of the children's lunch and placed the jug of cider in the basket. More shouts from Robert's men carried on the wind. "They must be working hard."

He crossed his ankles. "We'll be ready when the Sassenachs invade."

"Ye expect them this far west?"

His fingers toyed with a twig. "It's a matter of time. The attack on the MacCarthys was just one of many in recent weeks."

"I pray this fighting will end soon."

He tilted his head to the side. "I figured a healer would be averse to violence."

"I am averse to *senseless* violence. I loathe King Edward and his murdering soldiers. We have lost so many good men, and clans have suffered. I often wonder if there is any chance of peace between our countries."

"Och, that's a dream we all hold, but I don't see it coming to pass. My men and I will be ready when the enemy arrives."

Squeals from the water caught their attention. Isobel jumped up and down and ran to the other side of Androu. Sticks in hand, the children raced across the field.

Nichola turned toward the top of the hill and shouted, "I'm taking them down the river where it's shallow."

Cameron waved and watched them disappear around thick trees. "Isobel and Androu are so precious."

Robert touched her shoulder, and her head turned to him. "I thank ye, lass."

"Well, do not thank me yet. The true test will come this evening. That is when her difficult breathing spells occur most often."

"Aye, but I appreciate ye trying to help her." His fingers slid down her arm to hold her hand. "Ye're quite a healer."

His warm touch and praise staggered her, knocked her off guard. "I've longed to hear those words. I've studied under our clan's healer since I was five years of age."

His head cocked to the side. "Ye knew at such a young age ye wanted to learn the healing arts?"

His thumb rubbed circles on her hand and a deep longing to feel his touch elsewhere on her body caused her insides to tighten. She cleared her throat. "Aye, my mum said she saw a talent in me early on whether I was setting birds' broken wings or tending a baby squirrel that had fallen out of its nest. She encouraged my education."

His dark eyes softened. "She must have been some kind of lady to raise such an independent daughter."

138

Cameron searched his face. He did not smile in ridicule. He seemed sincere.

"Mum demanded Da support me and my sisters in our quests for happiness. My older sister, Heather, oversees the workings of the castle, and my younger sister, Lindsey, manages the stables, breeding and selling horses. Then, there's Elsbeth." Cameron chuckled. "My baby sister recoiled at the violent Scottish rebellion and has vowed to save misplaced and orphaned children…" Her voice trailed off, her chest clenching. How she missed them.

He glanced at their entwined fingers, and his thumb stroked her knuckles. "I'm afraid we had a poor start." His gaze returned to her eyes, and he tugged her toward him as he whispered, "I'd like to make amends. Thank ye for helping my clan."

His lips pressed against hers in a feather of a kiss. She closed her eyes, and his hand slipped around the nape of her neck, pulling her closer. Her palms splayed on his chest, and he wrapped his arm around her waist. She lost herself in his embrace.

He leaned her back, laying her against the blanket as he kissed her passionately. He cupped the side of her face, and his tongue found hers in an enticing dance.

The muscles of his thick chest and broad shoulders rippled beneath her fingertips. How she would like to feel his naked skin, the soft hair covering his torso. She moaned as his hand moved to her bodice and cupped her breast. Her nipple pressed against the fabric, and he rubbed the sensitive tip. A tingling sensation coursed through her body, and she longed to feel his hand on her bare skin.

His lips left hers to trail down her neck. She tilted her head to the side giving him access, but his mouth dipped lower to replace his fingers at the tip of her breast. When his lips closed over her clothed nipple, the warmth of his mouth penetrated the soft fabric. A bolt shot through her, and a dull ache throbbed at the apex of her legs. His hand traveled down her side, and a draft swirled around her skin as he lifted her skirt. His palm brushed her calf, over her knee, still higher to her thigh. When he touched the thin material of her undergarment, she sucked in a breath, and his mouth returned to hers.

"Easy," he whispered.

"But the children, Nichola…"

"Are well away. Relax. No one can see us." His fingers slid underneath the fabric and traced her nether lips.

"Ohh…" She sighed, gripping his shoulders. Sensations she had never experienced sprang forth, and she wantonly pressed her hips into his warm palm.

"I got one," Androu shouted from down the river. "Robert, come see!"

Robert lifted his head and stared into her eyes as his fingertips caressed her sensitive flesh.

Her breath came in quick puffs. Heat crept up her neck and spread across her cheeks.

"Forgive me. I had hoped for a few moments alone, but this is not the best place to express my *gratitude*."

He eased his hand from her heated flesh and kissed her gently while lowering her gown. He exhaled and straightened, then extended his hand to her. She grasped it, and he tugged her upright.

He stood and winked at her, then turned and jogged down the hill.

She closed her eyes and tried to still her breathing. Oh, Lord help her, she couldn't resist him.

~~~

After their delightful adventure, Cameron took a bath, gave Isobel another brew, and helped her into bed. She steeped herbs in a bowl suspended over the fire in Isobel's room. The steam emitted a vapor she hoped would keep the little girl's breathing passages clear.

The lass yawned and stretched, sleepy from the excitement of the day.

140

Cameron kissed Isobel's cheek and tucked the blankets around her neck. "Good night, sweetling. Sleep well."

In no time, Isobel's steady breathing—no rasping or wheezing—drifted across the room. Cameron sighed with relief and curled up in a chair in front of the fireplace. What would it be like to have a precious little one?

Robert's child would resemble Isobel with her large brown eyes and dark wavy hair. He would love his bairn as he did his siblings. He not only protected them, he worried about their happiness. Although he could be stern and forbidding, he had a loving side toward his family and clan. What would it be like to hold his affections? With those sweet thoughts, she tugged her robe to her neck, closed her eyes, and drifted off to sleep.

~~~

Cameron awoke to find Robert kneeling in front of her chair. He grinned lazily while lightly stroking her calf in small circles, gradually sliding his hand higher to the back of her knee. Transfixed by the coursing sensations, she voiced no objection to his attentions. In fact, she reveled in them.

"What are ye doing sleeping in Isobel's chair?" His deep voice rumbled in the silence.

"I wanted to be here in case she needed me."

His gaze rested on her breasts. Covered in a light robe, her nipples pressed against the soft fabric. She crossed her arms, but he grasped her hand and kissed her palm. The dark stubble on his chin scraped her flesh, and butterflies flittered in her stomach.

"Isobel had a wonderful day. I thank ye for caring for her." His warm breath sent shivers through her body.

"She's a sweet lass, and I pray she continues to improve. I'd best return to my chamber. I think she'll be fine tonight."

"Aye, she seems well." Robert stood and tugged Cameron from the chair. He held her hand and led her out of Isobel's room and down the hall.

Her pulse raced in anticipation over whether he would kiss her goodnight. Her breath quickened at the thought of him holding her with what little clothing she wore between them. When they stopped at her chamber, he turned toward her.

His pupils widened, and his nostrils flared.

She trembled with need, anxiously awaiting his kiss. He leaned into her, and her pulse beat faster. She raised her lips to meet his, but he reached around her and opened the door.

Her stomach dropped as disappointment flooded her body.

Robert looked over her shoulder. "Yer fire died down."

He walked to the hearth and threw in a bunch of peat. Flames curled around the dry moss inviting her to warm her hands. She held her fingers to the red and gold blaze.

Robert faced her. Tension strung tight between them.

"Ah lass, ye break my will," he breathed out and tugged her into his embrace. He rained kisses on her forehead and the side of her face before settling on her eager mouth.

His essence engulfed her. He let out a feral growl as his hands roved across her back and down to her bottom. He squeezed her bum and lifted her against the rigid length pressing into her stomach. His hand skimmed her waist, inching higher to cup her breast. Her sensitive peak stood taut against his warm palm, and she sighed.

"Ye know I want ye, lass." He nuzzled her neck. "Will ye let me love ye tonight?"

Robert's words came to her in a fog of desire. She ran her hands over his broad shoulders feeling his massive muscles bunch. Her nipples brushed his chest through her gown, and heat pooled between her legs. Her mind spun as his hands roamed her body. It felt heavenly to be in his arms—in the arms of the man she loved.

Trying to shake the haze of passion, Cameron knew she should make him stop. Where would this lead? If she let him continue, she risked getting with child. She would be a fallen woman bringing shame to her family. Truce or not, her father

142

would perish at the thought of her lying beneath his hated enemy.

But it felt right.

Would it be so wrong to lie with the man she loved? With plans not to marry, but to pursue the healing arts, she might never have this chance again.

Robert trailed kisses across her face and down her neck. He gently slid her gown off her right shoulder and nibbled her skin. His teeth scraped, sending shivers through her body, her every nerve screaming for his attention.

He tugged her gown. The material skimmed her nipple before he ran the pad of his thumb over her peak. Exquisite sensations shot straight to her core where a dull ache throbbed and grew in intensity.

Robert cupped her breast, filling his rough tanned hand with her bosom. "Ye're beautiful," he whispered while rubbing the tip back and forth.

He slowly slipped the gown off her other shoulder, then lower to her waist. His gaze caressed her naked breasts before he bent and flicked his tongue across the rosy tips. When he suckled her, her legs grew weak. Her breathing came in short, rapid bursts.

Now was the time to make him stop.

Her body protested at the thought.

She could not make love to a man who had kidnapped her and held her prisoner. Could she?

~~~

Cameron's innocent green eyes, wide with passion, mesmerized Robert. He nibbled on her kiss-swollen lips.

"Ye didn't answer me." His fingers drifted down her neck, to her breast and toyed with the pink tip. "Will ye let me love ye tonight?"

He held his breath. The fire crackled and popped. She trembled against him.

"Aye," she whispered.

Heart pounding, he captured her mouth once again. It had been some time since he last had a woman, and he wanted to go slow, but his every nerve was on fire. He enveloped her in his arms. His eager palms slipped down her back, underneath her gown. When his fingers skimmed her bare bottom, his manhood jerked painfully. *Oh, Lord.* Her cheek fit his palm, and he squeezed her firm flesh. His hard cock pulsed with need.

Cameron's hands crept under his tunic, and he sucked in a breath. He yanked the shirt over his head and dropped it on the floor. She skimmed her fingers over his chest, and her eyes darkened with desire.

He picked her up, and she rested her head against his shoulder. He eased her onto the bed and slowly kissed her while running his palms across her soft breasts. His member strained against his trews as his lips nibbled her soft skin, sliding lower to her collarbone and further to her nipple. Her fingers entwined in his hair, holding him to her breast, encouraging him.

Flicking his tongue around her nipple, he gently suckled while easing her gown past her hips, expecting to hear the word for him to stop. When she moaned and lifted her hips, he deftly drew her gown down her legs.

He rose on his elbow. Her naked body was a virtual banquet he craved to devour. Her eyes were wide. With what? Fright?

He ran the back of his finger across her face, along her neck and further to her breast. Little goose bumps rose on her skin, and her nipples stood stiff.

"I'll not take ye, if ye don't want me to." His fingers grazed her soft belly, and his hand splayed open, delving through the dark curls covering her sweetness.

She sucked in a breath and tensed.

He cupped her, exploring the softness nestled between her thighs. "Ye're so beautiful, lass. Try to relax."

Her hips moved against his hand. He slowly inserted the tip of his finger, and ran it up and down her folds. Her slick moisture told him she wanted this, wanted him. He separated and spread her inner lips, his finger dipping into her hot sheath.

Cameron grabbed his arm. "Robert? Perhaps we shouldn't..."

He stilled and gazed at her. Chest heaving, her green eyes darkened, intense.

"Shhh, it's all right." He slowly circled her sensitive nub with his fingertip. "I won't do anything ye don't want me to do."

Robert enjoyed watching Cameron's face while he pleasured her. Her gaze turned sultry, her skin flushed. She hesitated, but soon loosened her hold on his arm before sighing and closing her eyes.

His gaze raked her body. He slid his finger in and out of her warm haven, and he was anxious to replace it with his throbbing shaft. A groan escaped his throat. He suckled her breasts while inching another finger in, stretching her to receive his member, his thumb circling her nub. His mouth nibbled her collarbone, up her neck to her plump lips. She opened her mouth, and his tongue met hers in an intimate dance while he eagerly untied his trews. His engorged cock sprang free. Afraid to make sudden movements for fear she'd stop their lovemaking, he eased on top of her.

She placed her trembling arms around his neck.

"Ye taste so sweet." He kissed the side of her face, her eyes and nose. His fingertip continued to circle her core. "We'll take it as slow as ye like."

Unmistakable desire radiated from her face. "That feels...so good."

"Ye like my touch," he whispered against her lips.

"Aye," she breathed out.

He nibbled her soft ear lobe while nudging her legs farther apart with his knee. "Open for me."

When she complied, he fought the overwhelming urge to drive into her warmth. The tip of his cock glided up her slick folds. *Keep it slow. Don't rush.* When she tilted her hips to him, he almost lost control. He trembled in anticipation.

"Put yer legs around me." His voice was thick with desire.

At his encouragement, she wrapped her thighs around him, and he slowly inserted the head of his throbbing cock. Sweat broke out on his forehead. When he pushed in further, the barrier protecting her innocence blocked his entrance.

He stilled, gritted his teeth. "Are ye sure, lass? If ye want me to stop, ye need to tell me now."

Oh, Lord. Would he be able to end it if she said the word? He held his breath.

She arched her back underneath him. "No...please, don't stop."

Unable to withstand the sweet agony, he flexed his hips and thrust into her. At her sharp intake of breath, he groaned. While he relished the fact he was her first, he hated hurting her. He strained not to move until she became accustomed to his size.

Placing his hands on either side of her face, he kissed her soft lips. "Are ye all right?"

She nodded.

He looked into her passion-filled eyes and kissed each one closed. He had never taken a virgin, and he worried at her silence. "Ye know the first time for a woman is painful, but I promise, I won't hurt ye anymore."

Her eyes drifted open, and her brows scrunched. "I thought there was more to it. I...I don't want ye to...to stop."

He chuckled. "Nay, lass. We've just begun."

When she closed her eyes and relaxed around him, he moaned from pure pleasure. *Slow, take it slow*. He drew out only to fill her again. Reaching between them, he gently massaged her special nub while pushing in and out, building to a faster pace.

Her breathing became erratic, her skin flushed.

"Robert..."

Her body trembled with the rush of her explosion. He pumped into her, finding pleasure in the spasms of her orgasm. Feeling the beginning of his own climax, he thrust once more

146

and spewed his seed into her womb. He slowed his movements, her muscles milking his spent member.

Suddenly realizing what he'd done, he rolled off her and pulled her next to him. She nestled her head on his chest, and he wrapped his arm around her. What was wrong with him? Never before had he emptied himself into a lass. Never before had he forgotten to take precautions, and he contemplated the ramifications. He was not concerned about getting Cameron with child. In fact, he basked in the thought of her bearing his bairn.

The thought he had never felt this strongly about a lass hit him squarely between the eyes. He struggled with his actions and berated himself for losing control. He was *always* in charge of his emotions. He never did anything without fully studying and understanding the consequences.

She eased away from him and padded across the room to the water basin on the side table. Shadows from the hearth danced across her slender back as she dipped the edge of a drying cloth into the water and cleaned her virginal blood from her legs.

Virginal blood he spilled.

She turned toward the bed, and his cock filled. Disheveled curls caressed her breasts and hung to her slim waist. He glimpsed the dark vee nestled between her thighs, before she covered herself with the drying cloth.

She dropped the cover as she slid back under the blankets into his outstretched arm. Nestling against his chest, his fingertips rubbed her arm's silky skin as he fought to control the urge to make love to her again.

Troubled by this evening's turn of events, he moved to leave her bed, but her soft even breathing indicated she had fallen asleep. Her warm sated body fit snuggly against his. Her small hand lay on his chest, and he inhaled the lavender scent of her thick hair.

Perhaps just a few more moments…

~~~

147

Late in the night, Cameron awoke nestled in the crook of Robert's arm. She relaxed in the safety of his strong embrace. She had lost herself, given in to passion. How would he treat her now that he had breached her maidenhead? Perhaps the act of taking her meant nothing to him. Was she only a means to slate his lust? He never uttered words of endearment. It was clear he desired her, but he had not led her to believe he had feelings for her.

He kissed the top of her head, interrupting her thoughts. His finger tipped her chin to meet his mouth in a sweet, passionate kiss, and she wantonly responded, reigniting the fire between them. She breathed in his musky essence as he stroked her breasts, running his hand lightly over the sensitive peaks. Heat spread through her core, her muscles tightened, and the familiar dampness gathered between her legs.

When he placed her hand around his member, she squeezed slightly, sliding her palm up and down the soft velvet skin. Robert moaned, encouraging her to explore him.

He eased his hand between her legs, opening her thighs for his touch. When she spread her knees, he cupped her and gently slid his fingers through her slick folds. Cameron's breath quickened. He circled her nub while slipping a finger into her warmth. She raised her hips, eager to join with him.

"Ah, lass, I can't take much more." He positioned himself between her legs and kissed her breasts, suckling on the rosy tips. His hot mouth nuzzled her neck, and he buried his large member.

She ran her hands over his broad back, then lower to the steely muscles of his rear end. His hips pushed his thickness in and out, and she closed her eyes at the exquisite feeling. Her palms skimmed his muscular arms and broad shoulders as his essence surrounded her, his dark hair cloaking her in a cocoon of pleasure.

The low groan emitted from his throat exhaled on a breath against her neck. He filled her, stretching and massaging her sheath with every stroke. Waves of ecstasy poured through her, and she cried out in bliss, her spasms squeezing him.

148

"Cameron," he breathed against her neck, and his muscular body shuddered. For a brief moment, he relaxed, before moving off of her. He lay quiet, but held her against him and stroked her hair.

With her head resting on his chest, she once again considered her wanton actions. She had offered no resistance to his lovemaking. Indeed, she had encouraged and welcomed his touch, delighting in his assault on her senses.

What must he think of her?

~~~

Deep in thought, Robert lay with Cameron nestled against him. Taking the MacDougall lass shook him to his core. He knew better, but he let his baser needs dictate his actions. Would she feel remorse in the light of day?

Shortly before dawn, she stirred. Her leg draped over his, and her arm rested across his waist. She felt good snuggled next to him, and he instantly became aroused. As she would be sore from their earlier lovemaking, he gritted his teeth and tamped down the urge to take her again.

"Lass, are ye awake?"

Cameron stretched and yawned.

"Good morn." He kissed her upturned mouth. "I have to leave ye now. I don't want any questions as to why I'm in yer bed or slipping from yer room."

"Oh, aye, thank ye. That would be hard to explain."

He hesitated. She had the most beautiful green eyes. He ran his thumb across her silky cheek. His heart dropped. It could not have been any heavier if a cockatrice had turned it to stone. She had been innocent. What had he done? His stomach roiled and tightened into a knot.

He took a deep breath and exhaled. "Before I go, I would ask ye a question."

She raised her eyebrow. "What is it?"

He looked at her long and hard. "Do ye have regrets over my loving ye last night?"

149

Cameron placed her fingers against his lips and shook her head. "Nay, Robert. No matter what happens from this point on, I'll never have regrets about last night."

She may not have regrets, but I do. A lump stuck in his throat.

He kissed her forehead and slid off the bed. While dressing, he studied her disheveled hair, her sultry, sleepy eyes. The blankets barely covered her breasts. Even with guilt flooding through him, temptation beckoned him to take her once more. He shook his head. He had to pull himself together.

She gazed at him, and he gently kissed her. Would she still feel the same and look at him with affection when she realized their lovemaking changed nothing? He could not give her up. She was not going anywhere.

Chapter Ten

Cameron buried her head under the blanket and shut out the morning sun streaming into her room. She sighed. It was well past time to be out of bed. She sat and dangled her legs over the side of the mattress. Sore nether parts conjured images of her wanton behavior. She squeezed her eyes shut.

Making love with Robert had been a special time she would forever cherish. His rough, large hands, accustomed to wielding a sword, had been gentle. Memories of her initiation into the acts between a man and woman caused heat to creep across her cheeks. The things he did to her—the way he touched her, *where* he touched her.

Shameless.

She shook her head. What must he think of her willingness, nay her *eagerness* to lie with him? She savored the ecstasy found in his strong arms and wondered what it would be like to lie with him each night—as husband and wife? To have his bairn and watch him love their child as he did his siblings? What would it be like to give her heart to him unconditionally?

She scoffed at her thoughts. What happened last night could not take place again. Given their situation, it was best for both of them.

Robert had asked if she had any regrets.

She swallowed hard. Regrets? Only that she couldn't enjoy him more. The night in his arms had passed too quickly. After he left this morning, his scent remained for a time on the linens, and she wrapped herself in his lingering warmth. She didn't fool herself into believing their act meant anything more than a tumble to him.

Robert made no promises. It was one night of passion. Her thoughts turned to Da—his soft brown eyes filled with sorrow and shame. She prayed he would not learn of her recklessness. "I can't think about that now," she muttered while sliding off the bed.

After washing her face, she donned another borrowed gown and smoothed the wrinkles around her hips. She ran her hands over her stomach. What would she do if she were with child? Her chest clenched. She would be an outcast, bearing a bastard child. Could she stomach the shame? What choice would she have?

She knew how to rid a woman of an unwanted bairn. She had administered a concoction to bring on the monthly bleeding to women, but only to those who after birthing many children were well past the age of safely bearing more. That was not an option. She would not take a brew to rid herself of a child. If she found herself in a motherly way, she would deal with the consequences.

She dismissed those troubling thoughts, slipped her feet into her shoes and decided to take refuge in Nichola's garden. Like many times at home, she hoped to find solace working with the plants—getting her fingers dirty and helping the herbs grow.

Cameron strolled down the stairs to find Lachlan lounging on a chair next to the hearth in the main hall. Apparently, Robert entrusted him with the duty of watching her today. She squared her shoulders, determined to ignore his presence.

The bustle of servants occupied with preparing the noon meal enabled her to slip unnoticed through the room and down the side hall. She prayed she would find the garden empty.

She stepped through the door, and a light breeze welcomed her, blowing tendrils of hair about her face. Tilting her head to the sky, she breathed in refreshing cool air. The wind rustled willow leaves, filtering sunlight through the branches while providing shade for a carpet of bluebells. A light fragrance wafted from the bobbing, blue flowers surrounding and encroaching on an old stone path. A worn bench beneath the tree beckoned visitors to sit.

Foxglove, the creamy white petals not yet peeking through their tight buds, would soon burst out in clusters along

152

the trail. Nichola had quite a garden full of healing plants, including wild basil and garlic.

Cameron knelt beside the hairy foxglove leaves and pulled several weeds. She dug her fingers into the soil and yanked on the roots. Broadleaf grasses commingled with ungainly wild basil. The more weeds she unearthed, the lighter her mood became. The little garden blossomed and her spirit along with it.

"There ye are, slut."

Startled, Cameron twisted her neck to look over her shoulder. Rosalind glared, her black eyes filled with menace. Her finger pointed accusations, her stance rigid. Cameron stood and faced the woman.

"Robert and me 'er betrothed, and ye're spreading yer whore's thighs for 'im."

Cameron's breath caught. She brushed her shaking hands on her skirt and swallowed.

The woman lunged. Sunlight glinted off a large blade. Cameron's pulse raced. She jumped back, but not before Rosalind sliced her forearm. The slash burned. Blood seeped through her torn sleeve.

"I saw him leaving yer room this morning. I willnae give him up to ye!" Rosalind charged again, the knife locked in her fist.

Cameron screamed. The woman brought the blade down. A large pair of hands grabbed Rosalind's arm seconds before the dagger sank into Cameron's chest.

Legs wobbling, Cameron staggered and caught the edge of the bench to regain her balance. Blood oozed down her fingers and dripped on the flowers she'd just tended.

Lachlan shook Rosalind and wrested the knife from her fingers. "What the hell's the matter with ye?"

"She's spreading her thighs for Robert."

Lachlan's face darkened, his blue eyes turning black. He grabbed Rosalind's wrist and turned to Cameron. "Are ye all right?"

She trembled uncontrollably, stunned not only by the violent attack, but from Rosalind's declaration.

"I'll have Aine tend ye."

Cameron's gaze shot past him to Rosalind. The vicious maid cocked her head to the side. She looked down her nose, her mouth pinched in a smirk. How Cameron would like to wipe the sneer off her smug face. "Nay, I'll manage. 'Tis not but a wee scratch."

"Ye are sure?"

She squared her shoulders and narrowed her eyes at Rosalind. "Aye."

Lachlan shoved the woman to the door. "Get inside."

They disappeared into the keep. Cameron clutched her arm. Her legs gave way. She sank onto the wooden bench and closed her eyes. The woman's blade to her heart could not have hurt more. *Robert and me 'er betrothed.* The words reverberated through her mind.

Aye, she knew they had been lovers at some point, but *promised* to each other? *Nay.* Was Rosalind lying? Was Robert pledged to the maid? Had her plans to get with child come to fruition? The thought sliced through her middle.

If it was true, Cameron had behaved like the 'other woman' she loathed. The other woman that came between couples—the other woman Mum cried over.

How could she have let this happen? How could she have fallen into Robert's arms like a whore? She *knew* better. Tears spilled, and she quickly brushed them away. Her arm ached, but the pain paled in comparison to the anguish in her heart.

~~~

Robert sequestered himself behind closed doors, relieved for once to have ledgers to review. He remained away from prying eyes, and aye, away from Cameron. He berated himself for taking her innocence, for losing control. What demands would she now place on him? No doubt, she would

154

insist he return her to her father. She would expect no less for the loss of her virginity.

He leaned an elbow on the desk and dropped his chin to his chest while rubbing the back of his tired neck. A long sigh escaped. In his mind's eye, his hands covered her soft breasts, his tongue tasted her sweet nipples, and his cock pushed into her warm haven. He groaned, hard with need for her again. She'd bewitched him.

A loud knock at the door broke his thoughts. He straightened and raked a hand through his hair. "Aye, come in."

Lachlan thrust the door open and shoved Rosalind inside to stand before the desk. She struggled against his grasp on her arm.

Robert glanced at the maid and then at Lachlan. "What is it?"

"She attacked Mistress MacDougall with a knife." Lachlan tossed a blade on his desk. The weapon skidded across the surface.

Robert's stomach lurched as if Eton had kicked him. He locked eyes with Lachlan. "Is she hurt?"

"She received a nasty cut on her arm. I don't know how deep it was, but she was bleeding."

His head pounded. Every muscle strained not to grab Rosalind by the throat and choke the life out of her. His breathing quickened. He stood and leaned forward on clenched fists, barely able to control his anger. "What do ye have to say for yerself?"

"She has no business in yer bed. Ye know I'm the only one who can satisfy ye." Rosalind broke from Lachlan's grasp and sidled around the desk and next to Robert. She brazenly reached for his crotch, but he grabbed her wrist. She winced, her other hand pushing against his grip. "Ye're hurting me."

"Ye listen to me and hear me good. Ye're to stay away from Cameron MacDougall. If ye so much as think about going near her, I'll banish ye from the clan." He shoved her from him. "Do ye understand me, wench?"

"But, Robert," she wailed.

He slammed his palm on the desk with a resounding bang. "Stay away from her, or get the hell out!"

"Ye willnae find what ye need from that scrawny bitch," she screamed, and ran from the room.

"Don't let her out of yer sight." Robert stormed from the solar. He hurried up the stairs, and down the hall that led to Cameron's chamber. Lachlan said she had received a nasty cut. He should have had Rosalind flogged and thrown out. Praying the wound wasn't severe, he knocked on the dark oak door.

"Come in."

He entered the room. Cameron stood next to the bedside table. She glared over her shoulder at him. Her eyes were not teary as expected. No, they blazed fury. Her rolled up sleeve exposed white skin marred with a long red gash. She turned back to the table and rifled through her basket.

He placed his hand on her shoulder. "I'm sorry, lass. I hope ye're all right."

She lurched away from him. "All right? Are ye daft?" Her eyes widened, sparks emanating from the green depths. "I was attacked by a woman with a knife. A woman I learned is yer betrothed."

He jammed his hands on his hips. "What?"

"How can ye casually stroll in here after betraying her?" Her breath hitched. "After betraying me? I would never have lain with ye had I known."

"My *betrothed*? What are ye talking about?"

"Yer betrothal to Rosalind."

"Rosalind is *not* my intended." How could she think he was to marry the maid?

"Ye made love to her."

"Nay, I didn't make love to her. She offered herself, and I didn't refuse. She came to me an experienced woman. She knew full well I would not marry her."

Cameron searched his eyes.

156

"There's a big difference from what ye and I shared." He stepped closer, bent his head so his mouth touched her forehead. "Ye and I made love, lass."

He cupped her chin and tilted her face toward him, but she wrenched away.

"Don't." She held up a hand. "There's no difference between what we did and what ye did with Rosalind."

She turned her back on him and removed a jar from her basket.

Robert dropped his arms to his sides and exhaled. "Let me see it."

When he clutched her elbow, she tried to pull away. "I can do it myself."

He held firm. "Even healers need help now and again. Let me see it."

She reluctantly yielded.

The wound was red and irritated. His jaw tightened. He should throw Rosalind out. "She got ye good, didn't she?"

"She was crazed."

Robert dipped a cloth in a bowl of water on her bedside table. "Aye, she was." He gingerly cleaned the dried blood around the gash. "I wouldn't have lain with ye if I was promised to another."

Cameron's head jerked up. Her eyes widened, and her brows rose. "Truly?"

His dark gaze met hers, and he paused. "Truly." He patted her arm dry. "Does it hurt?"

Cameron exhaled. "Not as much as it did."

"Now what do I need to do?" He nodded toward her basket. "Tell me what salve ye use."

"I can put it on…"

He shook his head. "Nay, I'll do it for ye."

She squirmed as if his touch made her uncomfortable.

He reached for a jar she had placed on the table. "Is this the one?"

"Aye."

He smeared the salve over the cut, applying it liberally, and wrapped a cloth around her arm, tying the ends to hold it in place.

Cameron tugged her arm back, and he dropped his hands to his sides. She turned her back on him, replaced the jar in her basket, and gathered the supplies.

He ran his hand down her arm. "Lass…"

She stiffened and flayed him with silence. Was this a tactic to make him feel bad? He took a deep breath. "Rosalind's been warned. If she ever so much as —"

She whirled toward him. "What? Attacks me again?"

"My men are on alert. They'll watch out for ye."

Cameron yanked her sleeve over the bandage, and planted her hands on her hips. "Well, thank ye verra much, but I don't want to be watched. I'm tired of being held prisoner. Ye have punished my da long enough. Let me return home where I won't be in fear of a blade finding its way into my chest."

The thought of her leaving him sank into the pit of his stomach like a boulder. He could not let her go. He would not give her up.

"No."

158

Chapter Eleven

Graham Castle
August 1297

Another six weeks passed, and Cameron rarely saw Robert. He left before dawn and returned well after the evening meal. She told herself it didn't matter. He had not fooled her into believing he cared for her. Their one night of passion was just that. But the emptiness his absence left in her chest refused to subside.

She missed him—his laugh, the bond between him and his men, his interaction with Nichola, Androu and Isobel. Closing her eyes, she recalled his touch, his caring manner when he tended her arm. A dull ache spread through her head, and her fingers massaged her temples in small circles. After weeks of Robert avoiding her, it was clear he had no room for her in his life.

She stood from the chair before her hearth and smoothed her grey woolen gown. With thoughts of him still racing through her head, she grabbed her basket and headed to the village beyond the castle gates. Glancing to the right and left, she thought she might be alone, but when Michael fell in step behind her, there was no doubt Robert continued to have her guarded.

The afternoon ended with her giving instructions to a woman on caring for her son's infected leg wound. She wiped perspiration from her upper lip as she made her way past the cottages lining the dirt road. With Michael following close behind, she paused by a grassy field filled with children, running and playing, Isobel amongst them.

A boy had wrapped a cloth around his eyes, his hands stretched in front of him, feeling for the other children. Isobel squealed and raced away when he ventured near.

Cameron's heart swelled. She continued to treat the child's breathing difficulties, and Isobel flourished from the daily potions. The time between her breathing attacks grew. In

159

fact, they were now rare. She was a different lass with a renewed outlook on life.

"Mistress MacDougall!" A man's shouts broke through her pleasant thoughts. "Mistress MacDougall!"

"I'm here," Cameron yelled. She hiked her skirt and ran toward the bailey.

A crowd had gathered. Lachlan caught a wounded man as he fell from his horse. He lowered him to the ground.

Cameron dropped to her knees beside the man. Blood matted his dark hair. He squinted through one eye, the other mangled from an obvious blow to the side of his pale face. His breath hissed through a hole in his chest. Blood soaked his frayed tunic, and dirt stuck to the edges of the crusty fabric.

"What happened?" Cameron opened his shirt and gasped. His entrails were exposed.

"Shite," Lachlan breathed out.

"Waaasss sher…" the man struggled to speak.

Cameron leaned down, placing her ear to his mouth.

"Wasss yeer cla..clan."

No! She straightened, and her stomach tightened. The man's lifeless eye stared at her. His words echoed through her mind. She had known it was only a matter of time before this happened. How would Robert react? Would he storm into MacDougall Castle and lay waste to her family?

Lachlan closed the man's eye. "He just rode in, barely holding onto the saddle."

"What was his name?"

"Harold. He worked a northern plot of land for Robert."

She picked up her basket. Her hands shook uncontrollably, and constrictions in her throat prevented her from speaking. Thunder rumbled in the distance, and the wind picked up as fat raindrops splattered the dirt.

Lachlan addressed the men crowded around them. "Help me carry him inside."

Tears stung her eyes. She fled up the bailey stairs, into the keep, and down the hall to her chambers. Leaning against the closed door, she dropped her basket, put her face in her

160

hands and sobbed. What would happen now? Robert once threatened to destroy her clan. The thought pierced as if his sword plunged into her heart.

Her eyes flew open. Perhaps he wouldn't know who attacked Harold. After all, only she heard his muffled, dying words. With all of the English soldiers roaming the countryside, mayhap Robert would think the enemy attacked.

Pushing away from the door, she numbly walked to the hearth and sank in the chair before the fire. She wiped tears from her face, wrapped her arms around her legs and stared into the flames.

A loud rap sounded on the door.

"Come in."

Several lads struggled into the room with a large bathing tub. Three others followed with buckets of hot water.

Who would have requested this for her? Nichola?

The boys deposited the tub in front of the fireplace and poured in the water. Steam rose from the surface and Cameron sighed, anxious to sink into its warmth. If only she could wash away her troubles so easily.

"Thank ye," she said when the lads turned to leave the room. After closing the door behind them, she undressed and climbed into the tub. She picked up a wedge of soap and lathered herself, taking solace from the heat of the water.

Lightning flashed and thunder rumbled, the turbulent storm matching her inner turmoil. What was she to do? The vicious attack on Harold caused her stomach to heave. Bile rose in her throat. Da wouldn't have done this, but Harold clearly accused her clan. It was more important than ever she leave and put an end to this senseless violence. She could not sit by and watch the nightmare of losing loved ones unfold.

Someone knocked and the door opened. Tessa ambled into the room. "M'lady? I brought ye some fresh clothes."

"Thank ye." Cameron was surprised to see Tessa. The woman had made it clear she didn't welcome Cameron into Graham Castle.

Tessa placed the clothes on the chair and picked up the drying cloth, holding it open. Cameron rose and flung water from her hands as the old woman wrapped the warm cloth around her. "Did ye enjoy yer bath?"

"I did." Cameron paused and tilted her head. "Did ye send it for me?"

"Aye, m'lady. I wanted to thank ye fer helping my grandson, Neyll. It was my daughter, Fiona, ye were with today."

"Oh, I see. I didn't realize yer relation."

"He's much better, and we've ye to thank." Tessa eased a clean chemise over Cameron's head. "I'll ask the lads to remove the tub." She picked up the discarded gown and turned toward the door. "Let me know if ye need anything. Thank ye again, mistress."

Tessa shut the door and the chamber fell quiet. The rain subsided, although thunder still rumbled low. Cameron curled up in a chair before the fire.

She could not keep her clan's attack from Robert.

As much as she loved her da, she would not lie to Robert. She'd have to convince him Symon led the attacks. He must give her father a chance to explain.

On shaky legs, she stepped into the gown Tessa left and ran a brush through her hair while rehearsing her words. She swallowed the lump that threatened to choke her and went in search of Robert.

～～～

Eton's hooves clattered over the wooden bridge leading into the bailey. Robert returned with Kendrick and a small group of men who drove Graham cattle to pastures where the grasses were plentiful. He was dirty and tired, irritable over his constant thoughts of Cameron. He had intended to stay away from her to lose interest. But if anything, it only heightened his awareness of her when he did see her. He longed to take her in his arms, hold her against his body.

Lachlan strode across the yard. "I'm glad yer back."

162

Robert swung off his horse and handed the reins to a stable lad. He pulled off his gloves and slapped them against his leg. "What is it?"

Lachlan followed him toward the keep. "It's Harold. He rode in this evening, bloodied and dying."

Robert stopped and faced him. "Dying?"

"Aye, the right side of his face was bashed, and his guts hung out his belly."

"What the hell happened?"

"I don't know." Lachlan rubbed the back of his neck. "He came in alone. Couldn't speak when he got here. Bubbles frothed out his chest."

"Shite! Sassenachs?"

Lachlan shrugged his shoulders. "Could've been. Or the MacDougalls."

Robert narrowed his eyes. The MacDougalls? Alastair would not strike with Cameron here. But then again, he didn't know Robert held his daughter. Mayhap it *was* the MacDougalls. The thought dropped into his stomach like a boulder.

He strode through the hall to his chambers, poured a large mug of mead and guzzled the burning liquid. His eyes watered, but he splashed more of the amber fire into his cup and emptied it again.

Arms braced on either side of the table, he dropped his head between his shoulders and closed his eyes. *Another attack.* He would ride to his northern property on the morrow and find out what happened. If Alastair was involved, Robert would end the confrontation the old laird started once and for all.

Someone knocked and opened the door. Robert turned as Duncan shuffled into the room. "Tessa sent this up for ye."

Several lads hurried in with the wooden tub.

"She's warming yer dinner."

Robert nodded. "Tell her I'll be down after I bathe."

"Aye, m'laird," Duncan answered as he escorted the lads out the room and closed the door behind them.

The hot water soothed his aching muscles, but it did little to assuage his troubling thoughts. He hoped he wouldn't find evidence of the MacDougall clan attacking Harold. Cameron would never forgive him for destroying her family, but strike them he would if he learned Alastair murdered Harold.

The castle was quiet when he strode from his chambers and climbed the stairs to the battlements overlooking the bailey—a favorite place he visited when sleep eluded his troubled mind.

Lightning lit the night sky and thunder rumbled in the distance. The wind whipped around him. Torchlight danced wildly and flags fluttered, slapping their staffs. He crossed his arms over his chest and surveyed the quiet bailey.

Edward sent his forces into Scotland, encroaching on their soil, constantly patrolling and striking at the slightest affront. If Harold had encountered the English scum, then they were closer than he thought. It was doubtful Harold had done anything to incite an attack.

Light footsteps sounded behind him. A familiar whiff of lavender wafted past, and his stomach tightened.

"Robert?"

Cameron's sweet voice drifted over him. His back stiffened, and he squared his shoulders. Heart beating erratically, he closed his eyes briefly and took a deep breath.

She stepped beside him, and he turned his head, acknowledging her presence. She hugged her waist and rubbed her arms. "I thought I might find ye here."

Her eyes were puffy as if she'd been crying. He turned back, staring into the darkness. The lightning was no more powerful than the current stretching between them. His throat constricted. He had missed her.

"I need to talk to ye."

"What do ye want?" He had not intended to sound so harsh.

When she hesitated, he faced her, arms crossed. She nervously licked her lips, and his cock instantly reacted, stirring to life. He strained to control his traitorous body.

"I wanted to tell ye how sorry I was about Harold." She paused. "I didn't know him, but he didn't deserve to suffer such violence."

"Nay, he didn't."

She dropped her gaze to the ground, and a few stilted moments passed. When she raised her head, her green eyes shimmered with tears. "I also wanted to tell ye that before Harold died, he…"

Robert braced himself. "He what?"

Cameron's breath hitched, and a tear trickled down her cheek. "He told me it was my clan that attacked him."

Her words knocked the breath from him. He turned away to hide his shock. She knew who attacked Harold, and she told him, well aware he would strike her clan. Most women would have lied, kept this secret from him.

She clasped his upper arm. "I beg ye to spare my da. I know ye don't believe me, but he would not have done this. Regardless of what ye think, he's an honorable man."

"How do ye reconcile yer *honorable* father murdering Harold? Bashing his face in and virtually disemboweling him?"

She shook her head violently. "Nay, it wasn't him. It had to have been Symon. Ye've got to believe me."

"What I believe is yer da has yet to learn his lesson."

~~~

Lightning streaked the dark sky. Thunder followed, and rain pelted the castle. Cameron blindly stared through the open window overlooking the grounds. The blustery weather threw the wooden shutters back, and they slammed against the wall, but she barely noticed. She had sealed Da's fate with the man she loved.

The bedchamber door creaked open, then shut. She wiped moisture from her eyes and turned.

Robert stood just inside her room, his hands behind his back. His thick hair hung to his broad shoulders. His unbuttoned shirt exposed dark curls feathering his massive chest, and his brown trews ended at his bare feet. He was so handsome.

Lightning flashed, and he pierced her with an intense stare. Her pulse beat frantically and she trembled, goose bumps covering her arms.

He advanced toward her and stopped mere inches away. Every nerve screamed for his touch, but she stopped from throwing herself into his arms.

He leaned into her and breathed deeply. She closed her eyes. The heat from his body warmed her face. So close—she could turn and press her lips to his. Her heart thumped so loud, surely he heard it.

Cool emptiness slid across her face. Her eyes fluttered open, and she realized he'd pulled back, watching her.

Several moments passed.

"I've missed ye." His deep voice rumbled in his thick chest.

She swallowed. "I've missed ye, too."

His gaze skimmed her face, finally resting on her eyes.

"I want to thank ye for yer honesty." He traced a line from her shoulder down her arm to her hand, entwining his fingers with hers. He raised her hand to his mouth. The sweet sensation of his lips brushed her knuckles. Tingles shot to her core.

"I trust verra few." His eyes narrowed. "I cannot abide deceit."

She stiffened. "I told ye the truth, hoping ye would see reason."

He cocked his head. "Did ye not tell me it was yer clan that killed Harold?"

"I did." She trembled. "But I don't believe my *father* killed Harold."

"Whether by his hands or his men's—"

166

She squeezed his fingers. "Nay, I don't think Da is even aware of the attacks."

"Cameron —"

"Please hear me out." She implored him with her eyes. It was now or never. She *had to* convince him. "I have thought and thought about it. My da was grief-stricken after my mum's death. He nay longer seemed to care about anything so he relinquished authority to Symon. I warned Da he allowed Symon too much leeway. My cousin's a troublemaker, and he's been stoking my da's rage against yer clan at every turn." Cameron looked down for a brief moment. "I don't know how our clans' feuding will serve his purpose, but rest assured he has one, and it does not bode well for either of our families."

Her eyes pleaded with him. "The only way this makes any sense is if Symon ordered the attack, and the men thought they were following Da's orders."

Robert exhaled.

"Please think on what I've said before ye charge in with yer sword."

"All right. I'll think on it." He placed her palm on his chest. "I want to trust ye."

Quiet moments passed. He held her gaze. His heart beat steady against her fingers, his chest hair soft. She longed to slide her hand over his warm skin.

He tilted his head, shadows crossing his face. "Can I trust ye, Cameron?"

"Aye," she whispered.

He reached out and cupped her breast while watching her face. His thumb stroked the taut peak through her gown. Her breath quickened with the arousing sensations, and her will to resist dissolved.

He pressed his mouth to hers. Her body quivered, helpless to stop his advances. Giving in to desire, she opened her mouth. When she stroked his tongue, he suckled hers. Stars exploded behind her eyes, and her legs grew weak.

He eased the soft fabric off her right shoulder, then her left. His dark gaze drifted to her breasts. She longed to feel his

167

bare skin against hers. Throwing caution to the wind, she shoved his shirt from his muscular chest and dropped it on the floor.

She drank in his sculpted shape. His dark skin kissed by the sun glistened in the candlelight. Black hair covered his torso, and corded muscles crisscrossed his belly in tight ripples. Fingers skimming through the soft curls, her palms splayed and his warm flesh filled her hands.

He wrapped his arms around her, and the thatch on his chest and abdomen teased her straining nipples.

"Ye smell good, lass," he murmured, moving her hair to the side and nibbling her neck. He trailed kisses across her shoulders while deftly easing her gown past her hips to pool around her feet.

He captured her lips in a deep kiss and ran his hands across her back, down to cup her bare bottom. His warm palms squeezed her plumpness, and his hard member pressed into her belly. She wantonly rubbed herself against him, craving his touch.

He bent, swept his arm beneath her legs and carried her to the bed. When she scooted to the middle of the mattress, his eyes smoldered with desire, and her stomach tightened at the carnal promises they held.

Her heart beat rapidly when he untied his trews and his manhood jutted out the top. Her eyes widened, taking in his glorious form. Chuckling at her response, he dropped his clothes to the floor and stood nude before her. His shaft engorged fully at her inspection.

"Ye keep studying me like that, and I'll embarrass myself."

Heat flooded her face, but her gaze lingered. She drank in his brawny build as if her mouth was parched.

He climbed into bed and embraced her. The feel of his naked skin against hers sent feverish shudders of desire coursing through her. She snuggled next to him and ran her fingers across his chest and lower, to his flat abdomen.

168

He cupped the side of her face and brought her mouth to his. Hungrily kissing her, he worked his way down to her nipples, laving his tongue around each as they puckered to his attention. He playfully caught one between his teeth and nibbled, driving her wild with pleasure while at the same time, creating an ache between her legs. His hand inched through her dark curls to massage her need.

While he pleasured her, she boldly reached between his legs, and her fingers surrounded his hard member. She brushed the swollen head and he moaned, then grasped her hand encouraging her to slide up and down his velvety length.

"I can't wait any longer." He eased on top of her and nudged her legs apart, his thick manhood poised at her opening. Her sensitive flesh quivered in anticipation.

"Please," she breathed out.

Finally, with a thrust, he gave her what she craved, massaging her need with each slick glide. He sighed against her neck. "Ah, lass."

Her legs fell open, and she tilted her hips, encouraging him to fill her completely, savoring his every stroke. Brazenly, her hands cupped his taut bottom, his rear flexing and muscles straining.

He kissed the side of her face, his lips drawing a path to her mouth as his hand eased between them. His fingertips stroked her crux. A rush tingled up her legs, and she exploded in ecstasy. Throaty gasps slipped past her lips as muscle spasms pulsed, tightening around his member. He roared and pumped into her, finding his release.

Dropping his head to hers, he leaned on his forearms and kissed her lips. "Look at me."

His dark eyes, filled with passion, gazed at her. He plunged into her warmth one last time. She lazily closed her eyes again. When he pulled out and rolled to the side, cold air swirled her heated skin, leaving her body bereft and craving his touch. Drawing her against him, they held each other. The raging storm buffeted the shutters, much like the tumultuous pain battering her heart.

~~~

Cameron awoke with her head resting on Robert's chest, his arm draped around her. She smiled, remembering their night together, his caress, his kiss. Warmth spread from the pit of her belly. She dearly loved him. But her happiness was short-lived when she thought of her family.

"Robert?"

His fingertips rubbed up and down her side. "Hmmm...?"

The wind sprayed rain against the wooden shutters. Lightning flittered through the slats, the flash shining across the dark room. Deafening thunder boomed, the accompanying vibrations rumbling.

"Have ye given any thought to our conversation? Are ye going to send me home?"

Robert stilled. "I haven't had time to think on it." He began stroking her hip again, running his hand over her backside and slightly squeezing her bottom. "I've been a bit preoccupied."

Cameron rose on her elbow. "I want to see my da and sisters. They must think I'm dead. It's been months since ye took me."

Robert sat up, threw the blanket off and stood. He jerked on his clothes and leveled a dark glare at her while tying his trews. "I don't care what yer da thinks. He tried to kill my little brother and Duncan. Ye told me yourself it was yer clan that murdered Harold."

She rose on her knees. "But I've explained, I truly don't think my da knew about the attacks. I can't believe he would've had anything to do with either one of them."

"Enough!"

His harsh tone struck her as if his meaty fist had punched her gut. She eased back on the bed. Her bottom lip quivered, and tears flooded her eyes.

"I'll not discuss this further. I have the arrows fletched with yer Da's markers as proof. Duncan said Symon led the raid."

170

"Aye, *Symon*, not my father."

Robert shoved his arms into his shirt. "He's yer father's nephew and first in command, for God's sake."

"Ye promised ye'd think on what I said." Her voice cracked.

He scowled and turned to leave the room.

"Robert, please."

He looked over his shoulder. She kneeled on the bed, holding the blankets over her breasts.

Shaking his head, he walked from the room and closed the door behind him.

Cameron sat back. Regardless of how much she loved him, she refused to stay here as his mistress, while her father and sisters grieved over her. Da would not have ordered the horrible attack on Duncan, Androu, or Harold.

Her mind raced. She had to discover what Symon's plans were before someone else was killed. With the clans embroiled in fighting, it could only end in the destruction of one or the other. Cameron's pulse drummed in her ears. She could not bear that happening. She had to talk to Da and tell him her suspicions. He would put an end to Symon's murderous plotting and ensure the safety of both clans.

She would use Nichola to preoccupy Lachlan. She hated to take advantage of her friend, but when Lachlan looked Nichola's way, Cameron would escape and make her way home.

Chapter Twelve

Robert glanced at his men gathered at the solar table. "With Harold's attack and recent reports of soldiers in the vicinity, we must protect our borders."

Each one nodded in agreement.

"I'm taking a group to scout the area and encourage the tenants to move closer to the castle."

Lachlan leaned against the wall, arms crossed. "From what I hear, Edward has men on the MacCarthys' perimeter. It won't be long before they move in again."

"They've also been spotted off the Firth of Clyde, near Irvine," Kendrick added. "That's not but a day's ride."

"Where's Brandon McLeod? I thought he was leading raids against them?" Michael asked.

"He is, but our land is widespread, and he's more than got his hands full." Robert leaned back in his chair. "We'll be called upon in the near future to support the rebellion. I want to secure Graham property as much as possible before we receive that summons."

"The men'll be ready to ride when ye are," Kendrick said.

Robert stood and shoved back his chair. "There's one more thing." He turned to Lachlan. "I'm taking Kendrick with me, but ye and Duncan are to stay here."

Lachlan pushed away from the wall, his forehead furrowed. "Why? Ye need my help."

"I do. That's why I'm leaving ye here." He paused. "I've decided to stop by MacDougall Castle on my way home."

Lachlan's eyes narrowed. "She's gotten to ye."

"Cameron's gotten to *all* of us. From the start, she treated Androu and Duncan. She tends my baby sister and all of the residents living here." Robert leaned over the table. "She even healed *yer* wound."

The silence in the room was deafening. No one could deny his words or his claim.

172

"Cameron has asked me to let her father know she's not dead." He exhaled loudly. "She swears he doesn't know about the attack."

Kendrick frowned and crossed his arms over his chest. "Come on, man, ye can't believe that."

"I don't know whether to believe it or not." Robert straightened to his full height, hands on hips. "It's for Cameron that I visit Alastair and give him a chance to explain. If things don't go well, I want Duncan and Lachlan here to protect the clan."

He withheld the information about the attack on Harold. He would confront Alastair and hear his explanation first.

Lachlan rubbed the back of his neck and audibly exhaled through his nose. "Aye, if that's what ye want." He dropped his arms. "Ye can count on us."

The meeting broke and Robert walked through the main hall with Kendrick on their way to the bailey. Cameron sat with Nichola and Androu as they ate their mid-day meal.

Robert addressed Cameron. "We're leaving for the borders. Duncan and Lachlan will be here to see to yer needs."

She nodded, then looked down at her hands folded in her lap. She was upset with him. He hadn't informed her of his intention to meet with her father. If things went as planned, he would tell her when he returned.

Nichola stood and kissed his cheek. "Be safe."

"I'll see ye in a few days." Robert glanced at Cameron's bent head before he spun on his heel and marched out the hall.

Horses trotted down the dirt road carrying Robert and his men toward the Grahams' northern borders. Many tenants lived in isolated, outlying areas. He scanned the thick forest for signs of soldiers. Nothing seemed out of the ordinary. Had they not received word the English encroached on their land, he would never have known from the evidence of the peaceful surroundings.

The day was cool. A light breeze blew across the meadow rich with crops of wheat, barley and rye. Gilbert supervised the northern tenants' mill operation, grinding dried grain into flour for the Grahams. In exchange, they received shelter, food, clothing and essential supplies from candles to soap. The tenants worked the land, and Robert provided support and security.

The English grew closer every day, and he was surprised they had not run across them yet. When he and his men approached the outer lying structures, he recognized Gilbert tending the fields with several men.

They stopped their work to observe the approaching party. Gilbert shaded his face from the afternoon sun. Robert knew they were on constant alert.

He reined in Eton, jumped to the ground and pulled off his gloves while striding toward the men. "Good day, Gilbert. William, Alane."

"Laird." Gilbert's face relaxed. He dropped his tools and ambled over to Robert. William and Alane followed. "I didn't realize it was ye."

Robert shook each man's hand and patted Alane on the shoulder. "I hear congratulations are in order, man."

"Aye, thank ye."

"How's yer bairn? She's getting stronger?"

"She is, Laird. She'll be jes like her mum—a real handful."

The men laughed.

"What brings ye here?" Gilbert asked. "Is anything amiss?"

Hands on hips, Robert nodded. "We've heard of attacks in the area and wanted to check on ye. Ye're doing well? Yer wives and families?"

Gilbert wiped sweat from his upper lip with his forearm. "Aye. There's been a number of assaults on the coast."

"McIntosh jes north of us was burned oot," William interjected. "The soldiers are getting close for sure."

Robert surveyed the area. Relieved the English had not made it to them yet, he turned back to the men. "Pack yer

174

belongings and bring them into the castle. We have room for yer families and until this uprising settles, I'd prefer to know ye're safe within our walls."

"Thank ye, Laird. I know my wife'll be glad to hear that. She's been mighty scared with the English dogs getting so close to us," Gilbert replied.

"Good, 'tis settled then. On the morrow, start yer preparations. I'll leave some of my men to escort ye to the castle."

"Would ye care to join us for the night?" Gilbert asked Robert. "We have plenty of room, and my Ella's cooking stew."

Robert contemplated a night out in the elements, sleeping on the ground next to a campfire. Maybe the discomfort would get his mind off Cameron.

He clapped Gilbert's shoulder. "It's been too long since I slept beneath the stars. I thank ye, but I'll pitch my blanket on the ground tonight."

Robert recalled those words while sleep eluded him. Hands folded under his head, he gazed at the stars, scanning the dark sky...thinking of Cameron.

What would it be like to have her remain at his side?

As Laird, he required a wife to manage Graham Castle—to raise his children and attend his needs. His desire for Cameron was strong. A number of men he knew had no choice but to marry a shrew for the good of their clan. He was fortunate that was not his case. Cameron was an intelligent woman. He longed to be near her—even as she expounded on about her herbs and healing practices. Although he abducted her and held her against her will, she never failed to amaze him with her compassionate spirit.

He *cared* for her...

Whether he liked it or not.

She constantly invaded his mind—the scent of her hair, the feel of her soft skin, the spirit in her bonnie green eyes. He smiled, contemplating marriage to Cameron. She challenged

175

him on more than one occasion. Living with her would certainly be…entertaining.

And their marriage would seal a final truce with Alastair. He would not dare attack the Grahams with his daughter residing there.

The thought intrigued him. Why had he not come up with it before?

A perfect solution.

Permanently ensconce his enemy's daughter in his midst.

With the matter settled in his mind, the haze of sleep crept in. A streak of light flew across the night sky. A shooting star.

An omen for sure—but time would soon reveal whether good…or bad.

~~~

Graham Castle

The day after Robert and his men rode to the borders, Cameron found her opportunity to escape. She'd hoped Robert would listen to reason, but it would be up to her to take matters in hand. She must leave while he was away. It was now or never.

She wandered into the hall to retrieve her wrap. Servants cleared the midday meal, and Tessa hummed while scrubbing the heavy trestle tables. Lachlan and Nichola, deep in conversation, sat before the hearth.

Her chest tightened.

She would miss them, even the cantankerous Lachlan.

Taking a deep breath, she squared her shoulders, walked out the door and into the bailey. Her basket swung on her arm as she casually strolled down the road and slipped past the last house on the row and into the surrounding woods.

She glanced behind her. Several men carried water buckets into the stables. A woman strolled through the yard with a basket of dirty linens while children chased each other around the well. Fortunately, no one expected her to leave. She had been here for three months, and everyone was used to her frequent afternoon visits to the village. They'd finally relaxed their guard.

She hiked her skirt and hurried down the worn path. Soft needles covered the trail, cushioning her footfalls. Wind blew through the treetops, and leaves rustled to the ground. Any other time, she would have relished the beautiful surroundings and refreshing air. But not today. She must get as far away from Graham Castle as possible before dark.

The wind picked up and dark clouds formed overhead. She groaned. "Grand. A storm is all I need."

When Robert brought her to Graham Castle, they had passed an abandoned shack. If she could only arrive before the heavens opened. A fat drop of rain hit her face, and she quickened her steps. Within no time, wind pelted her with cold water. She pulled her wrap tight, tucked her chin to her chest and hastened down the path.

Mud squished under her shoes, and the hem of her gown, sodden and dirty, clung to her legs. She grew tired and tripped over loose rocks and stumps. What seemed like hours passed before she came upon the dilapidated shack. Worn out, soaking wet and trembling cold, her shoulders sagged in relief.

Rain poured over her as she studied the hut. Dark holes in wooden slats gave no indication of life. She inched her way through brambles and undergrowth and hesitantly stepped onto the wooden porch.

It creaked, and she froze.

Rain pelted the roof. She clutched her basket and peered through a gap in one of the planks.

No movement inside.

She pushed the rickety door. It squeaked and partially opened.

Thunder cracked. Cameron jumped and stepped inside the room. Pulse racing, her gaze darted around, anxiously searching for critters.

She ducked under thick cobwebs and brushed past grimy furniture littered with leaves, dirt and debris. Raindrops filtered through the thatched roof, trickling to vines curling between the wooden boards in the floor. Although the cottage was not sturdy, she supposed it would somewhat protect her from the elements. At least it would provide a measure of shelter for the night.

Cameron treaded softly on rotten boards to an old bed positioned alongside the wall. After placing her basket on the tattered mattress, she inspected the room. A broken grate set inside a small hearth stood blackened with soot. Several busted chairs scattered the floor, and a three-legged table had been propped against the wall. Broken crockery, thick with dust, lined a wooden shelf.

The damp air in the cabin chilled her, and she rubbed her arms. A blanket draped a chair. She shook it out, and her nose wrinkled as a rank, musty odor assailed her nostrils. The threadbare moth-bitten material would do little to keep the cold at bay. However, with no other options, she brushed off the lumpy mattress and spread the cover on the bed.

"I need to get out of these wet clothes." Chilled to the bone and apprehensive of her surroundings, she shivered. "Why didn't I think to bring another gown?"

She cringed and yanked off the soggy dress. Her head swam, and she held the edge of the table to steady herself. Her belly had been unsettled throughout the day, and her breasts ached. She needed her strength to get home, but her exhausted limbs screamed in protest.

She couldn't afford to get sick now.

Goosebumps rose on her arms and legs. She squeezed water from her gown and hung it to dry. Hoping the cloth she packed wasn't soaked, her numb fingers fumbled through the jars of herbs and augments to the bottom of her basket. The soft material felt heavenly. She eased it out and swathed herself in its warmth.

The lumpy straw mattress appeared less than inviting. No telling what creatures called it home. She nudged the cot, expecting to see it move of its own accord. When it remained still, she decided to chance it. Fatigued and disheartened, she climbed onto the bed and leaned against the wall. Her eyes were extremely heavy, the drone of rain lulling her to sleep.

Robert.

She assured him he could trust her. Her decision to leave destroyed any possibility to be with him. He wouldn't have her after he learned of her deception. She wrapped her arms around her legs. She would bear his disgust in order to save the Grahams *and* the MacDougalls.

How she would miss him. She put her face in her hands and sobbed—her emotions unusually heightened, overly distraught from tension. Her dream of becoming a respected healer suddenly paled. She no longer desired the solitude of a marriage-less existence, wandering through life alone, never experiencing the joy and love of a husband and children.

I wouldn't have lain with ye if I was promised to another. Robert's words echoed through her mind. Did he speak the truth? If they had married, would he have been faithful to her? Would he have committed himself to their union?

Her breath hitched, and she wiped her nose.

It no longer mattered.

It was too late.

~~~

Dawn broke with pale sunlight filtering through open slats of the cottage. Sore from a restless night on the makeshift bed, Cameron gingerly straightened. She was still dizzy, her stomach upset. Taking a breath in through her nose, she slowly exhaled through her mouth.

"Of all the times to get sick," she muttered while reaching for her clothes hanging on the chair. Careful not to make sudden movements, she eased the damp cold gown over her head. Chill bumps rose on her arms, and she shivered.

Sitting on the edge of the bed, she rummaged through her basket. She had managed to pack a hunk of bread and a slab of cheese with a small wineskin before she left Graham Castle. She really should try to eat something.

After shakily sipping on the water, she heaved, and bolted for the door. Falling to the ground on her knees, she retched, emptying the contents of her stomach. She trembled and wiped her mouth with the back of her sleeve. Her skin felt clammy, but not feverish. Had she eaten something spoiled?

Bile billowed up, and she gagged. With nothing left to expel, she slowly stood on shaky legs and grasped the doorframe for support. Breathing deeply, she shuffled back inside. When she tugged her wrap around her shoulders, she cringed. Her breasts were very tender.

Bells reverberated in her head, and she sank onto one of the chairs before the hearth.

"Oh nay," she breathed out, running a hand across her taut abdomen. "How long has it been since my last bleeding?" Massaging her forehead, she thought back. Realization hit. "Over two months. It's been over two months."

She swallowed hard.

Why hadn't she noticed? Her flow had always been timely, but with her abduction and the stress of captivity, would it have been unheard of to skip a month...or two?

Her bottom lip quivered, and she ran her hand across her firm belly. "A babe. I'm going to have Robert's bairn."

Her father's face flashed before her eyes. What would he think of her, knowing she gave herself to a man out of wedlock, his hated enemy? She would bring disgrace to him and her sisters. "Oh Da, what've I done?"

And what of Robert? He never uttered endearing words of love to her while coaxing her into bed. She fell into his arms willingly, and being a healer, she was under no misconception about the possible consequences. She had known the risk.

Her weakness had made the situation worse between their clans.

How ironic.

The midmorning sun streamed into the room and shone on her face. Her stomach had settled somewhat. She eased off the chair and stepped out-of-doors.

180

A light wind caressed her face. Green leaves glistened in the sunlight, raindrops dripping from overhanging branches. The noise of rushing water in the distance caught her attention. She rubbed her arms, warding off the chilly air and followed the sound.

An overgrown path wound its way downhill, meandering through the tall trees. Wind-swayed branches sprinkled water from the night's storm. The trail opened to a slight embankment with massive boulders resting in and around the swollen river's churning water.

Cameron eased onto one of the large rocks. She was going to have a baby—perhaps a babe with soft brown eyes and dark hair. The thought squeezed her heart. Her hand slid over her abdomen. Sweet images of her own little one ran across her mind's eye.

A lone dove fluttered overhead and landed on the rock next to her. Its head bobbed as it strutted across the stone. Moments later, another dove appeared—its mate. The two cooed as if sensing her melancholy. Mum always cherished the birds. *Doves represent love and gentleness*, she would say.

Peace suddenly enveloped her as if Mum wrapped Cameron in an embrace. A gentle breeze and the warm sun comforted her soul. Perhaps the birds truly were signs of peace and happiness.

Resolved to face the consequences of her actions, she held her head high. She would love her child. She already did.

When she finally climbed off the boulder, daylight had begun to fade, and she made her way back to the worn cabin. After forcing herself to nibble on the bread and cheese, she once again curled up on the cot and tried to rest. She would pack her belongings and head for home at first light.

~~~

After inspecting his borders, Robert sat atop Eton, searching the hills and valley below. Thunder rumbled in the distance. Rain poured around him, water dripping off his cloak and onto his face. He swiped his arm across his eyes and squinted. Far to the west, a dark column of smoke ascended the trees. The rampant destruction spread farther into their homeland. Edward intended to bring Scotland to its knees— potentially killing every man, woman and child in his quest.

As much as Robert loathed the idea of relinquishing retribution against Alastair, he had no choice. For the good of his clan, he must end the feud—even if he had to force Alastair's hand into compliance by marrying the old laird's daughter.

Robert gave last minute instructions to Michael before he and Kendrick left for MacDougall Castle. The ride was long, but the rain eased up. The trip gave him time to consider what he would say to Alastair. He would need to choose his words carefully.

After discarding his first instinct to rush in with swords drawn, Robert would consider Alastair's explanation. Would he deny knowledge of the attack as Cameron suggested? Or would the old laird pompously boast of the deed? And if he did, how would Robert respond? Could he sink his blade into him—into Cameron's father?

Images of Androu's small body with bloodied arrows protruding from his leg and shoulder, and Duncan, frail and weak, barely surviving the assault flashed through his mind. Lachlan's words of Harold—*the right side of his face was bashed, and his guts hung out his belly*—rang through his ears.

His heart hammered.

He took a deep breath and briefly closed his eyes. While he wanted to race in and slay Laird MacDougall, he had to remember his goal and restrain his temper. With Edward breathing down their necks, each clan needed the support of the other.

Finally, he and Kendrick entered MacDougall land. Robert stopped and surveyed the castle. Nothing appeared out of the ordinary. People bustled about performing daily activities. He nudged Eton down the road and into the bailey. A clang of iron rang from the blacksmith, an aroma of baked

182

bread and pies cooling in windows wafted past. Children squealed. Dogs ran and barked, nipping at each other.

A bonnie lass clothed in lad's trews haggled with a couple of well-dressed men over a handsome stallion. Evidently, the men were not pleased with what she expected for the horse. Was *she* selling the animal? The idea was absurd. There were no MacDougall men overseeing the transaction, and she appeared to be in control. She accepted a sack of coins and handed the reins to one of the men.

Robert and Kendrick dismounted, and several lads ran to take their horses.

The lass watched the men ride out of the bailey with the horse in tow before she turned toward him. "Hello, I'm Lindsey MacDougall. How may I help ye?"

He should've known this strong-minded lass would be Cameron's sister. "We're here to talk to Laird MacDougall."

"Is he expecting ye?"

"Nay."

She drew herself up and folded her arms. "Who may I tell him is here?"

"Robert Graham."

"I see." Her blue eyes narrowed slightly, and she hesitated. Her questioning gaze raked his face as if determining whether to admit him or not. "Follow me."

She escorted them through the great room and down the stairs to Alastair's solar. "Please wait while I inform Da ye're here to see him."

She turned and left, shutting the door behind her.

Robert studied the well-furnished room. A heavy wooden desk and several chairs were positioned in front of a large window overlooking the lush grounds. Shelves filled with books and binders lined the walls, with a large fireplace housed the back corner.

Robert strolled around the room, his vigilance heightened.

Kendrick's hand gripped the hilt of his sword, his eyes alert and watchful.

A short time later, the door swung open. "Gentlemen, welcome."

Robert turned at the old laird's shaky voice. He took in Alastair's gaunt face, his deep-set eyes sunken into his wrinkled skin, his unkempt beard and hair. Apparently, Cameron's disappearance had weighed heavily upon him. Sympathy surged, but recalling the MacDougall arrows hardened his resolution.

Alastair extended his hand, but when Robert stood glaring, hands on his hips, the old laird quickly realized this was not a social call.

He dropped his arm while looking skeptically at Robert. "To what do I owe the pleasure of yer visit?"

"Tis not with pleasure that I visit ye, Alastair MacDougall."

The man visibly straightened. He stood rigid, frowning, his eyes guarded.

Stilted seconds passed before Robert spoke again. "I'm here to discuss yer daughter."

The laird's bushy brows drew together. "My daughter?"

"Aye, Cameron."

Alastair paled and advanced. "By Satan's hairy arse. Ye have her!"

Kendrick stepped forward, but Robert held up a hand, signaling him to stand down.

"Aye, I have her." Part of him wished the old man would attack. He would like nothing better than to beat Alastair for what he did to Androu, Duncan and Harold.

Laird MacDougall seemed to think better of the idea and paused. "What have ye done to her? If ye've hurt her, so help me God I'll see ye dead."

Robert glowered. His enemy stood before him...so close. All he had to do was... He breathed heavily, struggling to hold his temper. "She's not been harmed. She's treated well, and it's because of her that I'm here to tell ye she's safe."

"Ye bastard. Ye double-crossing bastard." Alastair's face contorted, and his eyes bulged. He clenched his fists and

184

took another step toward Robert. "Ye come in here spouting off about a truce between our clans, and then ye take my daughter? How dare ye tell me that ye have had her all these months? By God, I should run ye through where ye stand!"

"And how dare ye act outraged when *ye* are the one that went against the truce? *Ye* are the one that attacked my brother and captain, shooting them in the back." Robert could barely contain his fury. He jabbed his finger into Alastair's chest. "It was because of *ye* that I had to take yer daughter."

"What are ye talking about? What attack? We haven't fought yer clan since before ye came here asking for yer sham of a truce."

Robert rummaged in his tunic and tossed the arrows fletched with MacDougall feathers on the desk.

Alastair stared at them. His eyes narrowed, and his gaze swung back to Robert. "What's this?"

"*This* is what we wrenched out of Androu and Duncan. It's what they received in their backs while running from yer nephew on *Graham* land."

Alastair picked up one of the arrows with the distinctive red and black intertwined feathers. "There has to be some mistake. I know not of what ye speak."

"Aye, a mistake was made. Symon didn't finish what he started. He left them for dead, but we found them barely clinging to life. They live today because of yer daughter."

Alastair's face paled. His nostrils flared, and his breath became short and fast. "I swear to ye, I had no idea of this raid."

Robert studied Alastair's eyes. Cameron tried to convince him her father knew nothing of Symon's attack. Perhaps she'd been right.

Trembling, Alastair wobbled and held onto the desk. "I'll get to the bottom of this. I have Symon searching the countryside right now looking for my Cameron. When he returns, I'll find out what happened and deal with him appropriately."

Alastair's lack-luster eyes drooped, but he straightened his frame and pulled his hunched shoulders back. "I apologize for the actions of my nephew. With the loss of my wife, I delegated too many responsibilities to Symon. Obviously, that was a mistake. This should never have happened."

Robert studied the old man and thought of Cameron. His chest clenched at the thought of losing her. He could understand, if not forgive, how Alastair had allowed his preoccupation with grief over Rose's death to blind him to Symon's plotting.

"There was another strike just days ago. Ye may have sent Symon searching for yer daughter, but he's been on my land. He tortured and killed Harold, one of my tenants."

Kendrick's head jerked toward him.

"Shite!" Alastair dropped heavily in a chair. He rested his elbows on the desk and placed his hands on his head. "Are ye sure it was him?"

"Nay, but Harold made it to the castle only to die in yer daughter's arms. He said yer clan attacked him. I'm assuming from what ye say, it was not by yer order."

Laird MacDougall exhaled loudly and lowered his hands to the table. When he raised his head, his mouth had turned down. He aged before Robert's eyes. "I don't know what to say. Nothing I can do will atone for his actions. I can only ask ye to accept my deepest apologies and condolences. I assure ye, Symon will be whipped and banned in disgrace from my clan. I'll not have his kind amongst my people."

Robert nodded.

Stilted moments passed. The old laird rubbed the back of his neck. "I have to ask about my daughter."

"She requested I inform ye she's well so ye won't worry over her."

Alastair chuckled. "That's my Cameron…always thinking of others." He hesitated, then cleared his throat. "What are yer intentions? May I escort her home?"

186

Robert noted Alastair's deep concern, and he thought long and hard on his next words. "My intentions are to marry her."

Alastair's eyes widened. "Marry her?"

"I need a wife, and it would be good to join our clans." Robert's arms crossed his chest as he studied the aging laird.

"How does Cameron feel about this? I promised her mum all our daughters would have the husband of their choice."

"She doesn't know."

Alastair's eyes narrowed. "Ye appear to be a man of honor, one with courage. And it *would* be a good alliance for our clans."

"Do ye agree, Laird MacDougall?"

Alastair took a deep breath and slowly exhaled. "If Cameron consents, I agree."

He extended his hand. Robert looked Alastair squarely in the eyes and grasped the man's hand. They scrutinized each other. It would be a while before he trusted Alastair, but this was a promising start.

Now to win his bride's consent.

~~~

The day started out much the same as the one before, with Cameron on her knees retching. How would she endure this for nine months?

She wiped her mouth and took a deep breath. When she straightened, her hands shook, and her legs wobbled. She shuffled into the cabin and sat. A sip of water…then one more. A bite of bread—thick going down—managed to stay down.

Progress.

Slow and easy.

After awhile, her belly settled. It was time to go home. With any luck, she should be in her bedchamber before dark. Basket in hand, Cameron resumed her journey.

She followed the river snaking through the thick forest, a torrent of water coursing past. A stream broke to the right and

187

meandered east. It would empty into a loch not far from MacDougall Castle.

The midday sun had passed overhead some time earlier. Having walked quite a distance, her back and legs ached. Encouraged she made it thus far, she settled on a cold grey boulder, laid down and closed her eyes.

Cameron bolted upright. It was twilight. She had not intended to sleep. With her carelessness, she would have to navigate in the dark. She scrambled off the rock and onto the worn path. It wouldn't be long before predatory animals would be on the prowl. Once she regained her bearings, she hastened her steps toward home.

She had not ventured far when she heard a noise. She stopped and listened. Her head jerked to the right, then left. The jingle of horses' bridles and the clop of heavy hooves sounded loud in the quiet evening. Who would be in the woods at this time of night? Da had warned her of outlaws and hardened men, roaming the countryside and taking advantage of the unsuspecting. What would she do if one were to catch her alone in the forest?

Cameron hiked her skirt and ran off the path.

~~~

A streak of movement caught Robert's eye. He jerked his head around. Was that Cameron?

"Nay, it can't be." He bolted from Eton. Shrubs and brambles scraped him as he ran off the path and rounded a large tree. She sprinted ahead of him, but he caught up to her, grabbed her arm, and whirled her around to face him. "What the hell are ye doing here?"

She was out of breath and gasped for air. "Robert, it's ye."

"Aye, it's me." He wanted to shake her. "Answer me, damn it. What are ye doing here?"

"I was returning home."

Robert stared at her. "What?"

Her chin raised a notch, and her nostrils flared.

188

"Anything could have happened to ye." His voice grew louder. "Anyone could have come upon ye, and there would be nay telling what they would have done."

She frowned, her eyes narrowing to mere slits.

Defiant wench.

"Ye can't keep me locked up forever."

Blood pounded in his ears.

Cameron risked her life to escape him.

His body shook as he struggled to control his emotions. Had Eton kicked him in the gut, it would not have hurt more. She had given her word.

Jacqueline had used every method to manipulate and control him. Perhaps Cameron did the same. Niggling suspicions rose. Women were of the same ilk. He didn't trust them.

He grabbed her wrist and dragged her over fallen logs and through the undergrowth. Once he reached his awaiting horse, Kendrick handed Eton's reins to him. His eyebrow rose.

Robert tugged Cameron to him and deposited her on the saddle before he swung up behind her. Grasping her chin, he forced her to face him.

"Ye will return with me, lass, and ye won't *ever* leave again without my knowledge." He kicked Eton into a full gallop, heading home with Kendrick close behind.

~~~

They rode for several hours before their horses thundered into the bailey.

When they entered the yard, Nichola ran down the stairs to greet them. "Oh, Cameron, I was so worried about ye."

Robert slid off Eton, grabbed Cameron around the waist and set her on the ground in front of him. He didn't even look at her. He took her by the wrist and dragged her to the stairs.

"Not now, Nichola." Robert marched Cameron past his sister.

Cameron looked over her shoulder at Nichola and silently mouthed, "I'm sorry."

But she quickly turned, having to run to keep up with Robert's long strides.

When they entered his bedchamber, he pushed her inside and slammed the door. Hands firmly affixed to his hips, he leveled a piercing glare on her. The warrior, the true Laird of Graham Castle stood before her. She had known he would be furious and awaited his wrath. After a moment of brooding, he lowered his arms and slowly stalked toward her.

Determined not to cower and retreat, she raised her chin and returned his glacial stare.

"Ye told me I could trust ye," he said coolly.

She swallowed. "It didn't matter what I said. Ye never believed me about my da, so why would ye believe I wouldn't try to leave?"

"Ye lied to me."

"I had no choice. Ye abducted me! Did ye expect I'd accept my imprisonment without question?"

"I expected ye to keep yer word."

"Someone had to try to end this nonsense between our clans. Ye obviously weren't interested in doing so."

"Ye didn't give me a chance before ye went marching off, wandering through forests humming with outlaws." He threw his arms up. "Damn it, Cameron. Do ye not have any sense?"

Her hands balled into fists at her side. "I was fine until *ye* showed up."

Robert grabbed her upper arms and jerked her within inches of his face. "What would ye have done if a man not so taken with ye had shown up? Do ye think he would have seen ye safely home?"

Cameron trembled, but was determined to hold her ground.

He released her, turned to the side table and grabbed a flask. He snatched a mug and poured it full. "Did ye know just last week a lass was found not far from here? Someone had sliced her throat from ear to ear. She'd been raped and brutalized." He guzzled the contents of his cup and set it on the

190

table. "The locals say it was soldiers, taking their pleasure in torturing the young girl."

Cameron stared at his back, speechless.

He leaned on the table. His head dropped, and he exhaled. Finally, he turned and sat on the edge of the table, his large arms crossing his chest. "Have ye been mistreated, lass? Have I beaten and starved ye? Have I behaved so terribly that ye had to risk yer verra life to get away from me?"

"Nay, I haven't been mistreated, but I'll not continue to live here as yer mistress while my da thinks me dead. I *won't* do it." She trembled with frustration. "Ye wouldn't even listen to me about Symon. I had to leave before he attacked again. I need to talk to my father. Don't ye understand? I left to help yer clan and mine."

He paused as if considering her words. The fire in the hearth popped and crackled. Cameron's heart thumped wildly.

"Come here."

When she didn't move, he sternly repeated, "Come here, Cameron."

She jumped at his tone and hesitantly took a step closer. When his eyes narrowed, she took another few steps until she stood before him.

"I was returning from meeting with yer da when I ran across ye in the woods."

Cameron blinked several times. "What? Ye saw my da?"

"Aye."

"What do ye mean? When?"

"I considered yer explanation and decided to meet with him—for ye, Cameron." He inclined his head in her direction.

She placed her hands on his crossed forearms. "Is he well? Did ye see my sisters?"

"He's well, and I saw Lindsey." His brows rose. "Dressed in a lad's trews, bargaining with men over a horse."

Cameron chuckled. "I told ye she ran the stables."

He snorted. "Yer father knows ye're here, safe with me."

Cameron breathed a sigh of relief. She cocked her head to the side and studied him. "And did ye ask him about the attacks?"

"I did."

Once again, he paused.

"Tell me," she pleaded.

"He claims not to know anything about it, but he expects yer cousin does. He aims to find out."

"Oh, Robert. Thank ye."

He sighed and gathered her in his arms. She rested her head on his chest and closed her eyes, breathing in a whiff of mead on his breath. She could not believe she stood in his embrace. Only a few short hours ago, she feared she would never feel his strong arms surrounding her again.

He kissed her hair, and she raised her head. Looking into her eyes, he slowly bent and captured her lips in a gentle kiss. "What am I going to do with ye?" he whispered against her mouth.

Cameron ran her hands up his chest and around his neck. He picked her up, sat before the hearth and placed her on his lap. Holding her close, he tucked her head beneath his chin. The fire popped and hissed. A log rolled, and red sparks swirled up the chimney.

He tilted her chin. His dark eyes held concern. "Promise ye'll not lie to me again."

Her breath hitched. "I promise."

He seemed to search her eyes, then kissed her mouth—tenderly, not passionately.

She rested her head on his chest, his steady heartbeat strong in her ear. Quite some time passed with him cuddling her against him. Cameron slipped into blissful sleep snuggled against the man she loved, the father of their unborn child.

～～～

"Are ye awake, lass?"

"Aye." She had awoken sometime ago, fully clothed, lying in bed snuggled in Robert's arms.

"I know we didn't get along at the first, but I think we get along fairly well now."

Robert paused as if considering his every word. He ran his hand up and down her hip. "Ye've been good for Nichola to have someone close to her age to talk to and be with. And ye've been verra kind to Androu and Isobel. They really like ye, ye know?"

"I like them, too."

Silence stretched between them.

"What I'm trying to say is, I'd like ye to reside at Graham Castle."

Cameron rose on her elbow and peered down at him.

"I'd like us to wed, Cameron. I want ye as my wife."

Her heart leapt into her throat, and her eyes stung with the onslaught of tears. "Oh, Robert."

She leaned over and kissed him.

He rolled her underneath him and looked down at her. "Does that mean ye'll marry me?"

"Aye," she whispered pulling his head down to her. "Aye, it does."

Chapter Thirteen

The first light of dawn filtered through the bedchamber's shutters as Cameron lay in Robert's arms. Memories of their night together flooded his mind as he stroked her hair. She strove to please him. At his recollection of her tongue touching his swollen shaft, his jaw clenched.

Pure exquisite torture.

He'd endured her innocent explorations until he could take no more. With an animalistic growl escaping his throat, he had rolled her beneath him and slid into her tight passage.

Cameron stirred, breaking his arousing thoughts.

He tipped her chin up. "Good morn."

"Is it morning already?"

Robert chuckled. "It is."

He bent to kiss her, but her brows knit. Her eyes blinked several times. She pushed away from him, and grabbed her wrap as she ran from the room.

"What the hell?" He rose on his elbow and stared at the open door. Why would she bolt from his arms?

Minutes passed. Where was she? He threw aside the blankets, swung his legs over the bed and reached for his trews just as Cameron slipped back into the room and closed the door. She padded across the floor and climbed into bed.

"Are ye all right?" He dropped his clothes and settled next to her while running his hand down the side of her face. "Ye appear pale."

"I'm fine. I just needed to visit the garderobe."

He sniffed. "Ye smell like mint."

"Is it a crime to freshen yer breath?"

"Nay, but 'tis a strange habit to leap up first thing in the morn to chew mint."

They lay in each other's arms for some time. He stroked her hip while enjoying the feel of her against him. Anticipating a life with her by his side, a grin tugged at the corners of his mouth. "I'd like to announce our plans to marry. It'll be cause for celebration that'll do the clan good."

194

Cameron skimmed her hand over his chest. "Before ye do, I'd like to tell Da."

"He already knows my intentions."

Her hand stilled. "He does?"

"I told him I'd bring ye home after the wedding."

"And he agreed?"

"Aye."

"Well, did the two of ye set a date?"

At the inflection in her voice, Robert kissed her pouting lips. "Lass, I spoke to yer da about my plans because had I been in his place, I would have run the man through who was making love to my daughter without the sanctity of marriage."

Cameron rose on her elbow. "He knows we…that we…."

Her cheeks pinkened.

"I'm sure he suspected, but nay, I didn't inform him we're *well acquainted*." He squeezed her bottom.

She punched him on the shoulder and squealed when he flipped her underneath him. Mirth danced in her green eyes, her smile radiant. He brushed the soft dark hair framing her face and drew his finger across her plump bottom lip. "Ye're beautiful."

His manhood swelled and pushed against her thigh. He could not get enough of her. What magic did she weave? He kissed her soft, pliant lips. "I want ye."

"What are ye waiting for?" she whispered against his mouth.

Sweeter words had never been spoken.

~~~

Robert stepped out of the castle and stood at the top of the bailey stairs. Cameron waited several paces behind. The Graham clan had gathered and murmured amongst themselves, questioning why they'd been summoned.

He held up a hand. The crowd grew quiet, their eyes focused on him. "I have an announcement." He turned to Cameron and extended his hand. "I've asked Mistress

195

MacDougall to become my wife. And…" he paused and gazed into her eyes, "she's accepted."

The clan roared wild with excitement. "Hurrah," a man yelled.

Children jumped, several lads threw their fists in the air, whooping, clapping and shouting good cheers.

Tessa's hands covered her plump cheeks. "We're going to have a wedding!"

Cameron's chest swelled with the gracious welcome as Robert tucked her to his side.

Nichola, Androu and Isobel raced up the steps. Isobel threw her arms around Cameron's waist. "We'll be sisters."

Cameron embraced the little lass. "I couldn't ask for a sweeter one."

Nichola grabbed Cameron's shoulders. "There's so much to do. But first, let's talk to Tessa about a celebration tonight."

She hooked her arm through Cameron's and started inside.

"Come Issie, we'll need yer help," Cameron called over her shoulder.

Isobel's eyes widened, and her face lit up as she ran to take Cameron's outstretched hand.

Robert winked. There was that look, those dimples that caused her heart to flip over.

~~~

Everyone excitedly prepared to celebrate the marriage announcement, and the clan's thoughtfulness meant a great deal to Cameron. However, feeling a bit lightheaded, she decided to rest before the evening festivities.

The old healer threw a bunch of peat on the fire as Cameron entered her chambers. Flames curled around the moss, taking the chill out of the air. Several lads inched the wooden tub into the room.

"Place it in front of the hearth," Aine said.

196

A long line of boys struggled in, carrying heavy buckets filled with steaming water.

Aine turned, and her eyes lit. "Oh mistress, I didn't hear ye enter. Come in and relax."

"Thank ye, Aine. This looks heavenly, but ye've been so busy, and I hate ye've gone to such trouble."

"Och, 'tis nay trouble at all." She waved a hand in dismissal then shooed the lads out of the room. "Let me help ye with yer gown."

Aine lifted the dress off Cameron and hung it on the back of a chair. After stepping out of her underclothes, Cameron sank to her shoulders in the blissful heat and sighed.

"Do ye want me to assist yer bath?" Aine asked as she picked up discarded clothing.

"Oh nay, I'd like to relax here for a wee bit."

"Verra well. I'll leave this soap for ye." Aine winked. "Ye'll smell sweet for the festivities."

"Thank ye for everything."

"Ye're welcome, mistress. Congratulations again," she said before slipping across the room and out the door.

Deep in thought, Cameron drew circles on top of the water. She couldn't believe she would become Robert's wife.

I think we get along fairly well now.

She giggled. The large fearless warrior, always in control, seemed to struggle with finding the appropriate words.

Prickly heat slid over her face as she remembered the time that followed. He made ardent love to her, and although he never mentioned his feelings, he made her *feel* loved. She closed her eyes, marveling over the sweet memories.

~~~

"Are ye sleeping?"

Cameron raised her head from the back of the tub. "Oh, I didn't hear ye come in."

Nichola folded her arms over her waist. "Did my brother keep ye up too late last night?"

197

"I'm afraid there's another reason I'm so tired." Cameron stood and ran her hands over her abdomen. "I'm going to have a bairn."

Nichola's mouth dropped open. She gawked at Cameron's waist. When Cameron stepped from the tub, Nichola wrapped a drying cloth around her shoulders. "A bairn?"

Cameron took a deep breath and exhaled slowly.

"But..." Nichola's voice trailed off, her eyes wide with questions.

Cameron clutched the cloth tight. Heat crept up her neck and slithered across her cheeks. She lifted her gaze to Nichola's. "Robert and I...well, we made love."

"I had no idea... Oh, how exciting," Nichola exclaimed and lightly squeezed her.

"Ye're not mad?"

"Heavens, Cameron. Did ye really think I'd be mad?"

"I didn't know how ye'd take it—what ye'd think of me." She rubbed the drying cloth over her arms.

"I'm thrilled. As the clan will be when they learn of it."

Cameron grasped Nichola's hand. "Please don't say anything. Robert doesn't know. I hope to tell him tonight after the celebration."

Nichola squeezed Cameron's fingers. "I promise I won't say a word. Let's get ye ready. We have much to celebrate."

"Here ye are," Tessa bellowed while opening the chamber door. She walked in carrying a beautiful hunter-green gown that matched the color of Cameron's eyes. "Ye'll be bonnie in this."

Cameron ran her hand over the silky material. "It's truly lovely."

Nichola held out a cream-colored chemise. "Let's see how it fits ye."

After donning the underclothes, Tessa and Nichola slipped the gown over Cameron's outstretched arms. Cameron smoothed the soft skirt over her waist and down her hips. With wide eyes, she examined the dress. The tops of her breasts protruded over the neckline. Prickly tingles crept up her neck. "Do ye think it's decent?"

"Aye, ye look wonderful." Nichola giggled, playfully slapping Cameron's hands away from the bodice. "Don't be tugging on it. Robert won't be able to take his eyes off ye."

"Jes like a princess." Tessa clutched her chest. She bent and picked up the wet bathing cloth. "I'll have the lads fetch the tub directly," she said, before leaving the room.

Nichola brushed Cameron's hair. When she reached for pins, Cameron turned. "Let's not put it up. Robert likes it down."

"All right, ye're ready then." Nichola held Cameron's hands out to her sides. "Before we go below stairs, I want ye to know how verra happy I am ye'll be my sister."

"Oh, Nichola, I couldn't be happier." Tears welled in her eyes, and she shrugged her shoulders. "It's the bairn. I cry so easily it seems."

She and Nichola laughed as they made their way down the stairs and into the grand hall.

~~~

The room, loud with good cheer, laughter and music, had filled with Graham residents. Men, women and children enjoyed the large feast Tessa prepared. Tables brimmed with succulent meats and sauces, fish and poultry, vegetable dishes and sweet cakes. Ale flowed freely and everyone enjoyed the celebration—everyone but Rosalind.

She watched the revelry while leaning against the wall.

"If it hadnae been for that slut, Robert would've asked *me* to be his wife. Weel, I willnae sit by idly and watch her steal my place." Her eyes focused on Cameron. "Nay, I willnae let her have him fer long."

~~~

Nichola and Cameron made their way to Robert's table. When they approached, Michael placed his hand over his chest and shouted, "Here's to many years of blissful marriage."

199

The boisterous group cheered, and the men raised their tankards.

Robert wrapped his arm around Cameron's waist. His pulse beat wildly. She affected him like an untried lad.

"Brother, I'm so happy for ye. I couldn't have been more surprised or pleased."

He affectionately squeezed his sister's shoulder. Her happiness pleased him more than she would ever know. "I have yer approval?"

"Ye do." Nichola took Cameron's hand and the two chatted, Nichola full of wedding ideas.

Candlelight danced off Cameron's dark hair, and her green eyes sparkled. His eyes feasted on her white plump bosom spilling over the tight bodice.

"Ye'd best get yerself under control before ye throw her across the table and take her right here," Lachlan teased.

Robert turned and shook his friend's outstretched hand.

Kendrick slapped Robert on the shoulder. "Congratulations."

"Never thought I'd see ye with an anchor around yer neck." Lachlan chuckled, taking delight in goading him.

"Aye, but she's a velvet anchor." Robert glanced at her. The niggling feeling of distrust crept into his chest, and his stomach churned. He prayed that anchor's ropes would not tangle around his heart and drown him, but instead hold them steadfast and secured to each other.

Casting those thoughts aside, he motioned the men away from Cameron's ears. "I sent word for the MacDougalls to join us for the wedding. It's a surprise. She doesn't know they'll attend."

"She'll be verra pleased," Kendrick said.

"I'd like to toast ye, my good friend." Lachlan held up his mug. "May ye have a long marriage to the lass and many bairns to carry on for ye."

Kendrick raised his cup. "Aye, here's to ye and Cameron."

"Here's to all of us." Robert raised his tankard to his friends before turning it up and draining the contents.

Cheers interrupted them as a group of dancers gathered on the floor. Jacob strummed a lute, and Betsy played a harp. Cameron and Nichola ran to join the group. Holding hands, they glided, sidestepping around a large circle.

Michael broke away from the dancers and ran to the center, kicking his feet in time with the lively music. He jumped and twisted, landing in a squat only to spring to his feet and throw his legs out to the side again.

The crowd roared, cheering and laughing. The music tempo grew faster.

Michael ran to the dancers, took Nichola's hands and brought her into the middle of the ring. He twirled her around and around. Slowly, he dropped her hands and clapping in time with the music, backed into position within the circle of dancers.

Nichola spun on her toes. Arms wide, she sashayed across the floor. Swaying her hips and swinging her arms, she twirled, her blue gown flowing around her legs. She stopped in front of Philip, grasped his hands, and tugged him into the ring. She clapped and backed into place within the circle.

The music sped up with Philip leaping and twisting. He landed in a crouched position, coiled to launch high into the air. The dancers twirled around, singing and laughing while Philip sprang up, tucked his chin into his chest and flipped, landing solidly on his feet.

The crowd cheered as Philip whipped around to select the next dancer.

He chose Cameron, and Robert's chest tightened. The man took her hands and twirled her into the circle. Philip let her go, and she floated across the floor, her arms moving gracefully to and fro in front of her. She spun and glided in another direction. Her long dark hair flowed around her lithe body while she weaved in time with the fast tempo. She dropped her head back and holding out her arms, she swirled

201

around and around before finally gliding to a stop in front of Walter.

Cameron took Walter's hands and coaxed him into the circle. Robert's gut wrenched at her smile for the other man. Was he jealous? The idea was absurd. After all, it was simply a dance. But his reaction jolted him—hard. His jaw became rigid, and his muscles constricted, as if eager for battle. When she stepped back into the ring of dancers and the circle continued around Walter, his tension eased.

The dance continued until each participant had taken a turn in the ring. Michael and Gavin broke from the group and dragged Robert into the middle of the circle. Nichola tugged Cameron out of the loop and thrust the two together.

Robert took Cameron's hand, pulling her against his chest—her laugh, a balm to his soul. She gazed into his eyes before he lowered his mouth and kissed her passionately while wrapping his arms around her and bending her backward.

The rowdy crowd clapped and shouted cheers for their Laird and the new Lady of the Graham clan.

When he straightened, Cameron squeezed his fingers. Her face glowed pink, her eyes bright. "I've had a wonderful time, but I'm ready to retire. Will ye escort me to my chamber?"

Robert raised his eyebrow and placed a kiss on her hand. He wrapped his arm around her and glanced at Lachlan and Kendrick. "Gentlemen, if ye'll excuse me?"

"Aye, goodnight," Lachlan replied.

Robert followed Cameron down the hall and into her room. When he walked inside, she closed the door and stepped into his arms. He nuzzled her neck and ran his hands up and down her back.

He cupped her soft bottom and pulled her against his obvious desire. "Do ye feel what ye do to me?" he whispered while nibbling her earlobe.

Cameron wiggled out of his embrace and smiled. What was she up to?

He dropped his arms. Watching her, his eyes narrowed. Holding his hand, she guided him to a chair in front of the fireplace and gently pushed him down.

She's trying to seduce me.

His cock, fully aroused from her attempts, stood stiff and ached for her touch. He reached out for her, but she stepped back shaking her head, her lips pursed.

"Not so fast," she teased, untying the laces confining her breasts while swaying her hips to the music drifting up from the hall.

Robert's mouth watered. She peeled the fabric down revealing dark pink nipples outlined in her thin chemise. Her dress eased over her hips, past her shapely legs to pool at her feet.

When she stepped out of the gown, Robert caught a glimpse of her dark nether curls and his shaft strained against his trews. Groaning, he adjusted himself, and Cameron smiled, seemingly pleased at his discomfort.

The wench.

Scantily clad before him in her intimate underclothes, she knelt, removed his leather boots, and deposited them on the floor behind her. She straightened and brushing his chest with her breasts, she tugged his shirt off his shoulders.

He leaned back in the chair as his clothing fluttered to the floor. The sight of her small fingers untying his trews and opening his breeches had him gritting his teeth. His thick rigid member jutted through the opening. When she gasped and her eyes widened, his shaft jerked. His anxious anticipation had sweat peppering his forehead, his heart pounding. He tamped down the urge to seize her and sink into her sweetness. When she tugged his breeks, he raised his hips, and she eased them down his legs.

His manhood stood proud against his belly. When her gaze raked him, a beastly growl escaped his throat. She placed her soft hands on his knees and took in the sight of him. His cock throbbed at her scrutiny. She reached out and touched the drop pooling on the sensitive tip, and he groaned, steeling himself to submit to the sweet agony. Her gaze lingered briefly before traveling down his thighs.

What did she plan? Could he control himself to withstand her explorations? He swallowed hard, impatient to join their bodies.

Inching her way up his legs, her soft breasts brushed him, and she lowered her hot mouth over his cock.

"Shite," he hissed and closed his eyes, savoring the feel of her lips encasing him. Each stroke of her tongue was exquisite, intense. "I can't take much more," he croaked through clenched teeth. "Ye'd best stop before I lose myself."

He grasped her arms and guided her over his thighs. She straddled his legs, and the tip of his rigid length pushed against her hidden treasure.

Her eyes glazed over as she lowered herself onto his pulsing member and sighed. "Oh, Robert."

He almost lost control at the feel of her tight sheath surrounding him. He wrapped his arms around her and held her tight against him, his shaft fully embedded. He stripped her chemise off, tossed it to the side and buried his face in her luscious breasts. He gently raked his teeth across her nipples. "Ride me, Cameron."

Trembling, she rose and sank. Robert reached between them and massaged her core. He gazed between her legs at their joining. When his cock disappeared in her, he came close to spilling his seed.

But he wanted to give her pleasure, see her face when she lost herself. Her sharp intake of air signaled her impending climax. He took over, driving into her warmth. She grasped his shoulders, her beautiful breasts bouncing in his face. Her body suddenly tensed, and she cried out.

Feeling her muscle spasms, he held onto her hips and pumped into her until he exploded, shooting his stream into her womb. Rocking slowly, he eased in and out of her while her tremors lessened.

A few moments passed before he picked her up and cradling her in his arms, carried her to bed. She snuggled close to him, and they lay quiet for some time, catching their breath and holding each other. Sated and fully relaxed, he caressed her hip.

"Robert?"

"Hmmm?"

"I need to talk to ye about something."

Dread crept over him at her serious tone. "What is it?"

She grasped his hand and guided it to her abdomen. "Ye're going to be a father," she whispered.

Robert stilled. Aye, he knew there was a chance his seed had taken hold, but he hadn't given it much consideration.

"A babe?" he asked, smiling as the thought sunk in. He ran his hand around her firm abdomen. "I'm going be a father."

"Ye're happy then?"

"I couldn't be more pleased."

Their foreheads touched. She closed her eyes and whispered, "I love ye, Robert Graham."

She didn't wait for his reply, but kissed him gently.

Cameron's declaration shook him to the core.

Did he love her?

He never held deep feelings for any woman, not even Jacqueline. At one time, he had thought he loved her, but after finding the same gratification from other women, he soon realized he only craved her body.

However, Cameron never failed to amaze him. While some women would have used pregnancy to rope him into marriage, she informed him of her condition after he asked her to become his wife. She brought out disturbing feelings. Aye, he cared for her, but he asked for her hand to seal a final truce with Alastair. As his wife, she would ensure her father kept his word...*right?* Those *were* his intentions.

But the gut wrenching pain that coursed through him when he thought Cameron wanted to leave him...did that match his intentions?

Deep in thought, he embraced her for hours, listening to her steady breathing while she slept. Could he give his heart to her? Could he trust her?

His mind screamed *caution*.

Chapter Fourteen

Graham Castle
October 1297

Cameron's wedding day finally arrived. She stretched then scooted farther under the blankets. A month elapsed since Robert proposed. Time crept by with her anxious nerves standing on end. She rarely saw him. As Laird, he was busy with the workings of the castle, training his men and meeting with other clans. Rumblings of nearby skirmishes increased the time he spent away.

But tonight he'd be hers. Anticipating his loving, her stomach tightened. A knock on the door startled her wicked thoughts. She rose on her elbow. "Aye, come in."

Tessa bustled into her chamber with Isobel on the old woman's heels. "Guid morn, mistress."

"Good morn."

Isobel jumped on the mattress. "Ye're marrying Robbie today, and we'll be sisters."

Cameron kissed the little girl's soft cheek. "And I can't wait to be part of yer family."

Tessa placed a tray of bread and cheese on a table next to the hearth. "I brought ye a wee bit to eat."

"It's time to get up." Isobel bounded from the bed, skipped to a trunk of borrowed clothes and threw open the lid. "I'll find ye something to wear."

"Come, let's get ye ready fer yer big day." Tessa motioned to a bench. "Why don't ye sit by the fire while I brush yer hair?"

Cameron selected a slice of cheese and sat in front of the warm hearth. No longer sick upon waking, she nibbled on the light meal. "Ye spoil me terribly."

"Well, it's yer special day to be spoiled."

"Here's a chemise." Isobel leapt up, clutching it in her fist.

"Thank ye, sweetling." Cameron placed the underclothes in her lap while Tessa arranged her hair.

A short time later, someone knocked on the door. Nichola peeked in the room and entered carrying a beautiful cream-colored dress. Isobel ran to meet her, lifted the skirt off the floor, and helped Nichola bring the garment to her.

"We'd be honored if ye'd wear our mum's gown today."

"Mum married Da in it," Isobel added.

Cameron stroked the fine fabric. "Are ye sure?"

"Aye, please." Nichola laid the gown on the bed.

Cameron swallowed emotions thick in her throat. Her chest constricted with thoughts of her own mum. If only her father and her sisters could be here. Casting the sad thoughts aside, she wiped the tears clouding her eyes. "I'd love to borrow it."

"It'll be lovely on ye." Tessa motioned. "Come, lass. Ye donnae want to keep the laird waitin'."

By the time they finished, Cameron felt like a queen. The gown was simple, but elegant. Embroidered silver thread wove intricate designs around the neckline, and a matching belt worn low over her hips hung down the skirt. The same pattern of thread bordered the hem of the long flowing sleeves. Across her forehead, she wore a beautiful silver circlet adorned with sapphires symbolic of the Graham clan. Her hair, embellished with streams of flowers laced through her long dark curls, trailed down her back.

Tessa sighed. "Ye're a bonnie bride, mistress."

"Aye, ye're just like a princess," Isobel exclaimed.

"Are ye ready?" Nichola's eyes were wide with excitement.

Cameron took a deep breath. "I'm ready."

She and Nichola made their way down the long flight of stairs leading into the bailey. "We aired out the old church and decorated it for yer wedding. The whole clan is seated in the chapel."

Cameron's heart squeezed in sudden jitters. The whole clan, her new family.

Isobel skipped ahead and ran up the chapel steps. "She's here! She's here!"

"Shhh…shhh…" Several voices hushed the lass and hands yanked her inside.

"Do ye like the flowers in yer hair? They came from my garden."

"Oh, aye, they're quite lovely."

Someone cracked open the door and Aine peered out. Her face lit, her eyes grew wide, and she ducked back in. "Get ready," she called and slammed the door shut.

"Let me help ye up the stairs." Nichola took Cameron's hand. When they reached the landing before the church, the doors opened wide.

Robert.

Her breath caught in her throat. He stood inside the vestibule's inner sanctuary. Dressed in a highland black and blue plaid, his powerful legs stood braced apart, strong hands clasped before his waist. Dark hair hung to his broad shoulders, and his eyes held promises for her alone.

Her sisters stepped from behind him.

Cameron gasped. A trembling shiver ran through her. "Lindsey? Heather?"

Tears of joy stung the backs of her eyes. The women ran to each other. Together they made a circle, the three of them kissing each other's cheeks, arms around one another.

Cameron straightened and gazed at Robert. *He* made this happen. He invited them. "Thank ye," she mouthed.

He gave her the smile that made her heart flutter and slightly bowed. "M'lady."

"Cameron?"

She whirled around.

Da's arms opened wide.

"Oh, Da." She threw herself into his embrace. "I've missed ye so," she choked out in a whisper.

He trembled and stroked her hair. "I've spent many sleepless nights worrying whether I'd ever see ye again." Slowly, he straightened, cupped her chin and smiled. "Lass, it's so verra good to find ye well."

"I love ye, Da." She held his wrinkled hands and smiled through the tears sliding down her face.

"And I love ye." He kissed her cheek, wrapped his arm around her shoulders and turned toward Robert, who patiently waited, watching their emotional reunion. "I think it's time for ye to marry."

Cameron answered unwaveringly, "Aye. It's time."

Her heart swelled with love for her husband-to-be, the father of their unborn child.

The Grahams and the MacDougalls were together at last.

Heather and Lindsey led Nichola and Isobel down the aisle and stopped next to the altar.

In a dream-like fog, Cameron took in the scene before her. Androu, Duncan, Lachlan and Kendrick stood to the right of a priest. The father stood waiting, a worn black bible clutched in his hands.

Da smiled and placed her fingers in Robert's warm palm.

When Robert escorted her into the sanctuary, everyone turned to face them. Her breath caught at the gathered clan. Fiona and Neyll waved. Glenda and Walter nodded encouragement. Ellen, Hume, and Tavish stood beside Bonnie and Marie. The chapel filled with cheerful residents gathered to welcome her.

The ceremony dashed by in a blur. She hardly remembered repeating her vows or hearing the father bless them as man and wife. The next thing she knew, Robert embraced and kissed her with the roar of the crowd spurring him on.

He nuzzled her neck. "I can't wait to get ye alone, wife."

210

His mouth found hers again and he groaned, melding her against him.

Hands clapped his shoulders and wrenched him away.

"There's time for all that later, man. Give the lady some air." Michael laughed while he, Lachlan, and Kendrick tugged Robert toward the keep. Her husband shrugged good-naturedly, and Cameron laughed at the men's antics.

Loving arms enveloped her, and she turned. "Oh, Muire, it's good to have ye here."

"I missed ye, child," the old healer said. "We were so worried, but look at ye. Ye're such a bonnie bride."

"Thank ye. I can't believe ye're really here."

Muire embraced her, then stilled. When she straightened, she ran her fingers down Cameron's arms and held her hands. "Ye're with child."

Cameron hesitated. What must she think of her? "I am."

Muire's gentle eyes displayed compassion, and relief poured through Cameron. "It will be wonderful to have another little Cammie."

Cameron squeezed Muire's hands before Lindsey and Heather stepped beside them. "We were really worried about ye, and to think ye were so close all this time, and we didn't even know it," Heather said.

Wanting to avoid discussion of her abduction and the hard feelings both clans struggled to get past, Cameron spoke up. "Let me introduce ye to Robert's family."

His siblings waited patiently next to the church benches. Cameron's arms encircled them. "This is Isobel...Nichola...and Androu."

Nichola extended her hand to the sisters. "Welcome to Graham Castle."

"I'm glad to see Cameron is safe after all these months," Lindsey replied coolly, her rigid stance and intense gaze accusing.

Nichola let her hand drop. "I understand. I'd feel the same about my brothers and sister." She glanced between Cameron's two siblings. "I'm verra happy our clans made amends, and I pray we can put our bad feelings aside and become friends."

Lindsey glared at Nichola.

Cameron stepped forward. "Lins, please."

She turned her angry and hurt eyes to Cameron. "Ye don't know what we've been through. Da almost lost his mind."

"Lindsey." Heather shook her head. "Not now."

Reluctantly, Lindsey's stance eased, and she exhaled.

"Please give this a chance," Nichola implored. "We've got so much to celebrate and be thankful for."

~~~

Rosalind slammed her tray onto the worktable in the kitchen. "The slut may have won this battle, but she willnae win the war."

Dara placed a platter next to Rosalind and reached over her to select a sweet tart. She arranged a few on her tray. "Ye're not daydreaming again are ye? The Laird has chosen Lady Cameron, not ye."

"She may have him now, but it willnae be for long. She got with child jes so she could force him into marrying her."

"Ye know it was not like that, Rosalind."

"Humph. Weel, babes often don't live."

Dara's head jerked toward Rosalind, her eyes wide. "What are ye saying?"

"Jes that bairns get sick and die. If that were to happen to 'miss high and mighty', she wouldnae have a hold on him any longer."

"Nothing will happen to her bairn, and ye need to quit dreaming about the laird." Dara looked back at the sweet buns. Frowning, she placed a few more on her tray. "Ye must really love him to still be pining over him."

Rosalind shrieked. "Ye fool, I donnae love *him*." She reached over Dara and selected several sweetmeats. "I love the power I'd have being his wife. I *deserve* to be Lady of this castle."

212

"Ye're still daydreaming all right." Laughing, Dara hoisted her tray onto her hip and left the kitchen.

"We'll jes see who's dreaming when the slut is nae longer around."

~~~

The afternoon wore on with the clan celebrating. Tessa prepared a grand feast, including roasted quail, boiled mutton and slices of thick venison. The succulent meat adorned large platters surrounded with dishes of salmon and trout caught from the nearby loch.

Robert placed more stewed cabbage and carrots on Cameron's trencher. "Tessa outdid herself."

"I saved room for the sweet tarts." Androu stuffed his mouth with custard, garnished with raspberries from the castle's garden.

The low roar of conversation, laughter, and clinking of utensils settled down when Blake and Walter blew into their bagpipes. The wooden instruments' smooth notes struck an emotional chord. The revelers quieted, listening to the sounds of the poignant music.

Cameron sipped on mulled wine. Robert clasped her hand and stood. She set her mug on the table and let him lead her onto the dance floor. After wrapping his arm around her, they glided, swaying to the beautiful, arousing melodies. She closed her eyes and relished the feel of his strong arms holding her against him.

Other couples joined them, but before long, Tavish and David picked up their flutes, transitioning the dancers into a fast-paced reel. The shouting revelers held hands, circling Robert and Cameron. The music grew faster. Laughter and cheers rang out in their exuberant celebration.

Robert held Cameron's hand and twirled her inside the circle of dancers. The group rushed in, holding their arms high, closing in on Robert and Cameron before drifting back, and dropping their hands, only to repeat the steps over and again.

The dancers then paired off into couples, stepping in time with the music.

"Sword dance!" Lachlan yelled.

Men shouted and gathered to perform the traditional dance, each placing his sword on the ground in front of him. Blake blew into his bagpipe signaling the beginning. Walter beat drums while the women scooted back, clapping to the fast tempo.

The men held their arms high. In unison, they bounced on the balls of their feet, kicked their legs to the side and landed next to their blades. Robert easily sprang in the air. For such a large man, he was very agile, impressing her with his speed and dexterity. The men intricately weaved in and out, hopping on one foot and then the other, twirling around while throwing their arms in the air. The beat grew faster. They shouted as the crowd cheered. With a final drum roll, the music suddenly stopped, and everyone applauded.

Da offered Robert a tankard of ale. "Good job, lad."

Breathing hard, Robert nodded before accepting the drink and swigging down the contents.

Da cleared his throat. "May I speak with Duncan and yer brother?"

Robert wiped his mouth on his sleeve. His eyes narrowed as if considering her father's request. He signaled Duncan and Androu from across the room, motioning them over.

"Aye?" Androu bit into another tart.

"This is Laird MacDougall. He wishes to speak to ye."

Da clasped his hands before him. "I want to apologize for the horrific attack on ye. Although I wasn't aware of it until recently, I *am* Laird of the MacDougall clan and as such, I'm responsible for the actions of my people. I want ye to know I flogged the men who attacked ye and banned them from our clan. I don't expect further trouble." He looked down at Androu and back to Duncan. "We've sealed a truce between our clans—a promise I intend to keep."

Duncan bowed and grasped Da's outstretched hand. "Yer apology is accepted. We look forward to living in peace with ye."

Da then extended his hand to Androu, and Cameron grinned when the lad accepted it.

Robert addressed her father. "If ye'd care to join me, I have a fine wine in my solar."

Cameron's heart leapt at Robert's offer—a beginning to amend the animosity between the two clans.

Da clapped Robert's shoulder. "Aye, I always savor good spirits."

Robert kissed her cheek. "Enjoy yer sisters' company."

"I will," she breathed out as he then walked from the room with her father ambling along beside him.

Nichola squeezed Cameron's hand. "I never thought I'd see the day."

Cameron's throat clogged. "It's a start."

The men disappeared into Robert's solar.

"Let's visit with yer sisters." Nichola looped her arm through Cameron's. The two joined Heather and Lindsey as they sipped spiced cider while lounging in front of the large hearth.

"Oh, Cammie, ye're such a bonnie bride," Heather said, when they approached.

"Well, thank ye." Cameron held her arms out to her sides and turned in a circle. "Nichola and Isobel let me borrow their mum's gown."

Heather straightened and glanced around the room. She stood, her eyes concerned. "Where's Da?"

"Oh, he's with Robert," Cameron replied. "They're sharing a drink."

"By himself?" Heather started around the benches.

Cameron placed her hand on her sister's arm. "It's all right. I want them to have some time alone."

Heather pulled away. "I should join them."

"Nay, Heather. Please." What was wrong with her?

Lindsey stood and addressed Heather. "It'll be all right."

Her sisters shared a look. Was something amiss? The truce was so very tentative. Did they fear Robert would harm Da?

"Robert will treat our father with the upmost respect." Cameron glanced between her sisters. "Let them have some time alone."

"But…" Heather smoothed the front of her gown, her blue eyes staring down the hall toward the solar.

Lindsey tugged their sister back down on the bench and shook her head. The women sat in stilted silence.

A serving girl arrived with a tray laden with mugs.

"Ahh, please have more cider." Nichola offered the sisters.

Cameron accepted a mug and changed the subject. "Tell me, where's our baby sister?"

She blew over the hot liquid before taking a sip.

"Elsbeth left a month ago with Sister Mary. The sisters are establishing a new abbey near Perth, and they asked her to join them," Lindsey answered.

Cameron's pulse skipped a beat. Elsbeth would be at the mercy of anyone who happened upon them. "What about the war? Is it safe?"

Heather exhaled. "I don't know. Da didn't want her to leave, but she wouldn't take no for an answer. She was determined to set out with the sisters and help protect the orphans."

"Da sent several men to escort them, but we haven't received word they made it safely," Lindsey added.

Nichola leaned forward. "Houses of worship should be safe from Edward."

Heather placed her mug on the table before her, worry reflected in her eyes. "Aye, she's right. I'm sure they'll be fine."

Thoughts of her sister in peril flooded Cameron's mind. "Please let me know when ye hear from her."

"We will," Heather agreed. "I know she'll be sorry she wasn't here to witness yer marriage."

Muire strolled into the room and sat beside Cameron. "We have more good news to be celebrating, aye, Cammie?"

Her sisters turned to face to her.

Cameron swallowed. She had not intended to blurt out her news. But the Grahams knew, and it would only be a matter of time before her family heard. How would her sisters react? Her trembling fingers splayed over her abdomen. "Aye, we do. I'm going to have a bairn."

Lindsey's mouth fell open, and Heather's eyes widened. Conflicting emotions passed across her sisters's faces.

Lindsey finally broke the silence. "Ye weren't forced were ye?"

Cameron sat forward. "Nay, nay, it wasn't anything like that. I know it's a shock. Things happened so quickly, but I love my husband, and this babe is truly a blessing."

"Of course it is," Heather agreed. "We were just taken aback."

Lindsey held up her mug. "Here's to the babe and many more."

Her father and Robert walked back into the room, and joined the women next to the fire. Heather relaxed with Da in the room. They laughed, and enjoyed the light atmosphere with talk of news from MacDougall Castle.

~~~

Robert glanced in Cameron's direction once again. He had watched her visit with her family the entire afternoon. Aye, she missed them, but he wanted her to himself. Standing from his chair, he placed his tankard on the table and strode to her.

"Would ye care to dance?" he asked in a husky voice, his thumb stroking her soft neck.

"I would."

He led her onto the floor before twirling her around and into his arms. As they swayed to the music, her green eyes sparkled with unmistakable joy.

"Ye're happy?"

"Aye, I can't believe my family is here. Thank ye, Robert. Thank ye so verra much."

He kissed her plump lips. "I'm glad ye're pleased, but ye don't intend to spend all night with them, do ye?"

He glanced over her head at her family still gathered by the hearth.

"Why?" Cameron smiled coyly. "Do ye have something better in mind?"

"I do." He danced in the direction of the stairs, scooped her into his arms and marched up the steps.

~~~

The MacDougalls remained at Graham Castle for three days. Cameron enjoyed their visit, but early the fourth morning Da announced they would return home. The horses and carts, loaded with the MacDougall's belongings, waited in the bailey.

Her father grasped Robert's hand. "Take care of my lassie."

"I won't let anything happen to her."

Heather hugged Cameron. "Please let us know how ye're doing with the babe."

"I will, but we'll visit ye soon," Cameron promised.

Lindsey, dressed in her lad's attire, mounted her horse. "See that you do."

With Robert's help, Muire settled next to Heather on the old wagon's rickety seat. "We're not far away, Cammie. Ye send word if ye need anything."

"I'll be fine." Cameron tucked a soft grey blanket around the old healer's legs. A sense of sadness swept over her at the thought she would no longer live at MacDougall Castle. A chapter closed, but a new one opened. With a deep breath, she lightly squeezed Muire's hand. "Take care of yerself and our family."

218

"I will, child. Don't fret over us."

A heavy hand grasped her shoulder, and Cameron turned. Da drew her into his embrace. She breathed in his familiar earthy scent. Memories of him comforting her as a wee lass flooded her mind. Her heart tugged.

He brushed a lock of hair from her face. "Ye send word if yer husband gets out of line," he teased, his eyes twinkling.

"I will, Da." She kissed his whiskered cheek.

He climbed onto the saddle and held his hand high. He winked at her and waved to the entourage. The horses trotted out of the bailey and the creaking wagon lurched forward, disappearing through the main gate. She hated to see them leave.

Robert tugged her to his side, and they strolled to the keep. "I'll take ye to visit before the bairn arrives. I'd like Muire to be here for the birth."

"I know it's silly to be upset, but I've always been close to my family. With them only a short distance away, I'm sure I'll see them often."

He stiffened. "I don't want ye to go off by yerself. Yer da told me Symon has his sights on Graham land."

"What?" Cameron stopped and faced him.

"He intended to pit the clans against each other. He schemed to gain control of Graham Castle with the idea yer da would need him to run his newly acquired lands."

Her mouth dropped open. "I can't believe he thought Da would go along with his plan."

"He didn't. He counted on our clans engaging in bloody conflict. The scary thing is, it could've worked. If Androu or Duncan had died..."

Cameron placed her fingertip on Robert's mouth. "Nay, don't say it."

He kissed her knuckles. His dark eyes clouded with worry. "Promise ye'll stay within the castle walls. Just because Symon's plan didn't work doesn't mean he hasn't got another."

Chapter Fifteen

Graham Castle
November 1297

Cameron awoke unusually early to find Robert dressing in the dark. The glow of the fire highlighted his muscular body as he stepped into his trews and reached for a shirt. He appeared deep in thought. What could be disturbing him?

She propped on her elbow and pushed an errant lock from her eyes. "Robert..."

He turned toward her and tugged his tunic over his head. "I'm riding to Kilmory today. Brandon McLeod sent a message to garner our support for the rebellion." He strapped the swordbreaker to his belt and grabbed a dagger off the bedside table.

"And he wants yer support," Cameron stated softly.

Robert picked up his cloak. "He *needs* our support."

"But why ye? Ye've put yer time in fighting for the rebellion. Isn't that enough?"

He paused and stared at her. "Nay. The enemy still ravishes and kills our countrymen."

She bent her head to hide the panic in her eyes, the fear settling in her chest.

"Brandon works with Wallace to run Edward out of Scotland. Lairds from clans south of Edinburgh gather to learn of their plan. I won't sit safely behind the walls of Graham Castle and let other men fight for our freedom."

No matter what argument she put forth, Robert was determined to join the fight. She wanted to be supportive, but she pictured her husband wounded or lying dead in a field of fallen warriors.

Her heart squeezed.

She pasted a smile on her face and raised her gaze to meet his. "When will ye return?"

"I won't be gone long, mayhap a week at most."

220

Cameron scooted off the bed and wrapped her arms around his neck. "Please be safe."

He gathered her in his strong arms and silently held her, stroking her hair. He kissed the top of her head and looked into her tear-filled eyes. "If there was any other way..."

Did his voice catch?

He took a deep breath and exhaled as he placed his forehead against hers. "Promise ye'll stay inside the castle walls. Don't go wandering about the forests searching for yer wee herbs."

"I'll be fine. Just take care of yerself."

He grasped her shoulders, startling her. His anxious dark gaze bore into her. "Promise me, Cameron."

"I promise," she whispered, her eyes wide.

His grip eased, and he ran his fingers across her swollen belly.

She covered his warm hand with hers and searched his face. "Robert, ye are telling me everything...aye?"

His silence frightened her.

"Robert?"

"I have no information, only a gut feeling. The rebellion is strong and resilient." He rubbed circles over her extended belly. "Edward is determined he will reign over our country. If he has his way, we'll be under his thumb, slaves to his commands." The muscles in his jaw clenched and his chin, covered with dark stubble, jutted out. "We won't let that happen." His dark eyes bore into her. "No matter what."

"What are ye saying?"

He paused. The fire crackled and popped. "We don't know what tomorrow holds."

Her pulse hammered.

"I want ye to know..." He cleared his throat and started again. "I want ye to know that I care for ye."

Her breath hitched. This was the first time Robert had uttered endearing words to her. Tears threatened to spill, and she hid her face in his chest. "Ye come home to me, husband."

She relished his strong body surrounding hers and committed it to memory for the long nights he'd be gone.

Too soon, he straightened. With his knuckle under her chin, he raised her mouth and kissed her. "I'll see ye in a few days."

He grabbed another knife from the chest at the foot of the bed, stuffed it into his belt and strode across the room. When he got to the door, he paused and turned.

"Remember yer promise, wife."

~~~

A week came and went, but Robert had yet to return. Where was he? Shouldn't he be home by now?

We don't know what tomorrow holds. His parting words echoed through Cameron's mind, and a foreboding wave of uneasiness encompassed her. Her troubled heart constricted with thoughts of the possible dangers he faced.

She tried to hold off anxious emotions, but try as she might the persistent apprehension pervaded her thoughts. She immersed herself in teaching Aine various healing remedies in addition to tending the clan's minor ailments. When Nichola requested her help with the castle's records, she jumped at the chance to preoccupy her mind and prayed the time until Robert returned would pass quickly.

With plans to check on the village residents, she donned a soft woolen gown and slippers, picked up her basket from the bedside table and strolled down the stairs.

"Take these rugs out back and beat the dirt from them. And when ye're done, remove these tapestries and clean them as well," Nichola instructed several lads.

Cameron had been relieved Nichola agreed to manage the keep, giving Cameron time to visit patients. "Good morn," she said as she approached the group.

"Oh, good morn," Nichola called over her shoulder. She handed an arm full of large cushions to a lass. "Air these pillows out, too."

222

"Ye're off to a busy start," Cameron commented, observing the activity in the hall. "I thought I'd see if ye'd like to go to the village with me. It's a lovely day, and I'd like to check on everyone."

Nichola hesitated and studied the large hall.

"Please?"

She turned and grinned. "Aye, I'll go with ye. Let me give instructions on what needs to be done while I'm gone."

"Wonderful. That'll give me time to talk to Tessa." Cameron headed toward the kitchen. "I'll meet ye back here in a few moments."

The kitchen bustled with activity. Tessa supervised the servants while they prepared the noon meal. "Take these to Gretchen." She handed several pots and pans to a couple of lasses. "Idla and Githa, chop the onions and carrots fer the stew."

Utensils clanged as the women placed containers and cookware on the worktable. Idla and Githa scurried off to retrieve the vegetables from the storage room. Walter caught Cameron's eye and winked as he turned a large roast skewered on a spit over a fire. Fat from the meat dripped into the flames and sizzled. A divine aroma filled the kitchen, and Cameron's stomach rumbled in anticipation.

Tessa dropped a mound of dough on a workbench.

"Good morn, Tessa."

The old cook glanced over her shoulder. "Ah, mistress, did ye sleep well last night? How are ye feeling?"

"I feel fine, thank ye." Cameron set her basket on the table. "I thought I'd visit the village. Do ye have any of yer sweet cakes that I may take? I know how much the wee ones love them." She perused the kitchen. "Oh, I see we have fruit left from this morning. May I have some apples?"

"Aye, we've got plenty." She looked over Cameron's head and bellowed, "Henry, bring the wooden basket."

"Aye, mistress," the lad responded before running from the kitchen.

"I'll have Henry go with ye, and he can carry yer food."

"That would be wonderful."

"If ye're heading into the village, will ye check on Fiona and Neyll fer me?"

"I will. Is anything amiss?"

Tessa waved her hand in dismissal. "Oh nay, I havenae had a chance to see them, and I want to make sure they're doing well."

Henry raced back into the room carrying the large basket.

Tessa wiped her hands on a cloth and stepped to a table lined with goodies. "Place it right here."

"I can't wait to taste one." Cameron selected a pastry and popped it in her mouth.

Tessa placed apples and nuts in the basket along with fresh pies and sweet cakes. "I grow fat jes looking at them."

Once the basket was full, Cameron turned to Henry. "Can ye manage this yourself, or do ye need help? There's a good amount of food here."

He picked up the basket. "I can manage it."

"Verra well, let's be off."

They found Nichola issuing last minute cleaning instructions to servants while grabbing her red woolen wrap off the chair.

"I'm glad ye can come. I'm anxious for a breath of fresh air," Cameron said.

"Well truth be known, I'd much prefer to go visiting than oversee the cleaning." Nichola laughed and hooked her arm through Cameron's.

The three descended the long stone stairs, walked through the bailey and along the road leading into the village. The sun shone bright. She raised her face, relishing the comforting warmth. Wisps of scattered white clouds drifted across the brilliant blue sky.

Several hours passed with the residents welcoming the three into their homes. Cameron depleted her basket of goodies, but she had one more stop to make.

When they approached the last of the houses, Cameron noticed Lachlan conspicuously hanging about. Nichola had glanced at him on several occasions. The two coyly eyed each other before Lachlan finally strode over.

Nichola beamed. "Good afternoon, Lachlan."

He returned her smile. "Aye, 'tis a good day." He nodded at Cameron and then looked back at Nichola. "I'm riding to the south field to check on the cattle. Would ye care to join me?"

Nichola's eyes grew wide with excitement, but just as quickly, her expression sobered. "I'd love to, but I'm helping Cameron."

"Nonsense, Nichola. Go enjoy the rest of the day. Henry and I'll finish up and head back to the keep shortly."

"Are ye sure?"

"Of course. I'll see ye tonight then?"

"Aye, I'll be there." Nichola kissed Cameron's cheek. She took Lachlan's hand, and he led her to his awaiting horse.

After visiting with Fiona and Neyll, Cameron and Henry walked through the inner bailey.

"Thank ye for yer help today, Henry. I couldn't have made my visits without ye."

"Ye're welcome," he replied, before racing off to the kitchen with the empty basket.

Cameron stretched her tired back on the way to the stairs. She slowly climbed the steps and strolled down the hall to her chamber. Once inside the room, she shut the door and leaned against it. Her back ached, and her babe kicked. Placing her hand on her abdomen, her eyes closed.

Where was Robert tonight? Would he come home safely? What would Brandon ask of him?

When the babe once again moved, Cameron pushed away from the door and stepped into the room. Robert's black and blue plaid tartan lay across the end of the bed. One of the servants must have cleaned it and left it for him. Someone knocked on the door as she trailed her fingers across the soft material.

"Come in."

The door opened wide and Gretchen hurried into the chambers.

"Is there anything ye need, mistress?"

"Aye, I'd like a sleeping potion. Will ye have Aine prepare one?" Cameron tugged her gown over her head and dropped it on the chair.

"Aye, mistress. Are ye not feeling well?"

She put her hands on her lower back and stretched. "I'm fine, but my back aches, and I don't sleep well with Robert gone."

"I understand. I'll ask Aine to ready it for ye." Gretchen picked up a blanket off the chair and folded it.

"Thank ye. I'll be down for the evening meal shortly."

Gretchen ambled from the room and closed the door behind her.

~~~

Cameron sat at the long trestle table surrounded by women from the village and their children. At the end of the evening meal, Dara served Tessa's hot apple pies. Cameron's lips closed over the heavenly treat, and she sighed in sheer bliss. "This is wonderful."

The women agreed and laughed, watching the children devour the sweet treat.

Rosalind sauntered into the room and gave Cameron a hateful glare. Cameron refused to be intimidated and stared right back at her. The maid picked up several empty tankards and stacked them on a tray. When she finished, she threw her head back and chortled as she pranced back into the kitchen.

Cameron shook her head. She would never trust that woman.

As the evening grew late, the children became restless, and the group broke apart to retire for the night. Cameron wandered into Robert's solar and sat in one of the chairs before the large hearth. The fire heated the room, and she bathed in the comfort from the warm blaze. The wood popped and hissed

226

with red and orange flames curling up and over the logs. She leaned back, and her gaze skimmed the dark wooden carvings above the mantle of a hunting scene filled with deer, rabbits and a boar.

"Here ye are, mistress." Dara placed a mug on the worn table next to her. "Gretchen asked me to bring this sleeping potion to ye. I hope it helps ye tonight."

Cameron caressed her swollen belly. "Oh, thank ye. I'm sure it will."

"Is there anything else ye need before I retire?"

"Nay, get some rest. I'm going up to bed before long."

"Verra well. Goodnight, mistress."

Cameron glanced at her sewing where she left it on the hearth the night before. She picked it up and held the garment in front of her, inspecting her last stitches. She'd sewn a little each night, and accumulated a few baby outfits and several soft blankets. She threaded her needle, and pulled it through the little woolen nightgown.

Nichola sashayed into the room.

"Well, where have ye been? I began to worry, but I knew Lachlan would take good care of ye," Cameron teased.

Nichola dropped in the chair next to her. She sighed dreamily, her hand over her heart, her eyes fluttering closed. "I had a wonderful time."

"Cameron?" Isobel called out.

"I'm here, in the solar."

Footsteps slapped against the cold hard floor. Isobel raced into the room, waving something bunched in her fist. "Look what I made for the baby."

"What is it?" Cameron took the small stuffed pillow from Isobel's hands. She had sewn two pieces of woolen cloth together creating an oblong shaped cushion with four legs.

"It's a puppy," Isobel explained. "Babies like puppies."

Cameron hugged the little lass. "Oh, 'tis lovely. I can't wait for the babe to see it. Every time I look at it, I shall think of ye."

"I'm going to make another one." Isobel's cherubic face lit up, and she skipped from the room, her dark curls bouncing around her shoulders.

"She's like a different child." Nichola watched her sister leave. "Full of life now."

"Aye, 'tis good to see her feeling better." Cameron looked at Nichola and raised her eyebrows. "So, tell me..."

"Tell ye what?"

"Don't ye play coy, Nichola Graham. Tell me how things went with Lachlan."

Nichola laughed and wrapped her arms around herself. "Oh, I think I'm in love," she said, her eyes dreamy.

"I thought as much." Cameron placed another stitch in the baby's gown. She glanced back at Nichola. "Are ye going to continue, or do I have to drag it out of ye?"

Nichola grinned. "Oh, Cameron, my heart beats fast when I'm near him, and when he holds my hand, his feels so warm and strong." Nichola paused. "And when he takes me in his arms, I just melt."

"Aye, it does indeed sound like ye're in love."

"He makes me laugh, and he comforts me when I'm worried or sad." She stared into the flames. "I find myself searching the room for him, and I'm disappointed if I don't see him." She turned toward Cameron. "And I think he cares for me, too."

"I've seen him watching ye."

"Truthfully? Ye've noticed? Ye're not just saying that?"

"I'm not just saying that." Cameron looked up from her sewing. "It's obvious he's interested in ye."

Nichola beamed. "We had such a nice afternoon. While I rode in front of him, he wrapped his arms around me." She paused, and her cheeks pinkened.

"Go on..."

"He's been a good friend to Robert for as long as I can remember. He's always shown concern for, 'Robert's sister'." She tossed her head from side to side. "But today was different." She grinned guiltily. "He kissed me on the mouth, and I could tell he enjoyed it." She wiggled her eyebrows. "It was *hard* not to tell," she added giggling.

Cameron laughed at her veiled remark. "Oh Nichola, I'm happy for ye."

"Aye, well, I'm glad ye are because I've got a wee favor to ask."

"And that would be?"

Nichola bit her bottom lip. "Lachlan feels awkward courting me. He's not sure how Robert will feel about it."

"Ahh...I see. Ye want me to speak to Robert for ye?"

"Would ye mind? I wouldn't ask, but Lachlan doesn't want to start trouble, and he's trying his best to resist me."

Cameron patted Nichola's hand. "I'll be happy to broach the subject with him."

"Oh, thank ye, Cameron." Nichola leaned back in her chair. "So, tell me about Fiona and Neyll. I'm sorry I wasn't back in time for dinner."

"Everyone asked about ye, but I told them ye were out." Cameron placed another stitch in the gown. She bit the thread in two and tied it into a knot. "We had a good visit. Fiona and Neyll joined us, and Rebecca brought Elizabeth. She looks like Tavish, such a sweet little one."

"This tastes nasty," Nichola said, as she put down Cameron's mug.

Cameron shook her head. "That's my sleeping potion. It doesn't taste *that* bad." She picked up the cup and sniffed the contents. A strong odor wafted past her nostrils, and her eyes flew wide.

Carrots.

Nichola sat forward. "What is it?"

"I don't know. Something's not right." Cameron stuck her finger into the brew and stirred. Bits of seeds floated to the top. Wild carrot seeds.

She gasped. Her hands shook, and she dropped the mug. It crashed to the floor, the contents splattering her gown.

Nichola sprang from the chair. "What, Cameron? What's wrong?"

"There were wild carrot seeds in it." She clutched her stomach, her child nestled beneath.

"I don't understand."

"The seeds are used to rid a woman of an unwanted bairn, but with that many seeds, it would most likely kill the mother as well."

"What? Who would do such a thing?"

"I don't know." Rosalind's malicious grin flashed before her. *Would she try to kill me and my bairn?*

A loud bang broke her thoughts as someone threw open the front doors.

"Lady Graham! Lady Graham!" a man yelled frantically.

Cameron leapt off the chair, ran from the solar and into the great hall. "I'm here."

Michael hurried to her. He bent over, hands on knees, out of breath.

"What is it?" Cameron's pulse beat wildly.

"It's Laird Graham."

She held her breath. Her legs wobbled.

"He's been captured."

The room spun. She staggered and grasped a chair to her right, her hand covering her mouth.

"Captured?" Nichola grabbed Michael's arm. "What do ye mean?"

"We intercepted a messenger on his way to the abbey in Cunningham." Michael handed Cameron a parchment.

Her fingers trembled as she unrolled it.

King Edward I, Lord of Ireland, and Duke of Aquit, demands urgent medicinal attention for elite Field Commander Wilson. Failure to do so will result in the immediate execution of captured Scottish prisoners arrested for instigation of crimes committed against our sovereign ruler and rightful King of Scotland.

230

She looked in horror at Michael. Her body shook. "Robert is one of the prisoners?"

"He and our men. The runner revealed the English soldiers are camped some ten miles northwest of here."

Cameron's head reeled. She placed her hands on the chair and steadied herself.

Robert.

Captured.

She swallowed hard, then straightened. "Get Lachlan and Duncan, and meet me in Robert's solar."

"Aye, mistress." Michael ran from the room.

Nichola faced Cameron. "What are ye going to do?"

"Heal the commander and free my husband."

Chapter Sixteen

"Nay!" Lachlan slammed his open palm on the table. "Ye're not going. Robert would flay every inch of my hide."

"Listen to me." Cameron stood and leaned over the worn wooden surface of the solar desk. "We don't have much time. I'll disguise myself as one of the sisters from the abbey. They won't know I'm Robert's wife."

"Ye're expecting a bairn," Nichola stated the obvious.

"I'm well aware of that. I'll add padding under my gown to protect and conceal the babe, but I *am* going." Cameron squared her shoulders. "Now quit arguing, and listen to my plan."

Duncan, Lachlan, Michael and Nichola stared at her as if she'd lost her mind. A log rolled in the hearth, sending red and orange sparks swirling up the chimney.

"Michael and I will don robes—disguised as members of the clergy. I'll tend the commander and render him, and as many other soldiers as I can, unconscious from my herbs." Cameron turned to Lachlan. "Ye will lie in wait until ye hear our signal. Then, ye can take out the rest of the soldiers and free Robert."

"Are ye daft?" Lachlan stood, and his legs shoved his chair back. "They won't let ye just walk in there and give them yer wee potions." He crossed his arms over his chest. "Do ye think they'll trust ye not to poison them? A Scottish lass, giving their commander a sleeping potion?"

"I'll inform him it's to ward off fever."

Lachlan threw his hands up. "Oh, that will make all the difference."

"What choice do we have?" Cameron stepped around the table. "We're wasting valuable time. We have to take this chance."

Lachlan stared at her. "I don't like it."

"Please. We can do this."

He exhaled loudly and raked his fingers through his hair. "All right, but when the fighting starts, I want ye out of there. Do ye understand?"

She nodded. "Michael, send word to my da. We need his help."

~~~

A loud knock sounded on the door. "The MacDougalls have arrived, m'lady," Michael called.

"I'll be right down." Da was here. Cameron sighed with relief. She grabbed her wrap and tossed it around her shoulders before hurrying down the stairs.

MacDougall men and their horses filled the bailey.

"Cameron!" Heather broke from the group and ran toward her.

Cameron bolted into her sister's outstretched arms. A tear escaped and slid down her cheek. "Thank ye for coming."

Heather straightened and held Cameron's hands. "We got here as quick as we could."

Beathan stepped beside them. "Mistress Cameron, it's good to see ye, but I'm sorry it's under these circumstances."

"Thank ye." She looked over his shoulder at the men gathered in the yard, then peered around her sister. "Where's Da?"

Heather squeezed her hand. "Can we go inside and talk in private?"

"Is he all right?"

"Aye, let's discuss this in yer chamber."

Cameron swallowed hard and led Heather and Beathan up the stairs and into the main hall. Dread filled her chest at what she would hear. When she entered Robert's solar, she turned and indicated a bench in front of the fire before closing the door.

Beathan crossed the room and sat. Heather dropped in the chair across from him. She took a deep breath and exhaled. "Da's not well. His mind is going."

Cameron eased next to her. "Oh, Heather..."

Her sister closed her eyes briefly. When she opened them, stress and sadness emanated from the blue depths. "He can't remember anything in recent history. I can have a conversation with him, but a few minutes later, he'll forget we even spoke. He lives in the past." She glanced at Beathan. "Fortunately, we've covered for him, and no one outside our clan knows of his ailment."

"I don't understand. He seemed fine a few months ago," Cameron said, remembering her wedding day.

"After ye exchanged yer vows, do ye recall I didn't like the idea of Da going off with Robert by himself?"

"Aye."

"It was because I didn't want Da to reveal his secret. It's clear his mind is failing." Heather looked to Beathan. "When he has visitors, one of us is with him, to cover for him."

Cameron's chest squeezed. "I had no idea."

"I'm sorry to have to tell ye like this, but ye need to know. I've managed to keep it hidden for some time, but…."

"Oh, Heather, I hate ye've had to deal with this."

Heather's lips tightened into a thin line. "We're coping. Lindsey is with Da now. She and Fergus will watch out and protect him." She lightly clasped Cameron's fingers. "But, today we're here to help *ye*. Tell us what happened."

Cameron explained about Robert's capture, and they read the intercepted note. "My plan is to gain the trust of this field commander, and then render as many of the soldiers insensible as possible. Lachlan will lead the group to free Robert and the men."

"I don't like ye going in there," Heather said.

"It's risky," Beathan added.

"It is. But what options do we have?" Cameron stood and paced. "Someone has to do it. I'm the logical choice." She turned toward them. "We're running out of time."

"All right, but I'm going with ye," Heather said.

Cameron stepped toward her, shaking her head. "Nay…."

Heather held up a hand. "We'll go together. I'll assist ye, and Beathan and the MacDougall warriors will follow Lachlan's orders."

Cameron's shoulders sagged. She did need her sister's help.

Dear Lord, please don't let me lead them to their deaths.

~~~

Cold rain drizzled down Robert's neck and seeped into his tattered shirt. The cuts on his face burned, and his right eye had swollen half-shut. The beating he'd endured was well worth the satisfaction of severely wounding Commander Wilson.

Leather strips cut into his wrists, rubbing against raw abrasions he'd received from hours of chafing while secured to this blasted wooden post. Pain coursed through his torso as the thongs pulled tight. His weight stretched his arms and shoulders as his toes barely touched the ground.

Robert's gaze skimmed the area. The Sassenachs had erected a wooden pen around him and his battered men. His rain-soaked troops huddled on the ground, shivering from the cold night air. Kendrick, bound and tied to the post next to him, suffered a severe wound to his head. Dried blood caked the side of his face.

A whistle shrieked, and the guards stood alert. "Riders approach," the lookout shouted.

The heavy clop of horses' hooves and a creaking wagon clattered nearby. Soldiers hurried to meet it and helped a priest and two nuns off the seat.

One of the sisters reached into the back of the wagon and grabbed a basket—a brown basket, just like Cameron's. His eyes focused on the woman. Shite! His heart leapt into his throat, and he couldn't hold in a gasp.

"Easy, man," Kendrick whispered. "Don't let it show ye recognize her."

His chest constricted. He couldn't breathe.

235

What the hell is she doing? Blood pounded in his ears. He wanted to jerk against his ties, the leather cutting into his raw skin. God in heaven, why would she risk her life? The life of their child?

Heather's face turned to Robert, her eyes skimming his injured men. The priest clutched her arm and escorted her beside the fenced enclosure. As he strolled past, his head rotated, and Michael locked eyes with Robert. The man held his hand up to the prisoners. "God bless, my children."

The soldiers led Cameron, Michael and Heather into the commander's tent. Kendrick glanced at Robert. "Have ye seen Wilson since we camped?"

"Nay, I sliced him open. He should be dead."

"I imagine she's here to tend him."

"Tavish," Robert whispered.

The man glanced at the guards then inched around a group of his men huddled on the cold ground. Mud clung to his clothes, drizzle dripping off his hair.

"Spread the word. Be alert. When given the chance to escape, be ready."

Tavish nodded and sidled through the throng of men, spreading Robert's order.

Robert's stomach twisted as if a band squeezed the life out of him. "Lord, I'll tan her hide when we get out of here."

~~~

Cameron ducked between the flaps of the tent. Candles lined the dim, dank walls. Raindrops filtered through the roof and dripped in muddy puddles on the floor. The enclosure emitted a damp, musty smell. A soldier stood to the side of the opening, a sword clutched in his hands. Another grabbed her basket and rifled through it. He tossed her small knife on the table.

Michael pushed the black hood off his balding head and piously folded his hands before him. "Sir, we're here to tend yer commander. The sister will need her herbs and salves."

236

A ragged cough rent the air, and the soldier thrust the basket at Cameron. He grabbed her arm, his fingers pinching her flesh, and shoved her toward the bed in the corner of the tent. "Sister or not, I'll be watching you," he threatened, his eyes intense.

A large, heavyset man with dark greying hair lay on a straw mattress. Sweat covered his unclean body, and his stench threatened her last meal. She put her hand to her nose and took a deep breath. The soldier pushed her again, and she swallowed.

She could do this.

What choice did she have?

She must do this.

She placed her basket on the floor next to the bed and moved the blanket from the commander's chest. Seepage, yellow stains mingled with blood, soiled the dirty bandage covering his side. She tugged on the binding.

The commander grabbed her wrist.

Pain shot up her arm, and she inhaled sharply as her gaze darted to his face.

His piercing malevolent eyes bore into her. "I'm not dead yet, bitch. You'd best not try anything."

"Ye must let me see the wound." Her wrist ached from his steely grasp. He released her, and she rubbed her pinched skin. Taking a deep breath, she reached for the bandage again. The cause of the horrible smell was evident when her trembling fingers peeled the soiled cloth away. A sword wound, dirty and putrefying gaped open.

"I need water and a bowl."

"I'll get it for ye," Heather said.

"No, you will stay here," the burly soldier barked, and then addressed the guard at the tent's opening. "Bring a bucket of water."

Cameron turned back to the commander. Sweat trickled between her shoulder blades and down the center of her back. Her disguise, the woolen scapular, a cloth worn over her shoulders with an opening for her head, cut off ventilation.

With padding underneath, a dagger strapped to each leg, and the billowing robes and hood, the heat was stifling. "After I clean yer wound, I'll apply a salve to help stop the rotting of yer flesh."

"Here's the water." The man dropped the bucket at Cameron's feet, the water poured over the rim. A bowl floated on the surface.

Cameron grabbed the dish, dipped it into the water and stirred in leaves from her jar. "This tea will help alleviate fever and aid in healing yer wound."

The commander's evil eyes narrowed into slits.

She emptied the contents into a cup on the side table and held it to his lips.

He knocked her hand away, and the concoction sloshed, spilling on the blankets. "Do you take me for a fool?"

"It's a simple brew. It won't hurt ye."

"If that's the case, you drink first."

Cameron glared at the man. "I'm here to help ye."

"Prove it's not poison."

She drank from the cup and wiped her mouth. Once again, she extended it to him.

He turned his head slightly. "I don't trust you."

"We drink from the same cup."

He conceded and downed the brew, his eyes never leaving hers. She took the empty cup and prepared a salve. Once complete, she cleaned his wound and began stitching his side.

A blow slammed the side of her head. Pain radiated from her cheek, and black splotches burst before her eyes. She reeled on her feet.

"Stop," Heather shouted as she clutched Cameron's arm.

Michael bolted toward her, but the beefy soldiers grabbed his shoulders. "Sir, ye'll not strike the sister. She tries to heal ye."

"She stabs me on purpose!"

Cameron steadied herself, her eyes struggling to focus.

"She tries to sew yer filthy flesh together," Heather yelled.

Cameron squeezed her sister's hand. "Nay, it's all right. I'll be more careful."

Heather's chest heaved and hatred emanated from her blue eyes.

Wilson settled against the cushions and glowered at Cameron.

Her ears rang, and her fingers trembled as she stitched the wound closed. She smeared the salve over and around it, but she could not bring herself to bathe his grimy skin. Let him lie in his own filth.

His eyelids drooped.

The burly soldier grabbed her arm, his grip bruising. "Why's he falling asleep? What did you put in your brew?"

"It was only a healing potion. Do ye forget I drank from the same cup?"

The man studied Wilson with concern.

"His wound is severe, and it makes him drowsy," she assured him. "He needs rest to heal."

He released his unyielding grip, and she rubbed her arm. She sank onto a bench next to the mattress, and her sister scooted next to her.

"Ye're all right?" Heather's fingertips brushed the side of Cameron's eye.

"Aye." She winced and leaned away. "I'm fine."

Before long, the commander slept. He tossed and turned throughout the night. Cameron continued to dribble her tonic into his mouth, praying it would rid the man of his high temperature. She had to keep him alive and gain his confidence. Only then could she administer the last dose to render him senseless.

He moaned and thrashed on the mattress, crying out in pain. This had to work. If not, the English would execute Robert and his men. She prayed Lachlan and Beathan were ready.

By morning, Wilson's fever finally broke, and he rested comfortably. Cameron sighed in relief, her muscles stiff from anxious moments spent treating the commander throughout the exhausting night.

Hands on hips, the guard smiled and nodded at Wilson. "He's going to pull through."

She turned and reached for Heather's hand. "We need a bit of privacy."

Another soldier opened the flap of the tent. "This way."

Cameron nodded at Michael, and the sisters followed the man, walking arm in arm through the encampment. Men mingled in groups next to fires set around the site. Others sharpened their weapons and laughed over bawdy jokes.

The soldier shoved Cameron and licked his thick lips. "You can piss behind them bushes. I promise I won't be looking."

Cameron's skin crawled. Horses assembled in temporary pens nickered at the women's approach. The sisters scurried behind the shrubs.

"Now I have to convince Wilson to let me treat his men's wounds, get them to drink my brew," Cameron whispered.

"Ye must be careful," Heather responded. "He and his guards keep a sharp eye on ye."

Once the women relieved themselves, they returned to camp. Cameron stole a glance toward clusters of beaten men crowded in a wooden makeshift enclosure. The prisoners huddled on the cold wet ground. She nonchalantly searched the group for Robert. Familiar faces, Tavish, Hume, Eduard…injured but alive.

Robert.

Her breath caught.

His arms stretched over his head, secured to a post in the middle of the compound. Blood caked the side of his bloated face, one eye swollen shut.

Her heart beat rapidly.

A shiver snaked through her at his intense stare. He recognized her. She wrenched her gaze from him and ducked into the musty damp tent.

The commander was propped against pillows.

"Well, there you are." He smiled, but his nostrils flared slightly in disgust. "I've decided you'll return to my home with me. Any healer who can conjure such miracles is worth a fortune to a man in my...business."

Cameron stiffened. "Surely a man of yer importance has many healers at his disposal."

He sneered. "None so talented."

Her pulse hammered in her ears, but she willed herself to remain calm. She picked up her basket, searched the containers and selected a jar. "Yer men need tending as well."

"Aye, I'd have you treat them, but they may not have your brew. Only salves for their cuts. I don't trust you to not poison my troops."

He was on to her. Out of the corner of her eye, she saw Heather straighten. "And yet ye wish me to accompany ye home?"

"I have need of a healer to keep my prisoners alive so I can extract information." He chuckled.

She wanted to launch onto him with her knife in hand. "As ye wish, but they won't have the benefits of the herb to purge fever."

"Only your poultice!"

Cameron jumped at his outburst. She and Heather began making the concoction. They crushed herbs into a sticky paste. Cameron extracted several leaves of valerian and mashed them into the mixture. She handed Heather a handful, and they mixed the sleeping potion into the salve.

"Ye may administer this to the commander's men," Cameron told Michael and Heather. "Make sure to smear it generously in the wound." When they left the tent, she turned to Wilson's guard. "I must open his stitches to drain the fluid buildup, and I'll need my knife to snip the threads."

"I'll do it." The man cut the ties holding Wilson's sutures, and the wound gaped open.

She spread the paste thickly over and around his injury, making sure to pack the wound's cavity.

"Careful, woman." The commander grabbed her arm. "Do you think to torture me?"

Cameron flinched. "Nay, the wound must be filled with salve."

"Enough!" He shoved her from him.

She stumbled backward and grasped the side table.

"See to the others. I've had my fill of your Scot's stench."

Cameron's hand trembled as she gathered her supplies. She picked up her basket and left the tent, worried she had not administered enough of her potion to Wilson's wound.

Scores of injured men lined up, with Cameron, Heather and Michael dispensing the sleeping salve. "Ye must sit and rest to ensure the wound heals properly," Cameron advised the soldiers.

After absorbing the sticky balm into their systems, the English became drowsy. Cameron inched her way to Robert and the prisoners, tending men as she crept closer. She backed into the wooden fence and stooped beside a young soldier. His badly cut arm soaked his uniform in blood, and he shook from feverish-chills.

She glanced over her shoulder and whispered, "Tavish."

He scooted next to her, and she produced the daggers she had strapped to her leg under her billowing robe.

He scooped them up and winked.

She nonchalantly eased closer to Heather and Michael and placed her hand on her sister's arm. "It's time. We must slowly make our way out of camp. Leave the wagon. Walk past it and keep going. Beathan will get us to safety."

~~~

242

The agonizing leather thongs holding Robert's wrists fell away. His shoulders ached from the excruciating position. He nodded his thanks to Tavish and rubbed life into his limbs. The man tossed him a dagger. With his arms no longer tied over his head, he eagerly awaited Wilson.

Three men guarding their confinement, relaxed against a tree. One slept while the other two appeared sluggish. What had Cameron done?

Lachlan sneaked up behind the enclosure. He wrapped ropes around the wooden structure and threw one to Robert. "Tie this to the post. When we charge in, we'll get the men to safety."

Lachlan slipped into the shadows.

Robert turned to watch Cameron. She stepped over a man, his legs stretched before him. Another leaned against a boulder, his head resting on his shoulder. Heather and Michael followed her around the perimeter of the camp, and they slowly walked past the commander's tent.

A loud bellow came from inside.

Cameron jerked her head over her shoulder. An enraged Wilson stumbled between the flaps.

"Satan's whore! What have ye done to my men?" He grabbed her wimple and yanked her to him.

Robert pounded on the fence, jerking on the boards frantically trying to reach her.

Michael jumped on Wilson, his fists pummeling the commander.

Lachlan's ropes tightened and wrenched the structure surrounding Robert out of the ground. Wilson's men struggled to their feet. Robert leapt over them and elbowed one in the face with a satisfying crack.

MacDougall and Graham warriors closed in from all directions. The sound of clashing steel reverberated through his head.

Wilson launched Michael away from him and struck Cameron's face.

Robert saw red, the roar in his ears, his own. He ran over to them, grabbed Wilson's coat and hauled him off his wife. The man stumbled back, but Robert advanced and sank his dagger deep into the commander's gut, yanking it high in his chest. He spat in the churl's face before the man's dead body crumpled at his feet.

Robert picked up Cameron and cradled her in his arms. Heather helped Michael, and they ran for the woods.

Once safely away, he knelt and placed his wife on his thigh. He cupped the side of her face. Blood smeared her mouth, and dark bruises marred her soft skin. "Ye're all right?"

"Aye."

He slid his hand across her stomach. "And the babe?"

"We're both fine." Cameron's fingertips touched his face, and he winced. "Ye need tending."

"Ye're the one that will need tending when I get ye home." He pierced her with a stern glare and handed her to Beathan. "Get the women to safety."

Relieved Cameron and their child were unharmed, Robert stormed into battle. His heart burst with pride at the combined efforts of the once feuding clans. They worked in unison as brother Scots. The English, caught off guard and drugged into a stupor, had little chance.

Robert wrapped one arm around Eduard and the other around Hume. The men leaned against him as they struggled to safety. Several MacDougalls rushed out of the darkness and loaded the injured men onto a wagon.

When Robert raced back into the fray, fires blazed out of control. Tavish supported Gilbert and David. Bleeding and battered, they limped out of the camp.

Robert grabbed a sword and blocked the blow intended for the back of Tavish's head. Sparks flew off the blades. Sweat rolled into his eye, and his vision blurred. He swiped his forearm across his face. The soldier circled him. Robert thrust at the man's chest. The soldier jumped back, but not before Robert sliced his uniform. The man tripped backward and

244

sprawled onto the ground. Robert sunk his blade into the soldier's gut.

He straightened and eyed the carnage. A smile spread across his face. His men and the MacDougalls dealt well with the Sassenachs.

Now to deal with his wife.

Chapter Seventeen

Five miles west of Graham Castle
November 1297

The rickety old cart groaned with each clop of the horse's hooves. Cameron clutched her basket as she sat wedged between Lachlan and Heather. Sweat dribbled down the side of her face, and her hair stuck to her neck and back. She had finally removed the stifling black robe, the scapular and the protective padding, but the cool night air did little to assuage her heart.

Robert fumed.

But he was safe.

She held her head high. Her plan had worked, and now he and his men were free of the English brutality.

She had turned toward Robert one last time before Lachlan helped her onto the wagon. He hadn't spared a look at her as he instructed the MacDougalls and Grahams to erase the signs of battle. The men gathered the soldiers' horses and confiscated their weapons, food and supplies.

Lachlan nudged her with his shoulder, breaking her thoughts. "Ye did good."

She swallowed thick emotions clogging her throat. A moment passed before she spoke. "Robert is furious."

"Aye, but ye knew he would be."

Heather patted Cameron's hand. "Ye did what ye thought best, and it worked."

The cart rolled along. The three traveled in silence for the remainder of the journey. It was late at night when they arrived at Graham Castle. Horses and a wagon full of injured filled the bailey. Men and lads ran to take their horses and help them inside.

Lachlan lifted Cameron off the seat. When her feet touched the ground, she turned to the stairs, but he held her hand for a moment. When she looked back at him, he smiled.

246

"All will be well, Lady Graham. Our laird is a lucky man to have such a strong ally."

Cameron's heart clenched. She prayed her husband would feel the same. She squeezed his fingers. "Thank ye."

Nichola ran down the stairs with Aine close behind. "Where's Robert? Did ye find him? Is he all right?"

"We found him. He has injuries, but he's well," Cameron reassured her. "He and the rest of the men will be home shortly."

Heather tugged off the billowing robe and stood beside Cameron.

Lachlan rubbed Nichola's back, and she hugged him to her side. "That's wonderful news."

"Mistress, ye need tending." Aine placed her arm around Cameron's waist. "Come with me, and let me see to ye."

She shook her head. "Not until I treat the men."

Aine hugged Cameron's shoulders. "Gretchen and I will care for them. Ye need to rest."

"Please, Cameron. Aine's right," Heather implored. "Think of yer babe. Ye've been through a great deal."

Cameron took her sister's hand. "I can't thank ye enough for yer help."

Heather smiled. "I'm verra glad it turned out as it did." She glanced over Cameron's shoulder at the MacDougall men and back at Cameron. "We'll be heading home as soon as all the men arrive here safely."

"Won't ye rest and have a meal with us?"

"Nay, it's only a short distance home, and I worry about Da."

Cameron embraced her sister. "Ye'll let me know how he is?" She straightened and peered into her blue eyes. "If ye need me...."

Heather held up a hand. "I'll let ye know. Take care of yourself."

"Come, mistress." Aine helped her up the stairs, through the main hall and into her bedchambers. "Ye rest while I fetch my supplies."

Aine hurried from the room and closed the door behind her.

Exhausted and sore, Cameron sank in the chair before the fire. She dreaded the confrontation with Robert, but she had done the right thing. Her bairn kicked, and she skimmed her palm across her swollen belly. Her husband was safe and their babe, as well. What more could she want?

She exhaled, and her shoulders slumped. She wanted the fighting to end. Edward, with his sights on Scotland, would stop at nothing. The episode with Wilson was only one of many to come. Robert would constantly face danger. Her pulse raced with thoughts of tonight's outcome. It could have easily turned out much differently—the possibilities horrid.

Robert had killed the commander without a second thought, his rage evident with the thrust of his blade. Even as he examined her for injuries, the fury in his glare spoke volumes. Fighting was in his blood. Her husband was a true Scottish warrior bent on eradicating the English, no matter the danger he faced.

Aine bustled into the room. "I brought ye a wee bite to eat and a sleeping tonic, mistress."

The old woman placed a tray of sliced venison and cheese on the table in front of the hearth and handed a mug to Cameron.

"Oh, this reminds me. I wanted to talk to ye about the last potion ye made for me."

Aine's brow furrowed. "Is there something amiss?"

"I found wild carrot seeds in it." Cameron eased a slice of cheese in her sore mouth.

The old healer's eyes flew open. "In the potion *I* made for ye?"

"Aye."

"But I only put a wee pinch of valerian in it."

248

"I don't think it was ye, but there's no doubt someone did. It smelled like carrots, and it was oily with bits of seeds floating on top."

"Oh mistress, I would never do such a thing."

"Tell me, how was it that Dara brought it to me?" Cameron picked through slices of apple and selected a piece.

"Let me think. I was going over my supplies, like ye taught me. I looked at all of the jars to see what we needed. Do ye remember telling me ye would take me on a search for herbs?"

"Aye."

"Well, I was checking our supply to see what we needed, and I asked Gretchen to take ye yer potion." She paused. "I heard her ask Rosalind to take it to ye, but she refused. Dara offered, and I thought no more of it."

"Ye say Gretchen asked Rosalind?"

"Aye, mistress. Do ye think she put it in yer drink?"

"Was she near it? Did ye see her handling it?"

"Nay, she was stacking kitchen linens."

Cameron exhaled. "Well, I don't have proof it was her, just a niggling feeling."

"M'lady, I hate to think of what might have happened to ye and yer bairn had ye drunk that potion."

Cameron rubbed her swollen stomach. "As do I."

"What should we do?"

"Will ye ask Dara about it? Maybe she saw someone tamper with it."

"I'll ask her straight away." Aine pointed to the cup in Cameron's hands. "I promise that brew never left my sight. Ye'll not be finding any seeds in it."

"Thank ye." Cameron drank the potion and set the cup on the table.

"Let's get ye cleaned up and into bed." Aine lifted Cameron's gown over her head and slung it on the back of the chair. She took a cloth out of the basin on the bedside table and wrung the water out, then dabbed at the dried blood on her split lip.

Cameron winced and jerked her head back.

"I'm sorry, m'lady. I don't wish to hurt ye."

"It's all right. It only stings a bit."

Aine washed Cameron's face and hands. "Bless yer heart, ye really got clobbered. Ye've got blackish-purple marks all over."

Cameron touched her sore cheek.

Aine smeared salve above her eye. "What happened?"

"The commander took exception to me."

"Ye poor dear." The older woman clucked and wiped her hands. She took Cameron's elbow and helped her stand. "Ye climb in bed and get some rest. Ye'll feel better in the morning." She drew several blankets over Cameron's shoulder. "Sleep well, mistress."

The old woman shuffled from the room and closed the door.

Cameron lay on her side, staring into the flames. She relived the nightmare of Robert tied to the pole, his arms stretched above his head. His handsome face was distorted from blows he had received. Wilson's black soulless eyes stared at her. She smelled his horrible stench and felt his blow strike her head.

When she closed her eyes, the terrifying image transformed. Robert cradled her in his strong embrace, and her head rested against his chest. But when she gazed up at him, his words reverberated through her ears.

Ye're the one that will need tending when I get home.

~~~

Robert strode down the dark hall and into his solar. He unbuckled his swordbreaker and leaned it against the chair, tossed his daggers on the table, and grabbed a bottle of mead from the cabinet. He swigged a mouthful. The fiery liquid seared a path down his throat. The next guzzle sent warmth radiating through his gut. He put the mead down and placed his hands on either side of the table, his head bent forward.

250

The confrontation with Lachlan was still fresh. Anxiety and panic had coursed through his body at the sight of an English soldier leading Cameron into the commander's tent. He'd entrusted Lachlan with the care of Graham Castle, and the lives of his wife and unborn child. His stomach roiled with fury. Lachlan defended Cameron's plan.

When had he become her champion?

After exchanging heated words with his most trusted man, his anger at Cameron dissipated, only to be replaced by fear. Perhaps that made him angrier still. She had risked her life and the life of their bairn. What if she'd been killed?

The thought pierced his soul unlike anything Wilson's blade could have inflicted. When the commander struck her, Robert felt the blow more powerful than any he had experienced. His chest tightened with the meaning he didn't want to admit...even to himself.

Did he love her?

She had risked her life...for him.

Cameron once whispered endearing words, but she no longer needed to. She showed him in everything she did.

A knock sounded on the door. He wiped his mouth on his sleeve and took a deep breath. "Come in."

Aine opened the door and stuck her head inside. "Laird, do ye have a moment?"

"Aye."

She stepped into the room and shut the door. "Ye know I helped raise ye, and I don't mean any disrespect..."

He leaned against the table. "Speak freely."

"I'm worried about yer wife and yer bairn."

He stood as his gut dropped. "Why?"

She ambled closer, her grey eyes intense. "While ye were gone, someone put seeds in her sleeping potion."

"Seeds?"

"Poisonous seeds."

He jammed his hands on his hips. "What?"

"Lady Graham found wild carrot seeds in the sleeping potion I made for her—seeds used to rid a woman of a bairn.

When she asked me about it, I didn't know where they had come from, but now I have a strong suspicion. Rosalind told Dara that oftentimes babes don't make it." She wrung her hands. "And that if that were to happen, she'd step into yer wife's place."

Fury shot through him. "Are ye saying Rosalind put the seeds in Cameron's drink?"

"I believe so. No one actually saw her do it, but I worry it was her, and she may try again. That potion could have killed yer wife along with yer bairn."

Robert shook with rage.

Women scattered from his dark scowl as he stormed through the hall and down the stairs to the servants' chambers. He marched to Rosalind's room. He didn't knock, but threw open the door and strode inside. He looked around, taking in the rumpled bed, the small table and chairs. He flipped back the blankets and rifled through the bedding. Not finding anything amiss, he opened the table drawer and fumbled through trinkets, a comb and brush.

Robert inspected the room. A wooden chest was at the foot of the bed. He flicked off the lid and tossed out Rosalind's clothes. His fingers closed around a clay jar. Opening it, he sniffed the contents.

Carrots.

The scheming bitch!

Rosalind stepped into the room. Her mouth dropped open and her eyes widened. "Robert…what are ye doing here?" Her face relaxed, and she giggled. "Never mind, I know why ye're here."

She reached for the front of his trews.

He grabbed her wrist and held up the jar of seeds. "What's this? Wild carrot seeds? Is this what ye gave my wife?"

She gasped and shook her head. "Nay, it was not me. Someone else must've put it in her drink," she cried. "Dara served it to her."

252

He paused, glaring at her. "I didn't say anything about a drink."

"W-well I assumed it was put in her drink," Rosalind stammered.

He squeezed her upper arm. "Ye're the only one who would harm my wife."

"Nay, many others want her gone. She's a witch. Have ye ever seen anyone heal wounds like she does? She's cast a spell over ye. But ye know *I* should be yer wife. It should be *me* having yer bairn, not a MacDougall for Christ's sake. She's the enemy, Robert. She doesnae deserve to be Lady of Graham Castle."

Robert grabbed Rosalind's shoulders, lifted her until toes barely touched the floor, and sneered. "I want ye out of my sight before I can't control myself and rip yer every limb off. If ye ever show yerself around here again, I'll not be responsible for what happens to ye. Do ye understand?"

Wincing, Rosalind nodded and glared at him.

"I should strip ye naked and flay ye within an inch of yer life." He shoved her toward the door. "Get out."

"But, Robert...."

"I said get out," he yelled and advanced on her.

She stumbled backward feeling for the door. Quickly turning, she ran up the steps with him close behind.

"Michael," Robert bellowed when he reached the top of the stairs.

Michael walked from the main hall, wiping his mouth on his sleeve. "Aye, I'm here."

"Take her to Cunningham and leave her."

"Tonight?"

"Aye, she tried to kill Cameron and my bairn. Get her out of my sight."

Michael grabbed Rosalind's arm and yanked her toward the door.

Robert shuddered with uncontrollable rage. He took a deep breath and raked a hand through his hair, wondering at the wisdom of his leniency of letting the woman live. He always finished his battles and rarely left surviving enemies.

~~~

Robert leaned back in the chair, but kept his gaze on his sleeping wife. The glow of firelight danced across her face. She lay on her side, her head resting on her hands. Dark shadows marred the soft skin of her face. Black lashes fanned out in contrast to her alabaster cheeks. His gaze traveled from a purple bruise surrounding her eye down to a split on her lip. He should have tortured the swine for daring to touch her.

Easing into bed behind her, he tugged the blankets over them. He molded his body to her back and embraced her. He closed his eyes. Her hair smelled of smoke, and his chest clenched. He'd come close to losing her.

A hard thump from Cameron's stomach caused his eyes to fly open. Another thump. Robert pressed his palm against her abdomen. A *big* thump. He chuckled.

"Aye, my son. With yer mum's spirit and courage, ye'll be a fine warrior."

~~~

Cameron awoke. Flames flickered around logs in the hearth, casting shadows across the room. Robert lay at her back, his arm wrapped around her stomach. She placed her hand on his. He intertwined their fingers and kissed the side of her head.

"Ye did a verra reckless thing, wife."

She stilled. A moment of silence passed.

"I had no choice," she whispered.

"Aye, ye did."

The fire popped and crackled.

"Ye had no business putting yourself in harm's way. Lachlan and yer da's men could have taken the soldiers without ye."

"Wilson asked for a healer."

254

"I don't give a damn what the bastard asked for. Ye didn't have to give him what he wanted. Lachlan knew where we were located. He didn't need yer interference."

Her stomach plummeted. He didn't appreciate her efforts. She turned toward him. "Aye, perhaps there were other plans that could have been used, but ye can't deny mine worked."

He took her chin between his forefinger and thumb. "Ye will not overrule Lachlan's authority when I've left him in charge. Ye hindered his plans. He's a warrior. He knows best."

"Aye."

Robert looked into her eyes. "I'm relieved ye weren't harmed any more than ye were. Ye could've been beaten, raped and killed for God's sake."

A log rolled in the hearth sending sparks up the chimney. She remained quiet, bracing for his wrath.

"I thank ye for what ye did."

Cameron's breath caught. He *did* appreciate her efforts.

"But ye will not do it again."

"Only if ye promise not to get captured again."

Chapter Eighteen

Graham Castle
December 1297

"Lady Graham, Lady Graham," Tessa called.

"Aye, what is it?" Cameron peered down the stairs at her. The sound of men's voices drifted up from the main hall.

"We've got company. Hamish and his men have come to visit."

Her heart lurched. There was only one reason the rebel leader would arrive. "Will ye prepare food and drinks?"

"Aye, mistress," Tessa replied, then headed to the kitchen.

Stomach churning, Cameron smoothed her hair and pasted a smile on her face before she walked into the room.

Robert handed ale to the men sitting beside the large hearth. "Gentlemen, ye know my wife."

She walked over to him, and he hugged her to his side.

"Good afternoon," Cameron greeted the rugged men.

Hamish extended his hand. "It's been a long time, m'lady."

She accepted his hand, and he kissed her knuckles. "Ye're looking well. I believe the last time I saw ye was at Da's tournament a number of years ago."

"Aye, those were fun times. Everyone always enjoyed yer da's games."

Cameron turned to the other men. "Welcome to Graham Castle. Please make yourselves at home while I have food prepared."

She glanced at Robert, and her chest squeezed with thoughts of why Hamish was at Graham Castle. Her face grew stiff, and she quickly excused herself.

What would Hamish ask of Robert? Her hands trembled, and she took a deep breath to steady her nerves. Wiping perspiration off her palms, she smoothed her skirt and opened the kitchen door.

256

Tessa leaned over the worn worktable and prepared a tray of meat and cheese for the men. She stopped what she was doing, wiped her hands on a cloth and wrapped her arm around Cameron's shoulders. "He's a warrior, mistress."

Cameron rubbed her swollen belly. "I guess ye think me silly."

"Nay, m'lady, I donnae think that. We all worry fer those we love."

~~~

Cameron's eyes fluttered open. The glow of the embers shone into the room. Robert added a few logs to the fire and stepped to the bed. Gazing down at her, he tugged his shirt over his head and dropped it on the chair. His massive torso and muscular biceps gleamed in the firelight. He dropped his trews and slid into bed, nestling her against him.

She rested her head on his chest, and he ran his hand up and down her arm. They lay quietly for some time before he tilted her face toward him. His silence confirmed her worst fears.

He was leaving.

A band of dread squeezed her chest, and her breath hitched. She gazed into his dark eyes as her fingertips touched his whiskered cheek. He bent and gently kissed her mouth, then pulled her body against his as he wrapped her in his embrace and held her close. She eased her arms around his neck, and the heat of his body penetrated her light gown. Her eyes closed, and she inhaled his musky scent, committing it to memory for the long nights she would face without him.

He kissed the top of her head, and she tilted her face to him. Tears clouded her vision. A drop escaped and rolled down her cheek. His calloused hand cupped the side of her face, and his thumb brushed the wetness. Her hand covered his, and she turned and placed a kiss on his palm.

He slanted her face toward him and lowered his head, his lips capturing hers in a soft whispered touch. When she eagerly responded, he eased his tongue into her mouth and tugged her gown off her shoulders.

He trailed kisses across the top of her breasts while continuing to slide her nightdress past her hips and to the end of the bed. His fingers grazed the tips of her sensitive breasts. She dropped her head back when he suckled her, easing his hand down her abdomen and lower to cup her mound. He parted the folds of her flesh. Her privates tightened, weeping for his touch as his finger glided up and down her slick cleft.

He eased on top of her and nudged her legs apart. Her heart raced. He hovered over her, his shaggy hair draping his powerful shoulders. His intense, passion-filled eyes bore into her. He inserted the head of his manhood into her passage and thrust his hips. She inhaled sharply, and her eyes closed with the exquisite sensation, stroking, pulling her into oblivion.

He made love to her, bringing her to an explosive peak while reaching his own pinnacle. He rested his forehead against hers and kissed her gently. His breathing slowed, and he rolled off, dragging her against his body and nestling her head in the crook of his arm.

They lay together, quietly holding each other. Cameron didn't want to break the magical spell between them, but she needed to know Hamish's news.

She traced circles on his chest. "What did Hamish want?"

Robert stroked her back. A few moments passed before his deep voice rumbled in his chest. "He needs help with the English. We suffered a major defeat in a skirmish two weeks ago. Brandon McLeod asks all clans to gather. The Grahams and MacDougalls will ride with the Campbells."

Cameron stiffened. She had known his answer before she asked, but hearing it struck fear in her soul.

"We've known this time would come. 'Tis why we've trained so hard."

She wanted to show her support and be strong, but her words lodged in her throat. Fearing her voice would break and throw her into a fit of tears, she wrapped her arms around him and hugged.

They lay together for a long time before Cameron heard his steady, light snoring.

Father, please watch over him. Keep him safe and bring him home to me.

~~~

The inevitable day arrived, and it was time for Robert to leave. Cameron helped him into his heavy cloak. Her throat constricted. She knew the Scots had no choice but to fight the invaders. She knew they fought for freedom, for the survival of their clans, their way of life. However, she also knew the danger, death and destruction her husband would face.

Determined to be brave, she held her head high and smiled through watery eyes. She slid her fingers over his broad shoulders. "So, ye've got everything?"

Robert's hand rummaged through his tunic, and he patted the dagger at his side. "Aye, I'm ready." He cupped the side of her face. "I'll miss ye, lass."

Cameron's breath hitched, and she closed her eyes, turning her face into his warm palm. She placed her hand over his as a tear slipped from her eye.

"Ahh...don't cry." Robert tugged her into his embrace. "We'll be fine. The men are ready."

Cameron nodded, her face buried in Robert's chest.

When he straightened, he ran his thumb across her cheek and softly kissed her forehead, then her lips.

"Come see me off," he said, taking her hand. He bent and picked up his swordbreaker. With his fingers interlaced through hers, he led her down the stairs and through the active hall where final preparations were underway for their departure.

"Good morn." Robert set down his saddlebag and scanned the Graham warriors he had selected and the MacDougall men who joined his troops. Under his command, the clans combined their efforts to thwart the English threat.

The men sat around the large wooden trestle tables in the hall. The room quieted. All eyes were riveted on their leader. He paused, glancing from man to man.

"Ye've trained long and hard. Each of ye holds the skills needed for victory, and I'm proud of ye." He paused. "We fight for our verra lives, lads. We fight for our freedom and our homeland. We'll wipe the scum from our land and someday we *will* live in peace." He looked at each man. "We've gone over our plan many times. Don't flinch. Don't hesitate or second-guess, and we *will* be victorious."

The men cheered and roared in agreement.

"Say yer goodbyes and mount up!"

The men quickly readied themselves. As Robert gave instructions to Michael and Duncan, Cameron watched families offering farewell to their husbands, fathers, sons and brothers.

Nichola and Lachlan stood across the room. The corners of her mouth tugged up, remembering Nichola's squeal when Cameron informed her Robert had been happy to learn of Lachlan's interest in his sister.

Lachlan strapped on his belt with his sword dangling against his leg. Nichola helped him into his cloak. He pulled her into his embrace and kissed her while running his hands down her back. Finally, he broke their kiss and picked her up until her toes barely touched the floor. When he set her before him, he cupped her cheek, and they spoke to each other.

Feeling she intruded on their privacy, Cameron pulled her gaze from the intimate scene. The men grabbed their gear and walked out the door.

Androu ran around the room, handing out sacks of food Tessa had prepared.

Isobel stepped up to Cameron and took her hand. Cameron tried to smile at the little lass, but it was almost her undoing when she saw the fat tears silently sliding down Isobel's cheeks.

Robert finished with Michael and stooped next to Isobel. She dropped Cameron's hand and launched herself into his arms.

260

"Ye be a sweet lassie while I'm gone, and do what Cameron asks of ye."

"I will, Robbie." She kissed his cheek.

Robert stood while rubbing Isobel's curls and held his hand out to Cameron. "It's time to go."

She clasped his strong calloused fingers, and he led her from the hall and into the bailey. His men mounted and awaited his orders. Robert secured his weapons and satchel on Eton's back before he wrapped her in his strong embrace. He kissed her forehead as he whispered, "Be brave. I'll be home soon."

Her chest squeezed. "I'll be waiting, husband. Come home safely."

He nodded then mounted Eton.

Cameron clutched his thigh. "Robert?"

He looked down at her.

"Take care," she whispered, choking on the words.

"And ye, wife." He winked and produced those dimples that still caused flutters in her stomach. Taking Eton's reins, he sat straight in the saddle and held up a hand. "Let's ride."

He turned his horse and galloped through the gates.

Nichola held Isobel's hand. They stepped beside Cameron and Androu, and watched the men disappear from sight.

Chapter Nineteen

Graham Castle
February 1298

Two months passed, and the weather turned warm for the time of year. Cameron stretched her tired back. Sweat trickled down the side of her face. She wiped her brow with her forearm and studied the long rows of leeks and kale planted in the south field. Her basket was already full of carrots and radishes. It was a bountiful harvest requiring every helping hand to collect and store the winter vegetables.

Gretchen and Dara worked the rows next to her. Their bent frames inched a foot at a time, diligently plucking carrots out of the ground and depositing them in a sack attached to their backs.

Gretchen tossed a handful of vegetables in her bag. "I heard Fiona's expecting another wee one."

"Aye, she is." Cameron shook her basket to make room for more radishes. "I checked on her yesterday, and she's doing well."

"Tessa's thrilled." Dara giggled. "She just loves bairns. Spoils 'em rotten."

Michael's whistle shrieked. "Riders approach!"

Cameron's heart pounded. She squinted against the afternoon sun. A breeze blew a curl onto her face, and she brushed it aside.

Men on horseback came into view.

Her breath caught in her throat.

Robert.

She dropped her basket, hiked her skirt and hurried across the field. Her large stomach prevented her from jumping over rows of plants, but she grasped her belly and ran. Her legs wouldn't move fast enough in the freshly turned earth. Tears streamed across her face.

He's home!

262

Robert bounded off Eton, bolted down the embankment and onto the field. His men jumped to the ground behind him. As if in a fog, sounds of women shouting with joy and men cheering drifted around her.

Robert swept her into his arms and spun her around. He set her before him, and his hands cupped her face. "Cameron."

"Welcome home, husband," she whispered. He captured her mouth. She closed her eyes, and lost herself in his kiss.

He straightened and held her away from him. His hand splayed over her swollen stomach. "Ye're well? And the babe?"

"Aye and ye?"

"Aye." He tugged her close and buried his face in her hair. "I missed ye."

"Thank God ye're home."

He kissed the side of her face, and she turned into him, capturing his lips with her own. His tongue slid into her mouth, and the stars she had sorely missed exploded behind her eyes. His hard body pressed into hers, and she reveled in the feel of him, in his earthy scent.

His mouth trailed across her cheek to her ear. "Ah, lass, I've never been able to resist ye."

"Well, ye'll have to control yerself until we get to the keep." She wiggled out of his arms, held his hands out to the sides and inspected him. She swallowed the choking emotions. "Ye look good, husband." She gazed at his twinkling eyes. Her bottom lip quivered. "I'm so happy ye're home."

Robert wrapped his arm around her. "Ye will show me how happy ye are to have me home—give me a *proper* welcome."

He scooped her up, and she threw her arms around his neck and kissed his cheek. Dodging others rushing around them, he marched to his horse. As if in greeting, Eton tossed his head and nickered.

263

"And it is good to see ye, too," Cameron called to the horse. Robert chuckled, lifted her onto the saddle and climbed up behind her.

She sat sideways, her arms wrapped around his waist, the side of her face nestled against his chest. She closed her eyes. His pulse beat strong.

He kissed the top of her head and nudged Eton into a gallop down the dusty road.

She grinned with thoughts of how she would *properly* welcome him home.

Chapter Twenty

Graham Castle
March1298

A month passed with little to no contact with Edward's soldiers. While Robert continued to train his warriors, the atmosphere at Graham Castle relaxed, and the clan breathed a bit easier.

Cameron awoke with her head on Robert's chest, her swollen belly resting against his hip. Their child could arrive any moment and with each day, her stomach grew larger.

Robert casually stroked her side, and she stretched up to kiss him. He put his hand under her chin to deepen the kiss, and his rough stubble brushed her mouth. Despite her reassurances, he refused to take their lovemaking past gentle caresses, avowing to control himself until after the birth. Although it was frustrating at times, she appreciated his concern for her and their child.

"I ride to the northern borders today. We are readying the fields for early spring planting. Ye can expect us back at dusk." He kissed her and threw back the blankets. "Stay in bed and rest. I want ye to take care of yerself."

"Aye, husband."

Several hours later, Cameron made her way downstairs and into the main hall. Nichola, Androu and Isobel sat at the large wooden table eating the midday meal. Shortly after she joined them, Lachlan approached Nichola. She excused herself, and they walked off together.

Cameron stirred the porridge Tessa had made and glanced at Androu and Isobel. "I could use yer help finding herbs. On the south line of the forest, there's an area full of healing bark and roots this time of year." She leaned toward Isobel. "And there are bonnie early spring wildflowers growing nearby."

Isobel clapped her small hands. "I want to pick wildflowers."

"Aye, we'll help ye," Androu said.

"Wonderful. As soon as we finish eating, I'll get my basket, and we'll be off."

"I'll ready my horse," Androu called over his shoulder as he ran out of the main hall.

A few minutes later, Cameron and Isobel descended the keep's stairs to find the lad had saddled his horse and awaited them in the bailey. He reached for Cameron's hand. "May I help ye up?"

What a little gentleman. "Oh nay, I'll walk."

Isobel jumped up and down. "I want ta ride. I want ta ride."

"All right, Issie." Androu bent and laced his fingers together. Isobel placed her foot in his hands, and he hoisted her onto the saddle.

Grayish-white clouds drifted across the blue sky, lazily making their way east. Cameron inhaled fresh air while tilting her face to the sun. With the winter months, beautiful days such as this one were a distant memory.

Cameron and Androu strolled down the road leading Isobel and the horse toward the bordering woods. It didn't take long before Cameron discovered an assortment of plants.

Androu helped Isobel down and then held up a plant lined with fine hairs surrounding little white flowers. "How about this one?"

"Aye, that's winterweed. We can definitely use some."

"I'll get some for ye." He bent and tugged the green fronds.

Isobel squatted next to a group of yellow wildflowers. She hummed a tune, her little head bobbing from side to side, her dark curls bouncing.

Cameron smiled before studying a bunch of ground ivy in front of her. She snipped several fronds and placed them in her basket.

A warning horn blared from the castle. Cameron jumped. The ground rumbled, the sound of approaching horses unmistakable. She shaded her eyes from the sun and searched

266

the castle grounds at the base of the hill. A large contingency of men thundered down the road and charged into the bailey.

"Who's that?" Androu asked.

"I'm not sure," Cameron responded.

Shouting and the clash of steel rang out. A small group of men on horseback rounded the back of the castle walls. One of the men pointed up the hill.

"Soldiers! They've seen us," Androu said. "And they're heading this way. We've got to get out of here."

Androu grabbed Isobel's upper arm. She dropped a bunch of yellow flowers, her eyes wide with fear.

"Wait, where will we go?" Cameron asked. "There are three of us, and I can't ride with this stomach."

Androu searched the area. "Quick, follow me."

He tugged Isobel and the horse behind him.

Cameron clutched her basket and hurried to keep up.

"There's an old cave farther up the hill. Issie, ye know where it is?"

"Aye, I've been there lots of times."

"Good. Take Cameron, and ye both stay hidden until I return."

Cameron grabbed Androu's hand. "I can't let ye go off by yourself."

"Robert asked me to watch out for ye and our sisters, and I plan to do that." Androu seared her with his dark eyes, so much like her husband's. He jerked out of her grasp. "Now hide yourselves, and stay there until I get back. Get in the cave!"

Androu swung onto the saddle and galloped toward the north field where Robert and his men worked, luring the soldiers away from her and Isobel.

Isobel took Cameron's hand and led her into the thicket. "Hurry, it's up here."

Sharp pains streaked through Cameron's swollen abdomen, and she grabbed her stomach. She took another step, and warm liquid gushed from beneath her gown.

"What is it?" Isobel asked. "Is it the bairn? Is it dying?"

"No, no, Issie. It *is* the babe, but it's not dying. I'm afraid it's on its way."

Isobel looked back to the castle.

Cameron's hand trembled. "No, ye can't leave. Ye must stay with me."

"But the baby—ye need help."

"We'll be fine." Cameron took a deep breath. "Help me into the cave."

Isobel put her arm around Cameron and assisted her into the dark recesses of the cavern. The sound of thundering hooves raced past their hiding place. Isobel put her hands over her ears as if the loud noise frightened her, and Cameron hugged the little lass to her side.

"Don't worry. They've gone past." She briefly closed her eyes and offered a silent prayer for Androu. *Oh Lord, please watch over and protect him.*

She glanced around and shivered. The cavern was damp and her gown soaked. In the distance, the sound of steel striking steel rent the air as she prepared to deliver her bairn on the cold wet floor of a cave. What more could happen?

A sharp pain sliced through her, and she grabbed her tight abdomen. Sweat broke out on her forehead and trickled down her face. Her belly twisted into a spasm. Waves of agony rendered her speechless.

"What can I do?" Isobel asked.

What could a lass of five years do to help? "Th-There's a blanket in the bottom of my basket. Spread it on the ground so I can lie down."

Isobel rifled through the basket and shook out the cover.

"I'm sorry, Issie. Ye're too young to witness this, but we have no choice." Another pain cut through her, and she doubled over.

~~~

The sound of horses' hooves pounded the dirt road leading to the fields. Robert shaded his eyes from the afternoon

268

sun. Half a dozen English soldiers rode in his direction. He walked to the clearing and stood, hands on hips, waiting and watching the approaching party.

"Laird Robert Graham?" the leader asked.

"Aye."

The man held a document in his gloved hand. "We're arresting your wife for witchcraft. King Edward strictly prohibits the use of magic, and crimes committed against the Crown are punishable by death. She will be tried and if convicted, she'll burn at the stake."

Robert shook with uncontrollable rage. "Witchcraft?"

"Yes." The soldier sneered, delight evident in his black eyes. "We have secured the castle and will interrogate the residents for claims of miraculous healing with enchanted brews and salves. My men have been dispatched to escort your wife to court as we speak."

"Before ye have proof?"

The commander smirked. "We have all the proof we need. The interviews are simply a...formality."

Robert took the cloth from around his neck. He wiped his face and shook it out, dropped it on the ground and bent to retrieve it.

Sfit! Sfit! Sfit!

When he straightened, all six soldiers were falling to the ground, arrows protruding from their lifeless bodies. The signal he devised had worked.

Robert ran to Eton. He would track the bastards down and rip them apart.

Kendrick, Brian and David dropped from their hiding places in the trees, bows and arrows in their hands. Michael and the men working the fields left their tools and hurried to the clearing.

Robert strapped his sword on Eton's saddle.

"What happened?" Michael shouted.

"Cameron's been charged with witchcraft. They've arrested her." Robert grabbed Eton's reins.

Kendrick leapt onto his horse's back. "Witchcraft? Who in the hell would have accused her of that?"

"Rosalind." Robert addressed Michael. "Get rid of the bodies and evidence they were here. Then get back to the castle. We're going to cut the soldiers off before they cross the border."

Brian and David jumped onto their mounts and thundered behind Robert and Kendrick down the road. They searched for marks—anything to indicate a trail. Dusk's dim light made tracking difficult, but the men pressed on, determined to find Cameron.

Hours passed. They rode for miles, looking, searching. The night air grew cold, and light snowflakes fell. Robert wrapped his cloak tight around his shoulders and moisture dripped from his hair into his eyes. Where could they be?

He stared across the silent horizon. Snowdrifts formed alongside the road. A group of soldiers riding warhorses would leave evidence—the churned ground, horse droppings, freshly broken branches.

There was nothing.

His heart ripped asunder.

He had to keep his wits. He could not let his emotions run wild, causing him to make rash decisions, become reckless and make grave mistakes. In these conditions, hoof prints would quickly disappear. Although the moon rose high, it didn't provide the needed light to find their trail.

Crimes committed against the Crown are punishable by death. The soldier's words echoed through his mind.

Lord, no. This can't be happening.

"Robert," a frantic voice shouted.

Robert spun Eton around. Androu led a group of men toward him, and Robert kicked his horse into a gallop to meet them.

"It's Cameron. I hid her and Issie."

"What?"

"When the soldiers started chasing me, I told them to stay in the cave."

270

"Aye, the group that was to escort Cameron to trial chased Androu onto the fields shortly after ye left." Michael nodded toward his brother. "He led them right into our hands."

"None escaped?"

Michael grinned. "Nay, we took care of 'em. After Androu explained what had happened, we came searching for ye."

"And Hume and Donald have been dispatched to ensure Rosalind will never accuse anyone of anything again," Tavish added.

Michael crumpled a parchment and extended it to Robert. "No one will ever know of their outlandish charges."

Relief flooded through him, his voice nearly cut off with emotion. "Androu, take me to Cameron and Isobel." Eton pranced, sensing Robert's urgency. "Kendrick, take the others and get to the castle. Prepare in case of attack."

Androu took off with Robert following close behind. They rode for miles, but finally rounded the back of the castle and galloped up the side of the hill. They picked their way through the underbrush and onto a dirt pathway.

"Issie!" Androu yelled. "Cameron!"

Robert slid off Eton and dropped to the ground.

"They're here! They're here!" Isobel called out.

Robert jerked his head toward her voice and froze. The clouds parted, and moonlight lit the cave's entrance. Light snowflakes swirled in the air. Cameron held a bundle in one arm, and Isobel's hand in the other.

"I told ye they were safe," Androu shouted.

Robert sprinted up the slope with his brother behind him. His legs, as if mired in quicksand, would not move fast enough. Isobel broke from Cameron, raced down the hill and threw herself into his embrace. He grasped the little lass to him.

She straightened and placed her hands on either side of his face. "Cameron had the bairn, and I helped."

"She had the bairn?" Androu asked, his eyes wide.

Robert turned to Cameron. She held a babe. Their babe. *His* babe. He swallowed hard. His breath caught and the back of his eyes stung.

Cameron smiled. Her damp hair hung in strands to her waist. Dirt and stains smeared her face and gown, but she had never looked more beautiful.

"Come meet yer son."

His heart slammed into his chest with an overpowering swell of love. He eased Isobel to her feet and climbed the embankment to the cave.

"My son?"

Cameron handed the little bundle to him.

"He's so tiny," he whispered, cradling the baby.

Androu and Isobel stood on either side, peering at the wee one.

"Aye, my son." The babe yawned, and Robert laughed. He glanced at Cameron. She was pale and appeared weak, but her smile radiated warmth. The babe began to fret, and Robert handed him back to her. She eased their son into her arms and kissed his forehead.

Robert smoothed the blanket around the babe. When Cameron raised her head, her beautiful green eyes reflected the emotions coursing through his body. He kissed her gently and whispered, "I love ye, wife."

~~~

Cameron had dreamed of hearing those four little words, but she never imagined the blissful joy they would bring. Tears of happiness welled, and her throat constricted. "And I love ye, husband."

He stroked her cheek with the pad of his thumb. "Let's get ye home."

"I'll bring yer basket," Isobel said.

Robert patted Androu's back. "Ye kept them safe. If it wasn't for what ye did..." his voice cracked, and he paused.

Androu threw his arms around Robert's waist, and her husband hugged his brother. A moment passed before Robert let Androu go, but finally he ruffled Androu's dark hair. The lad stood tall and beamed.

Cameron's chest tightened at the tender scene.

They started back down the side of the hill to the horses. Robert helped her and the babe from the embankment, but when he bent to lift her onto Eton, her brows scrunched, and she held up a hand.

"I don't believe I'd care to ride."

"Ye're sure? Ye appear weak."

"I'd be more comfortable walking *slowly* with ye by my side."

"I will always walk by yer side, wife."

She smiled, and he placed Isobel on his horse as Androu scrambled onto his saddle. Robert took Cameron's soft hand, and they headed back to the castle.

Nichola led Lachlan, Kendrick and many of the clan up the hill to greet them.

"Cameron!" she yelled, hiked her skirt and ran the rest of the way up the steep slope. Her hand clutched her chest and tears brimmed in her blue eyes. "The babe. Ye had the babe."

Isobel bounced up and down on the horse. "And I helped! I was the first one to hold him."

Kendrick slapped Robert's back and grasped his hand. "Congratulations, man."

"Thank ye," Robert replied, his heart soaring as he gazed upon his wife and son.

Lachlan stopped behind Nichola and placed his hands on her shoulders while peering around her at the small bundle in Cameron's embrace.

Nichola held Cameron's arm, her eyes wide. "Ye're all right?"

"Aye, meet yer nephew." Cameron tugged the blanket from the little one's face. His eyes blinked, and he yawned.

Nichola's knuckle stroked his cheek. "How precious."

Lachlan laughed. "Born in the caves of Scotland? What a fine lad he will be."

~~~

Cameron woke to the wails of her hungry babe. Smiling, she gingerly slipped from bed and over to the crib.

"Good morn, sweetling." She picked him up and held him close, stroking his little back. "Ahh, ye need changing."

She took a soft cloth from the stack Nichola left on the side table and placed the little one in a dry wrap. Cradling him in her arms, she whispered to him.

Robert rose on his elbow and rubbed his eyes. "How's my son?"

"Hungry." She kissed the babe's soft head, climbed on the bed and propped against the pillows. She eased her gown aside and brought his wee mouth to her breast.

Robert watched him nurse. He cupped the back of the baby's head and trailed a path down his arm. He chuckled when a little fist grabbed his finger. "He's already got a strong grip."

Their bairn made exuberant sucking sounds, and she giggled. "What shall we name him?"

"Douglas. Douglas Graham, after my grandfather."

"Hmmm, I like it. Douglas it is."

Robert gathered her and their nursing child in his embrace. Her heart swelled with love. The three of them lay in bed snuggling close and enjoying their special time.

Later that morning, Robert took Douglas downstairs to formally meet the clan while Cameron rested. She smiled hearing cheers and congratulations ringing throughout the keep. Her eyes drifted closed with sweet thoughts of celebrating the birth of the Laird's son.

~~~

The next night, MacDougalls and Grahams filled the great hall in celebration of Douglas's birth. Tessa prepared a feast, and ale flowed freely. Several men strummed the lute, their musical instruments adding to the festive atmosphere.

Cameron sat with Robert, Douglas and their families. Heather stuck to Da, and Cameron's heart was heavy at the reason why. Her strong father was aging before her eyes.

274

Nichola and Lachlan shared a bench next to the hearth, and Isobel and Androu played a game at their feet.

"So ye'll be here for a while?" Da asked Robert.

"Aye, I'll still lead skirmishes, but we're hoping France's King Philip will send troops to help us." He cradled a cooing Douglas on his thigh. "William Wallace thinks it'll happen. I hope he's right. We could use their help."

Cameron sipped her spiced cider and leaned back against the cushions. Duncan chuckled and slapped Fergus on the back. Fergus bent at the waist, hands on hips, his laugh resonating across the room.

Kendrick leaned toward Lindsey and held up his mug. She tapped it with her cup, and they both drank. *I wonder what bargain they struck?* Kendrick brushed an auburn lock behind Lindsey's ear, and she smiled coyly. Her little sister was growing up.

Douglas whimpered, and Cameron turned toward the sound. Robert nuzzled her baby. He tugged the blanket around Douglas's neck and kissed his forehead.

Dear Father, what miracles ye have brought me!

Both clans together, united. A loving husband, who encourages my healing arts during the day, and ensconces me in his lover's embrace during the night.

Thank you for reading Cameron's story! I hope you enjoyed it as much as I enjoyed writing it. I would love to hear from you. Please email me at mcfarland.lane@gmail.com.

Don't forget to check out Heather's story in *The Daughters of Alastair MacDougall* ~ Book II.

Heather

Bent on overcoming the belief he's failed his aging father, Laird Alec Campbell concentrates on proving his worth to his people. He provides for them and leads men into battle, vowing never again to disappoint his clan or lose his heart.

Bound by a promise to her dying mother, Heather MacDougall secretly leads rebel warriors in her quest to keep her clan intact and hold off those who plot to overtake her father's land. She fights to keep her secrets safe, while resisting the lure of the handsome young laird who challenges her defenses.

They can't deny their passionate attraction, but can their love survive their secrets?

And look for ***Lindsey*** to be released in 2014 with ***Elsbeth*** soon to follow.

Please visit my at http://www.romancingtheeras.com to learn more about me and my books.

www.ingramcontent.com/pod-product-compliance
Lightning Source LLC
Chambersburg PA
CBHW061554170626
46811CB00001B/201